MY KILLER ON THE LOOSE

BOOK ONE OF THE OBSESSIVE SERIES

LOUISE WILDER

Publisher: Louise Wilder 2024
Copyright © 2024 Louise Wilder

All rights reserved.

No part of this book may be reproduced, stored in a retrieval system, or transmitted in any form or by any means, electronic, mechanical, photocopying, recording, or otherwise, without express written permission of the publisher.

This is a work of fiction. Names, characters, businesses, places, events and incidents are either products of the author's imagination or used in a fictitious manner. Any resemblance to actual persons, living or dead, or actual events is purely coincidental.

This book is licensed for your personal enjoyment only. This book may not be re-sold or given away to other people. If you would like to share this book with another person, please purchase an additional copy for each person you share it with. If you are reading this book and did not purchase it, or it was not purchased for your use only, then you should return it to the seller and purchase your own copy.

Thank you for respecting the author's work.

Published: Louise Wilder 2024

This content is only suitable for 18+ readers.

*"I love you as certain dark things are to be loved,
in secret, between the shadow and the soul."*

- Pablo Neruda, 100 Love Sonnets

TRIGGER WARNINGS

This book is the first of my dark romance serial killer series. There are a few details which will be very relevant throughout the series, so you will need to read the books in order to be able to follow the story.

There are a lot of triggers within this book from chapter one, so please be aware before you embark on this journey.

Your mental health is important to me, and if at any point this book is too much, please do not continue to read it.

If you do decide to continue this journey with me, please be aware of the triggers within this book.

These include but are not limited to coercion, stalking, kidnapping, torture, bloody gore, graphic physical violence, murder, serial killer, death of a relative, sexually explicit content, sexual assault, STIs, anxiety, gambling addiction, attempted murder, car accident, depression, divorce, alcohol, emotional abuse, drowning and suicide.

> Reader discretion is advised because you have been warned.

PLAYLIST

Eat You Alive - Limp Bizkit
Addicted - One True God
Dark Side - Ramsey
After Hours - The Weekend
My Black Death - Strvngers
Oxytocin - Billie Eilish
Savages - Kerli
Desire - Meg Myers
I See You - MISSIO
Darkness Inside - Astyria
I Wanna Be Your Slave - Maneskin
Tear You Apart - She Wants Revenge
Taste of You - REZZ
Death of Me - Pvris
A Little Bit Dangerous - CRMNL
Like U - Rosenfeld
Power - Isak Danielson
True Colors - Zedd
Violent Delights - CHVRCHES
Serial Killer - Slayyter
Smoke - BOBI ANDONOV
Psycho - Asking Alexandria
Hatef--k - The Bravery
RUNRUNRUN - Dutch Melrose
Keep it Down - Migrant Motel

1.

"Oh shit, I am so sorry." El immediately apologised, shouting a lot louder than she realised after crashing into him, spilling his beer all down his front. She had yet again been carrying far too many books as she stormed through the house with her music turned up loud in her earphones. El was trying to drown out the noise from her sister's impromptu party.

Now, instead of being able to continue with her studying, El was on a quest to save her precious items from getting wrecked by the growing hoard of drunken revellers that her sister had bought home with her.

Her sister Dorothy, or Dotty as she preferred to be called, was the life of the party and always seemed to bring random strangers to their Cambridge family home whenever their parents were away on business or holiday.

Dotty was a third-year student at Cambridge studying politics, was popular, beautiful, and of course, fucking her lecturer, to the dismay of El.

Short for Ethel (their mother had a fondness for old-fashioned names), El crouched down to collect her now sodden books from the floor, cursing herself for not looking where she was going.

The stranger she had bumped into stood motionless, looking down at the mousey brown-haired girl on her hands and knees before him. He only briefly saw her eyes before she ducked in front of him, gathering her things. But they were already burnt into the back of his retinas from that brief glimpse. They were quite the sight to behold, especially with her eyes widened in surprise.

El had heterochromia, a trait she had inherited from her beloved grandmother, Enid.

One eye was a dark chestnut colour with an amber limbal ring, and the other was an ice blue aqua colour with a limbal ring of teal around it. They were stunning and something no one could resist when they looked at her, drawing them to her.

Their grandmother always commented that they showed her dark and light sides. She loved to demonstrate it with her own eyes by covering one side of her face at a time and frightening the girls with her "evil grandmother voice" when her brown eye alone was on display. Then she would switch to her innocent, playful side when her blue eye showed, and she chased the girls around, laughing and trying to tickle them.

Enid loved the attention they brought her and was quite promiscuous with the male company she kept. She regularly told stories of her escapades to the dismay of El's mother, Enid's daughter, Betty.

El, on the other hand, detested the attention they bought her. She often wore her tinted reading glasses even if she wasn't reading to stop the admiration of unwanted admirers.

El huffed as she gathered her books into a neat pile to carry them to her bedroom to try and rectify the damage done to them with her hair dryer.

As she stood back up before him, the stranger tracked her movements with his eyes. They settled immediately onto hers as he shifted awkwardly on his feet. He swallowed as he stood staring down at her petite frame, causing her to get nervous and flustered before turning her head away.

Tom was a six-foot-two beanpole, as his friends often called him whilst making jibes about his appearance. He was the epitome of a typical-looking student with his scruffy auburn mop of wavy hair that flopped down into his eyes, knitted jumpers from his ever-attentive mother and a pair of washed-out dark blue denim jeans.

He was in the first year of his four-year PhD English literature studies. His research for his thesis on "The Symbolism of Shakespearian Literature" had started at a full pace, taking up most of his time, and this was the first real break from it he had had in months.

Tom had just tagged along with the rest of his brother's friends as they all followed Dotty back to her home for "the after party". Tom was suspicious that his brother was yet again bedding a student as he recognised Dotty from when she had come out of Charlie's office, but he didn't want to broach the subject. He wasn't much for parties, but Charlie had insisted that he take a break and join them at the faculty bar for a few drinks, which had turned into a bar crawl to pick up Dotty.

Charlie somehow finished his politics PhD at Cambridge and became a lecturer in the subject. Tom was bound to follow his brother into academia. He was always seeking approval from their father, who was also a professor. Charlie was "the golden child", following in his father's political footsteps, leaving Tom to wallow in the shadows with his fondness for literature.

In her flustered state, El quickly scurried past Tom to head upstairs. He watched her walk by, her chin resting on her books to keep them steady. He couldn't keep his eyes off her as she awkwardly walked up the stairs. Tom followed her as her long, flowing black cardigan billowed out in front of him as she hurried up the cream-carpeted steps.

As El reached her bedroom, she realised she couldn't open the door with her hands occupied, but before she could put the books down, a long arm reached past her to open it. She followed the lines of bulging veins up his slender yet muscular forearm and looked up to see the guy from downstairs smiling at her as he gestured for her to enter.

"After you," Tom said politely.

She couldn't hear him as she still had her earbuds wedged securely into her ears, but the movement of his mouth, the pleasant smile he gave her after he spoke.

There was something about him. Something in his dark blue eyes caused goosebumps across her skin to rise on her arms and the hairs on the back of her neck to stand up. His eyes held a hidden depth to them like the Great Blue Hole off the coast of Belize. That dark blue sinkhole that cuts through the ocean and drags you towards it, daring you to take a peek at what's lurking in the darkness. Whether the goosebumps that now marred El's skin were good or not, she wasn't entirely sure, but whatever it was, she suddenly felt very self-conscious and nervous around him. The prickling feeling of her hair standing on end warned her there was something dangerous about him that shouldn't be ignored.

El smiled politely, trying to hide her nerves as she entered her room to place the books on her study table.

Her bedroom was like any other twenty-year-old's, or so she thought.

A double bed in the middle of the light-yellow coloured room, pushed up against the wall, with a sunflower pattern duvet and pillow set. Her clothes were neatly folded, sat in the middle of her bed and were ready to be placed away in her drawers and wardrobes. Posters of classical musicians adorned one of her bedroom walls to the side of her bed. Her violin case rested against the corner of her room next to her music stand. The music sheetbook opened to her favourite classical piece she had been practising earlier. The room was dimly lit with just her table lamp as she had been studying before she heard her sister laughing whilst bursting drunkenly into the house.

El had rushed downstairs in her PJs, wrapping a cardigan around herself, to grab her books before they were ruined by the "guests". She hoped to have the house to herself for the night, but apparently, that was out of the question.

El was the typical classics enthusiast, the nerdy girl who was the overachiever, the quiet one who didn't have time for lots of friends and socialising anymore. She liked things just so and hated chaos. If she were truthful, it was most likely why she didn't approve of her sister that much, but you can't choose who you're related to.

El took out her earbuds and placed them carefully into their case before turning around to see the guy standing in her doorway.

He watched her patiently with interest, waiting to see if she would invite him in.

Tom's eyes had already scanned over her entire room, taking in every little detail he could absorb about her. He always believed that a bedroom, someone's personal space of solitude, said more about them than an entire hour-long conversation ever could.

She was obviously a neat freak, with everything having a specific place it needed to live in. Her stack of books told Tom that as she unconsciously straightened them by lining up the corners whilst placing them down. Her room was exceptionally tidy for a young woman. She was also obviously a student by the number of textbooks, notepads, neatly lined pens, highlighters, and pencils on her desk.

Tom carefully took a mental note of what subject the books covered. Her bedspread told him what her favourite flower was and that she loved the colour yellow, but her black cardigan was what puzzled him slightly. It was the only darkness in a room filled with bright colours, which was strange. The neatly folded pile of clothes on her bed were all mainly bright colours; nothing was dark apart from that single piece of clothing that she had wrapped around herself. He also observed that she had very few photos, none of herself, just of family and a few close friends, it seemed. She was apparently a bit of a loner, much like himself.

"Erm... I'm sorry about your jumper... Would you?" El's voice was quiet as she spoke. She hesitated before quickly scurrying past him out of her bedroom and into another room up the hallway.

Tom's eyes followed her, but he didn't move as El promptly appeared from the other room, holding a navy hoodie over the crook of her arm. As she approached him, she took hold of it in her hand and held it out at arm's length, ensuring she kept her distance.

"This is my dad's, but... it's probably too big... but... erm... at least it's dry," she shrugged her shoulders, thrusting the hoodie towards the guy more and gesturing for him to take it as she tried to hide the nervous tremor of her hand, keeping her eyes focused on the material in her hand.

"Oh... You don't need to offer me your dad's clothes. Honestly, it's fine."

Tom smiled at her, not caring that his jumper was wet or that he now stunk of beer that would soon turn to that awful stale smell.

El waved it even more at him, just wanting him to take it.

"I insist. Dad won't miss it. He has lots of clothes," her voice was a bit more forceful now as she shoved the hoodie towards him and briefly looked up at him.

Tom looked from her eyes to her hand and back again. She didn't hold his eye contact for long. He knew he was making her nervous; he could see the slight tremble of her hand as she held the hoodie.

"Okay... Thank you," Tom said as he took hold of the hoodie with his long fingers.

El made sure not to touch him and focused on his hand, ensuring she didn't. She didn't like to touch most people, let alone strangers.

"Is there somewhere I can change?" Tom asked, hopeful that she would invite him into her room. El bit her bottom lip, mulling over the options quickly in her head.

Tom's eyes instantly focused on her mouth as he unconsciously licked his lips in response to her innocent action.

He wondered what she would taste like.

Could he make her moan by sucking on that plump piece of skin and grazing his teeth against it?

"There's a bathroom down there, the last door on the left."

El pointed down the corridor before she passed Tom and went back into her room, closing the door behind her. She didn't look up at him as she did it and kept her eyes on the white wooden door of her bedroom. He made her uncomfortable; she didn't want to be rude and hated rudeness, but she didn't want attention from a guy. She didn't want attention from anyone.

Tom sighed, and his shoulders slumped slightly as the door was shut in his face. She made it clear she wasn't interested, but he wanted to change that; he needed to change that.

After Tom had changed, he walked past her bedroom door, pausing to lean his ear against it to listen. He could hear her moving around her room, flicking through book pages and tutting before a hair dryer was turned on.

Tom sighed, briefly placing his hand on the door for a moment, taking a deep breath before turning away and heading back downstairs.

Tom worried that maybe it had been his fault that her books were ruined with his beer. If he had drunk it instead of walking around with it in his hand, or even if he had never accepted it when Charlie handed it to him in the kitchen of this stranger's house, he wouldn't have upset the girl who lived here.

But would he have even met her if he didn't have the beer in his hand?

In any case, he wanted to make it up to her and had already formulated a plan for what he would do. This shy, nervous girl with beautiful eyes instantly captured something within him to want to see her again. This plan Tom was formulating was the perfect excuse.

Tom walked downstairs into the booming sound of dance music, looking around for Charlie to tell him he was leaving. It was late, and he had a lot of work to do.

Charlie appeared out of the pantry, adjusting his trousers as Tom entered the kitchen. Dotty stumbled out behind him, giggling as she wiped the corners of her mouth with the back of her hand. Tom sneered in disgust at his brother, who smirked back at him.

"I'm leaving - see you tomorrow, Charlie," his words were short and curt as he walked away.

"Hey, man. Wait up!" Charlie called out before quickly turning back to Dotty. He grabbed her face for a quick peck on the lips before going after Tom.

Charlie had to jog to catch up to his younger brother, who was halfway down the street already.

"Where did you disappear off to?" Charlie asked as he wrapped his arm around Tom's shoulders, heading back in the direction of Tom's flat.

"Urgh," Tom shrugged Charlie's arm off him. "Don't breathe on me - you stink of alcohol and that girl."

Charlie chuckled, "Oh, I stink? Says the guy carrying a beer-soaked jumper." He shoved Tom playfully with his shoulder as he spoke, "So where did you go? I looked for you."

Tom shook his head, "As if you'd look for me... You were too busy getting your cock sucked."

Charlie laughed loudly as he threw his head back, slightly drunk. "Ha... Your just jealous that a girl wants to suck my cock."

Tom stopped abruptly on the pavement and turned to stare at Charlie.

"She's your student Charlie for fucks sake," his voice raised slightly as his anger bubbled.

"And what does that matter?" Charlie asked as he shrugged his shoulders.

"Do you realise how much trouble you could get in?"

Charlie sighed and rolled his eyes. "We're both adults' man. Chill."

"Chill? Are you fucking serious?" Tom seethed with anger. He couldn't stand that Charlie couldn't see that what he was doing was wrong. "She's what... ten years younger than you and your student... You're in a position of trust, and you're breaking that."

"Come on, man... It's just a bit of fun."

"You are such an ass, Charlie," Tom turned back around and kept walking with stomping steps down the pavement.

"Hey! Tom, stop!" Charlie called out to him.

"Fuck off, Charlie, and leave me alone!" Tom answered as he continued to walk without looking back at his brother.

"Don't be like that," Charlie jogged up next to him. He knew he'd pissed Tom off. Charlie couldn't understand why he was getting so upset about it.

"Look... I'll call it off with Dot if that makes you happy."

"Hmph... I doubt that." Tom stopped again and sighed. "Look... Just don't make it so obvious, okay? You fucking your student in private is one thing, but snogging her face off in public will get you in trouble when the wrong person sees you."

Charlie patted him on the shoulder. "Aww, is my little brother worried about me?"

Tom shook his head and chuckled. "Someone has to be... Now fuck off. I want to go home." He shoved Charlie in the chest and walked off, chuckling quietly.

They may have fought constantly as brothers often do with sibling rivalry, but they still relied on each other and trusted one another.

"Love you, brother!" Charlie called out after him, to which Tom replied by shoving his middle finger in the air. "I know you love me too, no matter what obscene gestures you make," Charlie's sing-song voice echoed behind Tom as he pulled the hoodie up around his head and kept walking.

...

El had managed to dry most of her books, but they were now stained with brown patches. She sighed. It was exceptionally late now, and she was exhausted as it was close to three in the morning. The music downstairs had gone quiet, so she assumed everyone had left. Grabbing her glass from her table, she headed downstairs for a glass of milk.

As she walked through the living room, El saw Dotty passed out on the sofa. She paused and watched her sister sleeping peacefully on her back with her legs flopping over the armrest. She took the blanket off the back of the sofa and gently placed it over her, ensuring she would be warm enough. El smiled quietly to herself before she went into the kitchen.

She sighed when she saw the state of it, her shoulders slumping in annoyance.

Beer cans and bottles were all over the countertop. Open packets of crisps strewn across the floor, covering the laminate in little sharp shards of salty goodness. She was tempted to start cleaning, but it wasn't her mess, so for once, she left it.

After pouring some milk, she tiptoed upstairs and got into bed, placing the glass next to her on her bedside table. She pulled the current book she was reading, Jane Eyre, onto her lap to read a little more. After a few paragraphs, she took a sip of milk and settled on her pillow. Sleep threatened to take over, and she hated falling asleep and losing her page.

El lay in bed looking across at her glass of milk in the soft light of her bedside lamp; she wondered if her father might notice that his hoodie was missing. She hoped not, as she probably would get in trouble for giving it to a stranger, even if he was cute but still kind of creepy. It would also mean she would have to drop Dotty in it for the party, which she wasn't prepared to do.

Hopefully, he won't notice, El thought to herself as she placed the bookmark inside her book to mark her place and placed the book back onto her bedside table.

El placed her hand over her stomach, where a dull ache had started. She rubbed her fingers across it in circles, hoping to soothe away the tension in her muscles from getting too stressed.

It eased off slowly as El relaxed, and her eyes grew heavy. It wasn't long before her eyes drifted shut, and she fell into a deep sleep, dreaming about a tall figure shrouded in shadows with piercing blue eyes watching her in the dark.

Meanwhile, Tom put some clothes on to wash, changed into his "special" clothes, and headed out to his car in the garage around the back of his building.

The garage was one of the reasons he chose this flat. He needed the privacy of seclusion and somewhere secure to park his car from prying eyes.

He knew where to go, so he quickly changed the number plates on his car and opened the garage door. Tom then edged the car out of the garage before leaving the engine running as he closed the garage door, locking it behind him. As he jumped back in his car, Tom's compulsions kicked in tenfold, and he sped off, driving out of the parking area behind the building and onto the road.

He had been so good for months, but that girl, that craving he tried to shove down inside, raised its ugly head again, making his palms itch, and his fingers twitch with excitement.

He drove an hour outside of Cambridge before reaching his destination, a secluded area of a quiet 'B' road.

As he pulled up into the tarmacked layby, the car opposite flashed its headlights. Tom knew the routine and did the same back before turning the car so that his headlights trained across the back seats of the other vehicle and turned his engine off.

Tom leaned across to his glove box and grabbed what he needed from inside it before waiting a few moments and getting out of his car. He left his headlights on to give himself some better lighting for viewing purposes before closing the door behind him and heading over.

The night air was crisp as it hit Tom's face, chilling his cheeks and nose as misted, fogged breaths escaped and vapourised into the darkness that the headlights didn't reach.

His feet crunched across the loose pieces of gravel that had collected on the tarmac as he walked casually towards the other car as a few pieces of litter blew across his path.

Tom slipped the items from his glove box into his back pocket as he walked towards the car that had started rocking side to side on its axles, his form cast in shadow as the headlights acted as a backing light.

In the back of the car, the couple had started going at it like two rabbits. Two naked bodies entwined as the woman lay across the back seat with the guy buried between her legs. Her tits bounced up and down as he thrust his cock into her with a fully exposed view of what they were doing.

Blood started to rush to Tom's twitching cock as he stood to the side of the car towards the boot and watched them.

He liked to watch. He enjoyed listening to them as they fucked. It didn't matter who it was. He just needed the release at this point, some sexual gratification before his other impulses took over.

However, this time, frustratingly, he couldn't get fully hard.

As he closed his eyes to concentrate on the moans and groans coming from the open car window, all he could see were her eyes looking back at him. He thought about her bottom lip as she bit it. The sounds that he could tease from her mouth as he fucked her.

As soon as she had looked at him, his whole world had been captured by her. She was in the centre, everything else of insignificance floating around her as she bathed in sunlight. Tom kneeled at her feet, doing anything to please her. He wanted to worship her.

As Tom opened his eyes, a furious rage built within him that it wasn't her in front of him.

These strangers, these disgusting people, tainted his world with their presence.

It should be her here.

It should be her here with him.

He squeezed his eyes tight and unclenched his fists. His fingernails had dug into his palms, but Tom didn't care about the pain; it helped to ground him in the moment.

As he took a deep breath, he calmly retrieved the latex gloves from his back pocket and put them on before opening the car door.

2.

"Oh god, have you seen this?" John tapped on the newspaper story he was reading as he sat in his conservatory, waiting for his Sunday roast to be served.

"There are some sick fucks in this world," he stated.

"Oh, language darling... is that really pre-dinner conversation?" Anne complained as she rolled her eyes, looking between Tom and Charlie as they sat at the dinner table opposite each other.

Their mother, Anne, walked back and forth between the kitchen, carrying the serving dishes and plates full of freshly cooked and steaming food. There were buttered and minted garden peas, baby-buttered carrots, roast potatoes, and roasted lamb now all placed on the dining table, ready to be served.

"If I want to say fuck in my own home, I am allowed."

"Tsk...Not in front of the boys, John," Anne sighed as she straightened out the tablecloth by smoothing her hand over it.

"Urgh... Anne. The boys are grown men, not children anymore," John protested, shaking his head as he rose from his leather armchair in the conservatory.

Charlie smirked at his father from his seat at the dining table as John walked to the table to take his place at the head of it.

On the other side of the table, opposite Charlie, Tom flashed a sympathetic smile to his mother. She put up with a lot from her husband but didn't seem to mind. After all, they had been together for over thirty years.

John slapped the newspaper down onto the table next to his plate, causing Anne to jump slightly as she stood, waiting to serve the dinner she had prepared.

"Two missing people's bodies were found, dragged up from a car in Rutland Water... Throats slit..."

"John! Enough! Please," Anne interrupted.

John huffed as he scraped his dining chair across the slate floor of their dining room before taking his seat and tapping his fingers against the newspaper.

"At least their families will get some closure now after they've been missing for a week. Shame about the kid, though," Charlie chimed in as he held out his plate for his mother to take and dish his food onto.

The story had been across the news for the past three days.

A couple had gone missing, leaving their child with their grandparents overnight, and never returned to collect them. It was a mystery as to what had happened to them until police searched a local lake and discovered their car with their bodies inside.

Anne took Charlie's plate, tutting, before placing the prepared vegetables onto it and passing it back to him.

"That poor child will have to grow up an orphan now... Such a shame."

"Exactly. Too many psychopaths walking around if you ask me," John scoffed before changing the subject. "Anyway, how's work, Charles? Those students giving you a hard time?" John asked as he took hold of the stainless-steel carving knife and meat fork from the table next to the plate of roasted lamb.

Tom choked and spluttered on his red wine, having to take another sip to clear his throat.

"Oh, dear... Would you like some water, pet?"

Anne instantly moved to stand behind Tom, patting his back gently with a worried look on her overly attentive face.

"No, thank you. I'm fine, mum. Just went down the wrong hole, that's all," Tom said before clearing his throat and turning his head to smile at her.

"That's what she said," Charlie chuckled before taking a large gulp from his wine glass and looking at Tom over the rim, raising a suggestive eyebrow.

Tom shook his head as he placed his wine glass back on the table, his fingers lingering on the stem as he looked down at his empty plate. Tom focused on the reflective gleam of light on the ceramic and how it changed slightly with the angle as he tilted his head, studying it. It reminded him of how things had looked a week ago as he had done what he had.

John just rolled his eyes at Charlie's innuendo as he plunged the meat fork into the lamb to hold it steady before he sliced the carving knife across the joint of meat, slicing it into thin pieces.

"Tom?"

Anne broke Tom from his memories as she gestured for his plate with her open palm. He smiled up at his mother gratefully as he passed it to her.

Tom's eyes roamed across the table as he absentmindedly fiddled with his cutlery. His eyes settled on the lamb as his father cut it slowly, dragging the carving knife across the flesh, splitting the cooked muscles and tendons in half. It oozed bloodied clear liquid as John sliced down through it with the blade, leaving a bloodied pool of juice underneath it on the silver serving plate.

Tom's grip on his fork tightened in his hand as his breathing deepened.

It hadn't been mentioned in the newspaper story that it wasn't only their throats that had been cut. Other details had been omitted by the police that only the killer would also know.

If someone were to look upon the bodies of the couple, they would see their empty eye sockets looking back at them, where their eyes had been removed and taken.

The police hadn't managed to find them and were drawn to the conclusion that the killer had taken them as trophies.

"Tom? Thomas?" His father's voice was getting increasingly frustrated, breaking Tom from staring at the meat.

"One or two slices?"

Tom blinked as he refocused on his father, releasing his grip on the fork and placing his hand flat on the table beside it.

"Oh... Two, please," Tom smiled at John, who just sighed and shook his head at his youngest son.

"You're not working too hard, are you darling? You seem distracted," Anne's voice was concerned as she passed Tom his plate back, which now had two slices of roasted lamb and generous helpings of vegetables on it.

"Pfft, he's always working too hard," Charlie smirked. "All work and no play makes Tom a dull boy... Isn't that right, brother?"

Tom just rolled his eyes at Charlie's comment, giving him a contemptuous look.

If only Charlie knew, his brother was anything but dull.

...

"Another book?" Dotty asked as she passed El another package over the back of the sofa she had collected from the doorstep for her. It was wrapped in yellow tissue paper with a sunflower delicately placed within the bright yellow ribbon holding it all together, just as all the others had been.

El traced the ribbon with her index finger before removing the sunflower and running her fingers over the smooth petals.

"That's three this week. Who is this admirer of yours?"

El shrugged her shoulders at Dotty's question. She hadn't asked his name and didn't know that Dotty was screwing his brother, Charlie. She didn't even realise that he had paid that much attention when he stood at her bedroom door.

Maybe I should have invited him in to change after all. At least I might have found out his name, she thought.

The day after she had lent him her father's hoodie, she had found it on their doorstep, washed and neatly folded in a brown paper bag with a brand-new copy of "A Global History of Ancient Worlds by Eivind Heldaas Seland". The textbook was wrapped in yellow tissue paper with a single sunflower poking out the top of the paper bag. It was a replacement copy of one of the books the beer had ruined, with a thank you note.

> *Thank you for lending me the top.*
> *It has been washed, ironed, and returned to you.*
> *This replacement of your textbook will make up*
> *for my beer ruining your copy.*

"Don't you want to know what his name is?" Dotty asked her sister. "I can probably find out, ya know."

El hesitated.

Did she want to know?

Was she really even that bothered who he was?

She was too busy to have someone new in her life.

What was the point in finding out his name?

"I can ask Charlie. He came here with him, so…" Dotty leaned over the sofa, placing her chin on El's shoulder. "You know you wanna…" Dotty's voice trailed off as her breath tickled against El's ear.

Dotty wanted her sister to have someone or something else in her life besides their family or practising her violin.

El took a deep breath before she sighed, letting her shoulders slump despondently.

"I'm too busy. I mean, it's nice, but…"

Dotty clicked her tongue against the roof of her mouth and stood back up, patting El on her shoulder.

"But nothing. I'm going to text Charlie and ask," she stated as she pulled her phone out of her back pocket.

"NO! No, please don't," El spun around on the sofa to look at her sister with pleading eyes.

Dotty let out an irritated breath but stilled her fingers from typing on her phone as she raised an eyebrow, looking at her.

She could see that El had that familiar panicked look in her eyes. Dotty didn't want to upset her, so she gave in, stuffing her phone back in her pocket.

"Fine," she sighed, "but if you change your mind, you just have to ask me."

El smiled briefly at her before she stood from the sofa and took the book and flower upstairs with her. She held the new textbook close to her chest as she entered her bedroom to replace her damaged copy of "Ancient Mythological Images and their Interpretation" and put the flower in the vase with the others the mystery guy had gifted her on her desk.

Only three more textbooks and the stranger would have completely replaced all the damaged books.

El swapped the books over on her desk, took the damaged one downstairs, and went to the recycling bin at the side of the house.

After placing the book inside the blue-lidded bin, she turned around, and a black car driving away caught her attention.

A flash of auburn hair in the driver's seat made her quickly hurry to the gate at the end of the path.

El squinted her eyes to see if it was who she thought it was as she held on to the metal gate and leaned forward, stretching her neck to get a better look.

The black car had stopped at the junction of her cul-de-sac for a moment before driving away.

Tom had waited in his car, hoping El would come out of the house to find the package on the doorstep. She was the one who had discovered the other two.

He just wanted a glimpse of her. It would be enough to tie him over until the next time he laid eyes upon her.

Unfortunately, to Tom's disappointment, Dotty had come out and found it. He sat clutching the steering wheel so tightly with displeasure that his knuckles had blanched white as he twisted his fingers around it, making the leather creak under his grip.

He waited a few moments longer before deciding it was time to leave. Tom could see the neighbour's curtains twitching in his peripheral vision as they looked out to see who was sitting in the car outside their house.

As he started to drive away, he looked one last time to see a flash of the mousey-coloured brown hair coming out of the side of the house.

He didn't stop, just in case she had clocked him, but El was by the garden gate looking down the road at his car when he looked in the rear-view mirror.

Tom's heart thundered in his chest at the slightest glimpse of her.

It took everything in him not to slam the car into reverse and speed back towards her.

But he knew he couldn't. He knew he just had to bide his time.

It wouldn't be long until the second year of his PhD studies would start, and he would need to teach undergraduate students. He had already learnt El's name from a Facebook search for her sister, Dorothy Martin.

Dotty was prevalent on social media, and more pictures of El were on Dotty's profile.

Tom had printed off all the images with El in them, carefully cutting out each photo of her to pin up in his wardrobe, creating a collage of the beautiful, mousey brown hair-coloured girl with contrasting, captivating eyes.

As he went through Dotty's account, it was clear that El wasn't active on social media.

El had a profile page, but it had no information on it other than her name and a single picture of her violin as her profile picture.

On the other hand, Dotty's page was full of information, including congratulating her little sister for top marks in all her A levels. She then had a post from the same month congratulating El for gaining her place at Cambridge.

The dates confused Tom. It was over a year later that she started university.

It bothered him that he couldn't find the answer as to why she had taken a gap year. Nothing stood out that seemed strange, and there was no mention of it on Dotty's page.

In fact, for that whole period, there had barely been a mention of El at all for almost the entire year.

It was easy enough for Tom to find out more about El. What she was studying, her university schedule, her grades, her birthday, everything he could find out about her from sneaking into the university registry office one night and hacking into the computer system. But still, there was nothing about this mysterious gap year.

It annoyed him that he didn't know and could not find the information about why from his own research.

Next academic year, El could be in his lectures. He could be her lecturer. The only problem was that he wasn't in control of the timetables for next year, and he had yet to figure out a way to ensure he would be her lecturer.

As Tom arrived at his flat, he headed inside and locked the front door behind him before walking straight into his bedroom and stripping off all his clothes. He stood naked before his wardrobe and opened the oak doors, revealing what was inside.

Taking hold of a box of matchsticks, he took one out and struck it, lighting some scented tea lights he had brought and placing them in the holders that matched the ones in El's room, filling the air with the scent of vanilla and jasmine which he had smelt coming from her room.

He blew out the matchstick flame and put it on his bedside table before sitting on the edge of his bed opposite the open wardrobe. His legs were spread wide, his feet flat on the floor, and his toes curled against the soft cream carpet before relaxing.

He straightened his back, his head facing forward as his eyes roamed over all his pictures of El.

Some were older, and some were new, but he wanted more. He would need to get some fresh photos of El, which meant buying a new camera. His old one would never do. The images would come out too grainy.

As his eyes scanned over the shrine he had built for her, his eyes rested on the mason jar usually used for preserving foods like jams and pickles, but this one was preserving something else entirely.

The candlelight danced across the glass, creating rays of light and shadows, changing the colour of the eyes inside.

If Tom squinted enough, they were almost the same colours as hers.

Not quite the right shades, but they would do for now.

His cock stiffened up against his leg as he thought more about her.

He would be back in the library tomorrow to wait for her. He needed to find out what her daily routine was.

Tom could picture it now as he closed his eyes, her different eye colours dancing in the darkness behind his closed eyelids.

One aqua blue. One dark chestnut.

He would remove a book from the shelf just as she did on the other side of the bookshelf.

Their eyes would meet, and she would smile at him before biting her lip. That beautiful plump lip of hers that he wanted to sink his teeth into.

Her desire was evident on her face as she moved along the row of books. Her unique, contrasting eyes were visible in the gap between the books and the shelf. Tom would follow her, finding her with a book in her hand, leaning against the end of the shelves, waiting for him.

She would be wearing a yellow sundress. Her mousey brown hair framed her face as her fingers lightly traced over the pages of "The Works of William Shakespeare".

Tom would stop in front of her, taking the book delicately from her hands.

She'd ask him to read to her one of his favourite sonnets. He wanted to impress her, so he closed the book and recited Sonnet 116 as she backed up around a darkened corner against the shelf.

> *'Let me not to the marriage of true minds*
> *Admit impediments. Love is not love*
> *Which alters when it alteration finds,*
> *Or bends with the remover to remove.'*

El would hang on his every word. Her desire growing with every syllable he spoke.

Tom kept constant eye contact with her, watching her writhe beneath him as he leant into her more, whispering the words as his breath ghosted across her lips and he dropped the book from his hand.

The thumping noise did not distract them from each other for a second.

> *'O no! it is an ever-fixed mark*
> *That looks on tempests and is never shaken;*
> *It is the star to every wandering bark,*
> *Whose worth's unknown, although his height be taken.'*

She wouldn't be able to take any more as her need for him would take over.

El would put her hands into his hair and grip it tightly at the roots, bringing him down before she pressed her lips to his.

Tom would continue the sonnet between kisses across her soft skin, whispering breathlessly against her lips and neck as his mouth brought her undefined pleasures.

> *'Love's not time's fool, though rosy lips and cheeks*
> *Within his bending sickle's compass come;'*

Tom would then move his hands under her dress, lifting it and pushing his knee between her legs to settle in between the warmth of her thighs as he stood between her legs. He would glide his hands down her body and grip the back of her thighs tightly before lifting her and resting her backside against a shelf, scattering books across the floor behind El.

> *'Love alters not with his brief hours and weeks,*
> *But bears it out even to the edge of doom.'*

He would kiss her neck, licking and sucking in that sensitive spot just below her ear that he knew she would love, before whispering the final words against her soft skin as he allowed his teeth to scrap against her flesh.

> *'If this be error and upon me prov'd,*
> *I never writ, nor no man ever lov'd.'*

El would palm his cock through his trousers before quickly fumbling to undo them.

His hard length would spring free, and she would groan as she felt him pressing against her bare core.

She would be ready for him, dripping with anticipation
as her juices ran down her legs before wrapping them around his waist. His fingers would dig into her skin as she rolled her hips against him, grinding her soaking folds against his pulsing shaft.

Leaning back, he pulled the top of her dress down to expose her breasts, plunging his mouth to her nipple as he sunk his fingers into her sex, readying her before replacing them with his cock.

He would use his thumb to add to her pleasure and rub her clit in sensual circles, bringing her the ecstasy she deserved over and over.

Tom could see her dilated pupils looking back at him, feel her skin against his body as he pounded into her, hear her moaning his name, taste her juices as he brought his fingers back to his mouth to suck on them.

His imagination drove him wild with desire for her as he pumped his cock furiously in his hand, imagining fucking her.

Yes, Tom. Fuck me. Make me yours, Tom. I always want to be yours and yours alone.

Tom's eyes flew open as he stood and stepped over to the wardrobe. One hand stroked her face on a picture of her, the other continuing to stroke his quivering shaft as he leaned his face as close as possible.

"I'll do anything for you, El... Anything," he whispered against her picture.

Just love me, Tom. Love me, and I'm yours.

He felt the welcomed tightening of the muscles in his thighs, the heavy pressure in his groin deepening as he slowed his movements, drawing out every fantasy feeling of her, wishing she would whisper the words against his ear.

I love you, Tom.

Instantly, his body jerked and spasmed as he unloaded into his hand, his lungs fighting for breath from hearing those words in his head as he groaned out loudly into the candle-lit room.

Her sweet voice had pushed him over the edge into the oblivion of pleasure, making him see stars as he juddered and fought to catch his breath.

The sweat beaded on his forehead and chest as he stepped back away to grab some tissues from his bedside table, wrapping the tip of his cock in the soft, absorbent paper.

Once cleaned, the screwed-up, sticky tissue thrown in the waste bin by his bedside table, Tom stepped back to the wardrobe and blew the candles out, watching as the smoke rose and swirled around the air, framing the eyes that were looking back at him in a soft white mist.

Tomorrow, El should be in the library. All he needed to do was wait for her.

3.

El continued to read, highlighting her text with her yellow highlighter as she concentrated on absorbing the words.

Latin was her weakest subject, and it didn't help that the library was so busy. She had purposefully gotten there extra early to try and get her favourite table in the corner, away from everyone, so that she could concentrate. At least she had succeeded at getting her favourite spot.

Still, after around thirty minutes of relative quiet, more students gathered in the library for cramming sessions, making concentrating increasingly tricky.

El placed her earbuds in her ears to try to drown out the distraction with some classical music, but with the constant movement around her, it just wasn't helping that much.

She sighed as she sat back in the chair, lifting her reading glasses to rub her eyes. She considered whether to give up and just go home; she had already been there for an hour and a half with little progress, the black words now starting to blur together into a jumbled mess.

Tom had been waiting in the library as soon as it had opened for El to walk through the doors, hoping that today she would. He watched from behind one of the computers near the entrance as he tried to get a few research papers together to go through later.

His heart leapt into his mouth when she appeared, catching his breath as his eyes tracked her movements.

El's mousey brown hair flowed around her face as she walked past him, not noticing he was there. She wore a light blue shirt with long sleeves and tight, faded blue jeans. Her yellow backpack was secured to her on her back; it bobbed up and down as she walked with purpose towards her desired destination. Her eyes were covered by her tinted reading glasses, much to Tom's disappointment. He craved the reality of seeing her unique eyes again and not just the fantasy he had created in his head.

Tom quickly saved his work and logged off the computer, grabbing his bag from the floor and stuffing his notes inside. His palms started sweating, and his mouth went dry as he tracked El across the library, ensuring she didn't disappear from his sight.

After El had walked in, she found a table in the back corner of the library. Tom managed to get a seat at the other end of the same table, diagonally across from her, without her noticing him. He sat down quietly and placed his bag next to his legs before taking out a few books, his notebook and pen.

He had kept his head down, pretending to be absorbed in his book whilst taking notes. But every few minutes, Tom glanced across at her. He couldn't help himself as his pen stilled against the paper of his notebook, creating a blob of ink on the page as it seeped into the fibres.

El was so close yet distant to him as she concentrated on her work, not noticing him there. He watched her every move intently during the brief glances he dared to take.

The movement of her fingers as she fiddled absentmindedly with the yellow highlighter in her hand, clicking and unclicking the lid with her thumb. How she would always take a deep breath before turning a page and tilt her head to the right as if she were chasing the words on the page.

Everything excited him as he observed her little habits and quirks.

Her eyes focused on every word she highlighted as her tongue darted out to wet her lips.

When she took a sip of water from her bottle, Tom had to adjust himself a few times, pulling at the material of his trousers underneath the table and shifting in the seat to widen his stance. He watched as her head tilted back, and her throat bobbed with every gulp she took.

El's hand gripped her water bottle firmly, ensuring she didn't spill anything onto the precious paper below her hand.

Tom couldn't help but imagine her hand wrapped around his cock, and her throat bobbing under his palm as she swallowed down every last drop of his warm seed that he spilt into her mouth, coating her tongue.

As he observed her sitting back in the chair, lifting her glasses to rub her eyes, he couldn't help noticing the scar on her arm as her sleeve dropped slightly, revealing it.

He hadn't seen it before as her cardigan had covered it whilst he was at her house, and as there were no recent pictures of El that he could find, this was new and must have happened in the period of missing information about El.

But now that she had stretched her arm up, the light blue sleeve of her shirt dropped slightly, exposing the faint red line that tracked up towards her elbow and out of sight under her sleeve. It intrigued Tom, making him wonder how she had come to injure herself badly enough to leave such a deep-set scar.

As she moved her hand away from her face and readjusted her glasses on the bridge of her nose, El's eyes travelled across the room, catching Tom looking at her. She quickly averted her gaze, looking back at her textbook as Tom swore internally to himself for getting caught staring.

It was now or never.

Tom needed to cover his tracks about being here, looking at her, staring at her. It was the push he needed to actually talk to her again.

He got up quickly, his heart hammering in his chest with nerves as he headed to her side of the table, crouching down next to her.

El was in panic mode as a sudden sinking feeling washed over her, causing her breathing to quicken.

This guy, this stranger, had been leaving gifts of replacement books outside her home. He hadn't even told her his name, and now he crouched beside her, making his presence known.

El froze, unable to string a sentence together as her anxiety kicked in, causing her throat to involuntarily tighten as she stared straight ahead. She hoped he would remain this anonymous guy in her head who left replacement books for her, like some kind of book-giving Father Christmas. Someone that she didn't need to connect with or acknowledge as a part of her life, a fantasy she could pretend was some benevolent creature that didn't require anything from her.

This all made it too real with him there.

Tom placed his hand flat on the table next to her book as he leaned forward slightly to get her to look at him.

"Hi."

El swallowed as she saw him mouth the word from the corner of her eye. He was near her but not too close; he gave her some space, at least.

She put her book down on the table, pressed pause on her phone to stop her music and removed her earbuds to place them in the open case next to her book before she turned in her chair to look at him, forcing herself to be polite.

With his height, he was basically at eye level with her as he crouched down, his knees splayed widely apart for balance. Tom used his hand on the table to steady himself, but he was effectively trapping her in her seat now that she faced him because of where he had placed it, caging her in with his body.

"Hi," he whispered again as he smiled at her, trying to hide the nervous excitement in his voice.

El focused in on his mouth as she watched his thin lips move, her heart racing with adrenaline as her fight or flight response clawed to kick in.

"I thought it was you. I didn't know if I should come over and say hello, but..." Tom swallowed nervously as his mouth started to run away from him. His free hand had a mind of its own as it gestured about as he babbled with excitement at talking to her. "I hope you don't mind me coming over or that I am very slowly replacing your books. If I had the money, I would get them all at once for you, but you know... student life, no money... Ehehe."

Tom wasn't about to reveal that he had already brought every replacement book for her immediately the next day after the beer-spilling incident. Or that he went to a craft store to match the yellow tissue paper to the colour of her bedroom walls. Or that he had found a florist with a constant supply of what he assumed were her favourite flowers, considering sunflowers were all over her bedspread, hoping she would appreciate the extra gift of apology.

That would just be weird.

Plus, Tom would use every opportunity to go to El's home, hoping to see her, meaning he had to play the long game and drag this out by leaving one book at a time.

"So, what are you studying? It must be classics or something similar as the books I'm replacing suggest, and what you're reading now," he gestured down to the open book on the table as he continued to talk. "Is that Reading Latin? God, I hated Latin in school, but I do love to read."

El smiled politely, but her eyes never met his, trying to remain as calm on the outside as possible as he continued the verbal diarrhoea assault on her ears.

Her anxiety was making her freeze like a deer caught in headlights, unsure of whether to turn and run or just take the hit and bullseye the windshield as her eyes danced around, trying to find an exit.

Tom constantly watched her, trying to get her to look at him as his head dipped and rose, but her eyes avoided his. He thought that perhaps she was just shy like she had been at her house.

He didn't notice her clenched hand around her pen, her nails digging into the fabric of her sleeve, or the rapid pulse in her neck as he continued talking at her.

"Oh, God... I just realised I haven't even introduced myself to you. I'm Tom, Tom Hendricks." He held out his hand to her as she looked down at it.

She swallowed as she looked from his hand to his eyes and back again, taking in the length of his fingers reaching towards her like some sort of olive branch.

El was an expert at suppressing her anxiety quickly in public. Most of the time, she would save it up for when she got home to have a meltdown in her bathroom in private, locked away from the world's prying eyes. There was the odd occasion when a panic attack had crept in and reared its ugly head whilst she was with others, but that hadn't happened too often recently, much to El's relief. It was embarrassing feeling like you couldn't breathe for no reason.

El thrust her hand quickly into his to get this over with as soon as possible as his fingers wrapped around and devoured her limb like a Venus flytrap.

Tom swallowed the itching urge to pull her into him and wrap his arms around her in a tight embrace. He feared that if he did, he might never let her go again, which was too soon. Tom needed her to want to be with him constantly.

Tom settled instead for softly tracing the veins and tendons on her wrist with his fingertips. He wanted to memorise every dip and rise in her body. Tom wanted to savour this feeling of her beneath his touch, not knowing when he would get the chance again. He tried to gauge her reaction to his wandering fingertips and how she felt about the sense of him touching her bare skin.

El didn't pull away, but her pupils widened slightly at the intimate gesture. Whether that was a good or bad thing, he didn't know. But at least she wasn't trying to pull away from him. That could only be seen as a positive for him.

"Oh, erm, it's nice to meet you, Tom. Properly," El's voice was quiet as she spoke.

Tom smiled at her, keeping hold of her hand as he began speaking. He was relieved she was finally talking and could refresh the angelic sound of her voice in his head, storing it away again for later use.

"And what might your name be? I feel incredibly rude leaving books for you and not knowing your name."

El swallowed the lump of nerves in her dry throat, unaware that Tom already knew exactly what her name was.

"Oh. It's El. Well, actually... it's Ethel, but I can't stand that, so it's always been El," her voice was soft and timid as she spoke.

Tom smiled at her as he readjusted his grip on her hand and shook it gently.

"It's nice to finally put a name to a face... El," he smiled again at her as he watched a slight smile tug at the corner of her mouth.

Tom was tempted to raise her hand to his lips and kiss her knuckles one by one, but he held that temptation back as he watched her shift awkwardly in her seat.

He reluctantly let go of her hand slowly, running his fingertips along the inside of her palm, savouring every touch he could get of her soft skin.

"Oh... Hendricks? Are you related to the politics professor, Charles Hendricks?" El asked as her eyes met his.

Tom clenched his teeth with a tight, forced smile across his face as he bobbed his head and sucked in a breath.

"Afraid so. I'm Charlie's brother," he chuckled.

"Oh? So that's why you were with him." El raised her eyebrow as she tilted her head with her vague statement that sounded like a question.

Tom furrowed his brow in confusion.

El watched his reaction and realised she needed to clarify her statement.

"Oh, sorry. It's just I wouldn't have put you two as brothers. You don't look alike," El nervously swallowed and looked away from him down at her hands.

"No. No, I suppose we don't," Tom chuckled.

It was true. Tom and Charlie didn't look alike at all.

Charlie was muscular with dark blonde hair, blue eyes, and full lips. They were similar in height, but that was about as far as the similarity went.

Tom shifted his legs to kneel in front of El. He still had his hand on the table but moved the other to rest on his waist to try and look more casual.

"So. Erm... I'm guessing Dot is your sister?" Tom asked, pretending not to already know the answer and just wanting to continue the conversation for as long as possible.

El tilted her head again as her brows furrowed in confusion at the name he had given.

"Dot?" El asked before she broke out into a smile of recognition as her nerves diminished slightly. "Ohh... you mean, Dotty... Yes, unfortunately," El muttered, making Tom chuckle. "Oh god... you won't tell Charlie I said that will you?" she asked in a panic as her eyes widened. El sought his eyes, hoping to see the familiarity of understanding what it was to have an annoying sibling.

"Your secret is safe... I promise," Tom placed his hand over his heart as he bowed his head.

As he looked up, an awkward silence fell between them as he stared into her unique eyes.

Being this close, he could see the difference in colour between them, but they were still obstructed by the tint in her reading glasses, making them look dull. Tom wished he could reach out and remove them from her face to have a better view of them, but he knew that he would be stepping over a boundary.

Tom could smell her now as he inhaled deeply. Her vanilla and jasmine scent was beautiful and intoxicating. He had first thought it was the smell of her room, but it was, in fact, El that he had smelt the first time he met her and not some scented candles that couldn't do the reality of her justice.

El sucked her bottom lip into her mouth before she started to chew on it as he continued to watch her. Her nerves crept back to rampage through her with the situation she now found herself in, but she could not break from his gaze.

Tom's eyes were flitting between her eyes and now her mouth, his lips parted slightly, and his breathing deepened as he watched her studiously.

El cleared her throat loudly to break the tension between them before she started to speak.

"So... erm... Tom."

"Shhhh! This is a library. Keep your voices down," a stranger across the table interrupted El in an irritated tone as he told her off for talking.

El's eyes snapped across to look at the stranger. She apologised instantly, mouthing the words sorry as she turned around in her chair away from Tom, shaking her head and chastising herself internally for disturbing someone else.

It appeared that El was developing a habit of being too loud while around Tom.

On the other hand, Tom glared at him for interrupting El. Tom's fists balled as he stared down the man, looking at them disdainfully. He wanted to fly across the table at this man for disrupting the continuation of their conversation, cracking his head open with the laptop in front of him.

El started tidying her things into her bag as quietly as possible, getting ready to leave as she felt the judgement from the stranger across the table burning into her, making her even more uncomfortable than when Tom had approached her, trapping her in her seat.

Tom's heart dropped as he saw she was preparing to leave.

"Erm... Where are you heading off to?" he whispered to her.

"Oh, erm... probably home before my lecture later," El didn't look back at him and continued with her task, neatly placing everything in her bag in its designated place.

"Can I give you a lift home?" Tom asked.

"Oh, no... honestly, it's fine."

"Shhhh!" The stranger was staring at them angrily with his index finger to his lips.

Tom's head jerked to face the guy again.

They were whispering, for god's sake. He scanned over this ignorant piece of shit and took in his name from his ID badge that hung from the lanyard around his neck.

As Tom was with El, he didn't say anything back to "Simon Stanton". Even though a rage burned in Tom to call him out for his rudeness and interrupting El. The itch to inflict pain and suffering on this man-made Tom's fingers twitch with dark desires to see Tom's own hands covered in this dickheads blood.

Instead, Tom turned his head back to El and forced a charming smile across his face, concealing his anger behind a curtain of pleasantries.

El quickly tidied everything away and stood from her chair, turning to see Tom kneeling before her, blocking her way.

If someone walked past now, it would almost look like Tom was proposing to her as he was down on his knees in front of her. That, or begging for her forgiveness.

"Er..." El stiffly stood with her bag in her hand before placing it over her shoulder and looking down at Tom.

A grin spread across his face as he looked up at her, unable to contain his happiness at being in this position of worshipping at her feet.

"Sorry, Tom? You're kind of in my way."

"Oh, fuck. Sorry," Tom apologised as he slowly stood up in front of her, inhaling in her scent as he passed her groin.

His mouth immediately salivated as her essence embedded itself in his memory, saving that for later use in his fantasies.

Luckily for Tom, El hadn't noticed him do it.

He stepped back to allow her to pass him and leaned down towards her ear to whisper as she walked by.

"Would you like a lift home?" he asked again, dropping the tone of his voice this time.

She paused and turned her head, tilting her chin up to meet his gaze. His deep, honeyed voice sank into her skin, making her feel a flutter of something as she looked up at him.

Tom's face was right in front of hers as he remained hunched over, keeping his face at her level. He held his breath as he looked down at her tempting lips, quirking a hopeful eyebrow that she would say yes.

El swallowed quickly as the flutters turned to nerves.

"Oh, erm... No, thank you. I prefer to walk."

4.

"There's no use in crying or shouting. No one can hear you out here, Stanton," Tom leered at him as he walked around the metal table that Simon was strapped to in the old derelict cottage. The snap of latex gloves pinging against Tom's wrist cracked through the air, adding an ominous sound to the already stifling tension as he refreshed his gloves.

Simon's naked body was restrained with leather straps across his wrists, upper arms, ankles, thighs, waist, throat, and head.

A single, one-hundred-watt light bulb shone down on his bare form from above, casting an eerily illuminating glow on the naked body underneath it, highlighting every twitch of restrained flesh as Simon's body trembled.

It had been a while since Tom had used the disused building that was once someone's home, but he was finding uses for it again now. He wanted to take his time with this one. Tom needed the seclusion for what he had planned. Tom wanted to shame Simon before taking his final strangled breath for his rudeness towards not only himself but, more importantly, El.

The old, abandoned cottage in the middle of nowhere within The Fens of Cambridge was the perfect place for this.

It was a desolate and cold place during early Spring, especially at night, as the cold air blustered along the man-made channels and dykes through the marshes, rustling through the long reeds and grasses.

"Please, please... I'll do anything you want... Please, please don't kill me. I'm begging you."

Tom laughed at Simon, his pleading falling on deaf ears. "As if your begging is going to change my mind. Next, you'll be telling me you won't say anything. You won't go to the police. It'll be our secret."

Simon sobbed out loudly. With his head strapped down, Simon couldn't move in the direction of Tom's voice as his tormentor walked around the table slowly to stand behind his restrained body. The only sound in the room was Simon's ragged breaths as terror gripped him.

"Please," Simon whined out into the room.

Tom slammed his hands down on either side of Simon's head, making him yelp and tremble, rattling the straps' zinc buckles against the metal table, causing the room to fill with the soft sounds of metallic clinking.

Dust particles jolted and swirled through the beam of the shining light as the sudden gust of wind stirred them up from their settled space.

Tom stuck his head over Simon's face quickly, his head blocking out the light from the bulb and shouted, "BOO!" making Simon squeal again and sob more. Tom just laughed. He enjoyed toying with them before the inevitable end.

"They'll catch you. They'll find out who you are," Simon sobbed as he tried to move his limbs to pull on the restraints, but it was all to no avail. His strength was wavering from the fear and shock ravaging his senses, sapping his energy. Simon shivered as a cold breeze blew through the drafty house, prickly at his skin to form goosebumps.

Tom laughed even harder as he watched Simon try and struggle. The men often turned to open threats when their pathetic cries did nothing to sway him.

"Oh, I'll be caught, will I? Well, they haven't caught me yet, and what, you must be number..." Tom paused as he leaned over him, tilting his head in thought as he started counting on his fingers. He remembered every single one. "Ooo... Nine? No, wait. Ten," he chuckled darkly. "Silly me, I forgot the last one was a double. Oh, you get to take me into double figures. What an honour that you have been bestowed. What an achievement, Stanton," Tom's voice oozed sarcasm as his darkened eyes pierced into Simon's wide pupils full of fear.

A soft trickling sound started echoing around the room, replacing the clinking of the metal buckles as liquid dripped from the tabletop to the floor, quickly creating a puddle of wetness on the stone beneath.

Drip – Drip - Drip.

Tom's nose scrunched up as the hint of ammonia flooded his nose, and he looked at the wet patch on the floor.

"Oh my. Have you pissed yourself, Stanton?" Tom sneered as he looked at the puddle in disgust and back at Simon. "What a dirty, disgusting boy you are. Not only rude, but you don't seem to be able to hold your bladder either," Tom chastised before he burst out laughing, looking back at the urine spreading slowly across the floor. "You need to drink more, Stanton. Your piss is rather concentrated. Dehydration leads to kidney issues, you know," Tom smirked down at Simon before hitting his fists against the table either side of Simon's head and stepping back. He walked away out of

Simon's line of sight. "Not that it really matters now anyway. It's not as though my advice will help prevent renal failure now."

Simon continued to sob as he spoke, his voice trembling with not only the cold but with terror as well. "What... What are you going to do to me?"

Tom stood at another metal table against one of the exposed brick walls of the old kitchen, running his latex-covered hands over the precisely placed blades and medical instruments. His fingers landed on a scalpel, and he smirked to himself as a deliciously wicked idea coursed through his mind.

The plastic cheek retractor gained his attention as well as Tom gathered his tools. The evil ideas swirling in his head as excited anticipation of what was to transpire caused him to take a steadying breath. He couldn't let his excitement of seeing Simon's death at his hands overrule the need to drag this out. Tom still wanted to create the perceived punishment he wished to inflict upon this rude bastard for his crimes.

"Well... That would spoil the surprise, wouldn't it? Or..." Tom trailed off as he slowly walked back over to where Simon lay in his own urine, the scalpel in one hand, cheek retractor in the other.

"I suppose I could tell you, but you'll have to keep it a secret," Tom chuckled to himself as he flashed the scalpel across Simon's line of sight, causing him to sob and tremble more as it reflected a glimpse of Simon's own fearful eyes back at him.

"Shhhh..." Tom cooed as he ran his thumb smoothly along Simon's cheek, wiping his tears away with a gentle touch as he spoke softly. "See... Just a little politeness is all that's needed to ask someone to be quiet."

More silent tears started to run down Simon's cheeks. "My... my family will know I'm missing. They'll... they'll look for me," he stuttered in between sobs as he sniffed.

Tom shook his head as he spoke calmly. "Oh, but Stanton, they won't. See, I know your secret. I've been looking into you for the past week. Your dirty little secret that got you sent away in the first place to rehab. It almost caused you to be disowned by your family. Is your father still ashamed of you? Does he know you still suck cock? I mean, I'm just surprised you managed to get back into Cambridge at all. The shame it must have brought to the Stanton family name. Not only did your father lose a son, but he lost his best friend too... My my, what a tragedy."

"How... how do you know that? No one knows that," Simon stammered, blinking back more tears.

Tom scoffed at the notion that he could not find out every little detail about the disgusting fucker that now laid bare before him, stripped of not only his clothes but his facade of lies too. Simon was anything but the model student he claimed to be.

"You were a drug addict, Stanton... You sucked your father's best friend off for cash to support your habit when your family cut you off financially... You went to rehab, then came trotting back to Cambridge, a new man. Well almost. You still suck cock every Friday and Saturday night. Still, shove that shit up your nose." Tom booped Simon rather harshly on the tip of his nose with his index finger before he continued. "Does your father know you pay someone to do your urine tests for you?" Tom asked as he tapped the scalpel on Simon's forehead, watching Simon's eyes widen in shock.

"I-I-I..." Simon stuttered, his pulse thrashing wildly in his neck.

"There, there, it's alright..." Tom cooed. "It'll be over soon, and no one will give a damn about you. They're just going to assume you've relapsed again and disappeared, just like last time. The only difference is, this time, no one will find you crawling in the gutter," Tom chuckled darkly as he ran the scalpel blade tip across Simon's nose, just nicking the edge of his skin, allowing a small trickle of blood to form.

Simon writhed under the blade, his arms shaking as Tom slowly dragged the blade's edge deeper into Simon's skin across his cheek, splitting his skin open like a valley across his cheekbone. It left a trail of blood to run down the side of his face into his hair and onto the table like the man-made dykes surrounding the cottage.

"Well, don't you look a pretty picture in red... It matches your eyes," Tom's tone was light and airy as he took in the sight before him.

"YOU'RE SICK! YOU SICK FUCK!" Simon screamed at him before he tried to spit at Tom, but the frothy white saliva just landed back on Simon's cheek, mixing with his blood and turning the bubbles red as they drifted down his skin.

A wickedly dark smirk spread across Tom's face as he walked around the table's edge. He climbed on top of it, up over Simon. Sitting back on Simon's chest, crushing him with his weight, Tom gripped Simon's jaw with one hand as he held the mouth restraint in the other. He squeezed his thumb and index finger into Simon's cheeks, pushing them onto his teeth, causing a painful pinching sensation, but Simon kept his mouth tightly shut.

"Now... Be a good boy and open wide, Stanton, just like you do every Friday and Saturday night... I'd hate to have to force you." Tom sneered down at him as he started to apply more pressure on Simon's cheeks. He dug his fingernails into his skin as the latex covering his fingernails threatened to burst under the pressure.

Simon gritted his teeth together, clenching his jaw, making Tom sigh before he placed the mouth gag on the table next to Simon's head.

Tom tutted, slowly shaking his head as he leaned forward to stare into Simon's fearful eyes.

"I tried to be nice."

Tom grabbed Simon's nose and pinched Simon's nostrils together, splitting the skin on the tip of his nose more as he held his jaw in the other hand.

"Now you're just being plain rude," Tom sneered as his hands shook with anger under the force he used to try and get Simon to open his mouth.

Simon's body started shaking as he held his breath, causing Tom to pinch harder. It wouldn't be long, and Simon would have to take a breath in and open his mouth.

Tom watched as Simon's cheeks started to turn purple and the veins in his eyes bulged, but Tom wouldn't give up. Tom gritted his teeth and growled in frustration before lifting his body up onto his knees and slamming his ass down onto Simon's chest, causing Simon to gasp as the wind was knocked out of him.

As soon as Simon opened his mouth, Tom pushed his cheeks onto his teeth, harshly splitting them inside to stop him from closing his mouth again.

Tom leaned over him as he let go of his nose and grabbed the mouth restraint.

"I was going to make this next bit quick, but... after that little display, Stanton," Tom snarled.

He pinched the gag together to make it smaller before forcefully ramming it into Simon's mouth, spreading his cheeks and jaw wide open as the plastic restraint sat against Simon's molar, preventing him from closing his mouth or speaking. The mouth gag even made it hard for Simon to swallow as his tongue flailed in his mouth.

As Tom leaned back, Simon started making a gurgling noise before coughing. The blood from where his cheeks were cut on his own teeth was running down the back of his throat.

"Ah ah ah... Let's not have you drowning in your own blood just yet."

Tom scrambled off Simon and leaned under the table, twisting a round lever. The table started to tip up, stopping Simon's blood and saliva from running down his throat and preventing him from choking on it. Once the table was fully erect, Tom locked the table into position by pushing a metal pin into the mechanism.

Tom's eyes scanned over the new upright position that Simon was now in as he had stopped gurgling on his blood. He placed his hands on his hips as he surveyed his victim with a satisfactory grin.

"Now that's better."

Simon looked like a baby bird begging to be fed as he started mumbling, but because he couldn't move his lips, Tom couldn't understand a word he was saying.

As Tom stepped around in front of the table, Simon coughed again, splattering blood across Tom's face.

"Now, that's not very polite," Tom chortled as he wiped the blood from his cheek with the back of his hand, smearing it across his face and glove.

Simon continued making incoherent noises as Tom smirked back at him, looking over his handy work.

Tom lifted the scalpel into Simon's line of sight and watched as his eyes widened even further in fear. Not knowing what Tom planned to do with him was even more terrifying as Simon continued to make garbled noises.

"Will you please shut up! It's very distracting."

It didn't work, and Tom became more irritated until he snapped. He stormed over to the table by the stone wall and grabbed a pair of metal forceps before returning to stand before Simon.

Without saying a word, Tom slowly pushed them into Simon's mouth and grabbed his tongue, clicking the forceps into place so that they pinched. The metal painfully bit into the end of Simon's tongue as Tom pulled it out of his mouth so that the muscle stretched to its limit.

Simon kept coughing and spluttering as more blood flowed into his mouth from his cheeks. The mixture of saliva and blood started to pool under Simon's tongue and around his bottom gums as he gagged on the sensation of being unable to swallow at all now with his tongue pulled forward. It gave Simon the most uncomfortable feeling of pressure in his throat as he retched and convulsed, trying desperately to ease the tension. But nothing helped.

Tom held up the scalpel directly before Simon's eyes, ensuring he could see it. If Simon had closed his eyes, Tom would have considered placing fishhooks into his eyelids with fishing lines attached to pull them back to keep Simon's eyes open. But it seemed that Simon's fear forced him to keep them open; he couldn't look away. The unknown was more terrifying than the reality before him. He needed to see what was coming.

Simon could see his own congealing blood had already stained the edge of the blade from where Tom had cut his nose with it as he made more choked noises.

Tom smiled at him sweetly before his features turned sinister. It didn't seem possible, but Tom's eyes were almost entirely black now as he tilted his chin down, casting them in shadow in the shade from his brow.

The whole room suddenly felt a lot colder as the anticipation of what was about to happen sucked the warmth from the room.

Tom took a deep breath, savouring the moment before he spoke.

"Now... Hold still..."

5.

El received another book from Tom last week, bringing the total to four now. He had even attempted to deliver this one right into her hands, trying to catch her at home. He even rang the doorbell and waited, but she wasn't there. No one was, so he had left it on the doorstep like the previous packages. He was conscious about her trying to work from a damaged book, so he put his selfishness aside to see her and left it there instead of taking it away with him.

Tom also had wanted to ask her out for a coffee or something, anything to get her to start to trust him more and spend more time with her without him needing to be secretive and spying on her. The incident in the library had caused him to want El to get to know him more so she would start to trust him.

Tom had realised that ambushing her in the library maybe hadn't been the best idea, but he couldn't help his impulse to get closer to her when she spotted him staring at her.

When Tom reflected on the encounter, replaying her every little movement in his head, he concluded that he had made her nervous. Tom didn't want that. He wanted her to trust him and have faith that he'd protect her.

El's parents had returned home now, so Tom had been extra careful not to sit in his car for too long outside their home. He would often park up outside late at night when all the lights in the house were off, hoping that El would come downstairs for a drink as she often did, but that seemed to have stopped these past few days.

Tom also had yet to find her in the library again or around the campus. It irritated him that he hadn't seen her in person for a few days. The pictures Tom had of El were no longer a suitable substitute for her actual presence, but they would have to do for now.

Now that he had spoken to her again in person, he wanted the chance to ask her out for something innocent. He had even forgotten to ask her for her number at the library. Not that he needed it, as he already had it, but he knew if a stranger happened to text her, it would probably put her off, and she might not even answer him. He didn't even want to pretend he had asked his brother Charlie to ask Dotty for it in an out-of-the-blue text to El. He knew El would then ask her sister, and Tom didn't want to be caught in that lie so easily. She'd never trust him then.

The matter with Stanton had distracted Tom's attention away from her, which annoyed him greatly. It had taken a few days to dismember Simon's body as he had needed to freeze him first to make it easier. The cuts were cleaner and less messy, meaning the cleanup was quicker. Dismembering a body was often a very bloody affair; even if you drained the body of blood, there were always residual fluids. Deep freezing a body prevented the spillage. With the cottage being so remote in The Fens, destroying the evidence was a lot easier as Tom could just deposit pieces of Simon's body into the watery marshes, allowing nature to take care of it. Water was always Tom's preferred method of disposal. It destroyed evidence as it seeped into the pores, washing it away.

But Stanton was dealt with now and disposed of, so it didn't matter. Tom's studies had also been playing on his mind, so he had been forcing himself to get back to it, hoping he might bump into El on campus.

It was nearly Easter break, and families, including Tom's parents, were planning holidays away.

"John?... John? Have you packed a flannel?" Anne called out from the bathroom as she scurried around their home, making sure everything was packed for their trip away to France in their caravan.

Once a year, every year, Anne and John would take the family to France for a caravan holiday. They would stay at various campsites, absorbing the local culture, as John liked to call it. They did hope to retire to France soon, so this was an opportunity to see where they could eventually settle. Tom had always accompanied them, but this year was the first time he wasn't going. He was responsible for housesitting and tending to their garden. Charlie couldn't be trusted to ensure everything was watered correctly, and as Anne and John didn't trust their new neighbours to do it, they had asked Tom.

Initially, when the planning began during the Christmas holidays, Tom would be going with them. But everything had changed.

Tom had fond memories of France, lots of fond memories over the past few years. Two, in particular, played through his mind when contemplating the trip. But he had said he was far too busy with his PhD. Housesitting would give him time to study. He also didn't want to think about being too far from El. That was the hidden agenda that really changed Tom's mind about the yearly trip with his parents.

Tom was starting to get withdrawal symptoms from not seeing her. He now carried a photo of her around in his pocket. A recent one he had taken of her walking home from the library.

It may have only been the back of her body with her yellow backpack, light blue shirt, and tight denim jeans on, but it was still her. The picture had already started to get worn around the edges from where Tom kept touching it in his pocket. Running his fingertips over it, again and again, fading the colours.

...

As Easter weekend started in full swing, El's family made their annual journey to their family gathering at her grandmother's house. Her grandmother had moved to a quiet village, Atherington, in Sussex, near the coast a few years ago. Enid loved the sea and wanted to be closer to it, often quoting its health benefits to her family.

The weather was pleasant but too cold for El to take a dip in it. She preferred to avoid jumping in the freezing cold sea water even though Enid encouraged it at all times of the year. Even on the morning of the traditional Boxing Day dip in the sea, she insisted on dragging El and Dotty with her, and as it was Christmas, they begrudgingly agreed to keep their beloved grandmother happy.

The usual family had arrived at Enid's home, with El's multiple cousins, aunts, and uncles. Like every year, arguments broke out during the family games night on

Good Friday. Monopoly was often a hotly contested game like it was in most homes. Too much alcohol was consumed, and people said things they shouldn't have as things got out of hand.

El stood on the beach looking out at the sea as she rubbed the scar on her arm, soothing the ache that the arguing had caused in her body. The wind whipped up her hair as she drifted off in thought. The night was chilly but not cold enough that she needed more than a light jacket. The house was only a few hundred yards from the beach, and she had had enough of the screaming matches for one evening. The noise brought back too many bad memories.

El hadn't noticed that her grandmother had come to stand next to her.

"Hello, love."

"Shit! Nan! You scared me," El exclaimed as she held her chest and turned her head to look at Enid.

Enid chuckled at her granddaughter. She loved to make her jump with fright.

"Had enough of the arguments?"

"You could say that."

"Me too... Are you warm enough?" Enid asked her. She had seen El rubbing her arm and had assumed it was because she was cold and not for any other reason.

El turned to look at her. Enid was carrying a thermos. Typical Nan, she thought, always thinking of others and how to cheer them up.

"I am a little bit chilly now," El admitted.

"Well... Good job, I bought this then." Enid unscrewed the cap and handed El a cup, pouring her some of the dark brown liquid from inside the thermos.

El took a swig, expecting a warm beverage. Instead, her throat instantly burned with the hit of scotch. She coughed and spluttered as Enid chuckled, rubbing her back to ease El's heaving chest.

"Nan! What the hell? I thought it was coffee or something."

"You're old enough now, pet... You could use a decent drink." Enid brought the thermos to her mouth and tipped it back, taking a big swig. "Ahh... Now that's better. Warms the cockles does a good scotch... And this is a good scotch."

El shook her head as she looked at her grandmother. She was a character, the life and soul of their family.

"Fancy a dip?" Enid asked as she screwed the cap back on the thermos, placed it on the shingles and started walking towards the sea. The tiny rocks crunched below her feet.

"Nan, it's nighttime and freezing," El protested.

"All the better to tire you out before bed." Enid laughed as she took her shoes off and rolled the legs of her trousers up to just below her knees.

"Nan!... Nan!" El called out to her. "Oh, for god's sake."

El quickly followed after her as Enid strode into the freezing sea up to her knees. As it was windy, the sea was quite choppy, with the waves crashing against her age-spot-covered legs. El was worried that Enid might fall over with the strength of the waves tonight as she kept her eyes on her.

"I can't believe you sometimes." El scolded her grandmother as she hurried to kick her shoes off, rolled her trousers up, and went to stand next to her.

El winced as she hopped across the shingles and into the freezing water. The cold instantly took her breath away as she made a silent "o" shape with her mouth, wrapping her arms around herself and rubbing her hands against her arms.

They stood silent for a while. The only noise was the English Channel splashing around them. Their legs and feet went numb from the cold. Enid reached across and took El's hand, squeezing it tightly as they looked at the horizon.

Enid didn't need to say a thing, and neither did El. She was always there for her. After last year, all El needed was for her grandmother to hold her hand. It made everything better. It made all those horrid, painful thoughts drift away, even if only for a brief respite for El's troubled mind.

Enid was the only one she had ever told the whole truth to.

Enid turned her head to look at the young woman standing next to her. She was so proud of the woman she was becoming after everything. El was strong and fierce. She just needed to show it more. If only she believed in herself just a fraction of how much Enid believed in her, she could conquer anything, take on the world and come out on top.

"Nan... I can't feel my feet anymore." El complained as Enid chuckled at her.

"Best we head back then."

...

Everyone was nursing their hangovers sprawled about the main house the next day. El had retreated into the summer house with her violin for some practice in the quiet. She didn't think her family would appreciate the noise early in the morning, but she had the compulsion to play.

As she stood barefoot, lost in the music, she didn't notice that her grandmother had come to stand in the doorway to watch and listen to her.

El played beautifully. She could have been a professional musician but chose a different path during her A-level exams. She loved music and wanted to refrain from tarnishing it by relying on it to pay bills. She knew a musician's life was a struggle and didn't want that. She was planning to go into teaching after her degree but had yet to fully decide if that was the path she really wanted to take.

As El played, she started to sway more with her music, fully committing to it as the tempo built. Like a single voice in a choir, something was missing from the music as she played alone. It just needed the other instruments to make it complete and sound as the composer had intended. She was playing Ludovico Einaudi, Experience. It wasn't a highly complex piece, but it was one of her favourites.

El was about three-quarters of the way through the piece when she felt a thump on the wooden floor rattle through her feet into her bones. She stopped playing immediately and spun around quickly to see what had fallen over when her eyes landed on Enid sprawled out on the floor.

...

"Tom! Tom! Are you here?" Charlie called out as he entered their parent's home.

"In here," Tom called back from out in the conservatory. The weather wasn't great during this Easter bank holiday Monday, and it had started to rain heavily. The pitter-patter of raindrops splashing on the windows echoed through the otherwise quiet room.

"Ah, there you are... What's up, brother? Doing much?" Charlie asked as he walked into the room.

Tom sighed as he drew his eyes away from his laptop. "If you must know, I'm trying to study."

"Ah," Charlie plopped down in a chair opposite, sighing before leaning forward to pick up some research papers from the coffee table, flicking through them absentmindedly.

Tom huffed as he watched his brother sift through his papers, turning their order into a complete shambles that Tom would have to re-sort.

"Why are you here? Are you bored?" he asked, annoyed at the interruption.

"Urgh..." Charlie puffed out a sigh. "God, is it that obvious?"

"Well, you're here, aren't you? You usually are in the pub on bank holiday Monday, drinking yourself into a coma..."

Charlie chuckled as he leaned back in the chair. "Well, I was supposed to meet someone this afternoon, but she's bailed."

Tom continued to click through the online journal he was reading while taking notes for his literature reviews.

"Mmhmm? Anyone I'd know?" he asked absentmindedly as he concentrated on the screen.

"Dot, actually."

Tom's hands paused immediately, his interest peeking at the mention of El's sister, but he didn't break his eyes away from the laptop screen. He wanted to keep Charlie in the dark about his growing obsession with this girl's family, particularly Dot's sister.

"Oh? Found someone better, did she? More her age?" Tom taunted, trying to get a reaction from his brother.

"Ha!" Charlie laughed before he clicked his tongue against the roof of his mouth, and his expression turned serious. "No... Her grandmother died or something."

Tom's eyes shot to Charlie as he sat, picking at his fingernails.

"Her grandmother died?" asked Tom, trying to hide some of his concern and sound more empathetic.

"Yes, a heart attack on Saturday morning."

"Oh wow... Is she alright?" Tom's voice was full of worry as his thoughts shifted to El.

"She didn't sound it on the phone. Said she had to stay with her parents and sister today. They were meant to be travelling back last night so we could see each other today, but they're returning later this evening," Charlie said as his shoulders slumped and he sat back into the chair. "I suppose there go my chances for a shag this week," Charlie huffed.

"Charlie! You are disgusting!" Tom scorned his brother's response. "They've just lost their grandmother, and all you can think about is not getting your cock wet!" Tom fumed at him as he slammed his laptop shut and stood from the chair, quickly storming away from his brother.

"Woah... Woah! Why are you getting so upset about it?" Charlie asked irritatedly as he stood from his chair.

Pausing in the doorway, Tom put his hand in his pocket, stroking El's picture unconsciously as he leaned the other hand against the door frame.

"For once in your life Charlie, show some compassion, for fucks sake." Tom walked away from him without looking back and grabbed his coat and car keys.

"Where are you going?" Charlie called out to him, confused as he took a step forward.

"You know how to lock up, yes?"

With that, Tom opened the door and left without waiting for an answer.

As he drove towards El's house, he couldn't stop thinking about her. What was he going to say? What was he going to do? Perhaps this wasn't a good idea, but before he could stop himself, he was already parked outside her home.

El's family were still out, as no car was parked on their driveway. Tom sat gripping the steering wheel tightly, looking out of the window down the road as he waited for her.

Tom hadn't realised he'd fallen asleep in the car or that it was dark outside. The rain had lulled him to sleep until he was woken by the bright headlights passing over him as El's parent's car pulled into their driveway, and his eyes flew open.

Tom's eyes tracked their movements as he sat watching them. He saw Dotty get out first, followed by her mother and father, but El didn't get out. Her father opened the back passenger side door and leaned down to talk to someone.

Tom could see a figure sitting there in the back. They were talking, and they kept shaking their head. El's father touched something on the ceiling before leaning back and shaking his head sadly. It was still raining outside, or perhaps it had stopped and started again, but as Tom watched El's father slowly close the door and walk into the house, Tom's heart juddered with an aching realisation.

In the back of the car, El was illuminated by the inside roof light. She was sat staring straight ahead, the most haunting blank expression on her face. She looked gaunt like she hadn't slept in days. Deep dark circles under her eyes, her hair a mess, and her mouth parted slightly, framed by chapped, dry lips.

Tom's heart broke as he looked at her.

He could see in his peripheral vision the curtains twitching in El's living room. Her family must be watching her from inside, hoping she would get out soon, but she stayed put. He had to do something; he couldn't just sit there and watch.

Tom grabbed one of the books from his glove box and stuck it under his coat before stepping out of his car. He slowly walked over to the car and looked down at El through the window. She didn't move. She didn't lift her head. She didn't do anything but sit staring forward and just breathing.

"Dotty, who's that outside?" Betty called to Dotty from her viewpoint at the bay windows, keeping an eye on El.

Dotty came to stand next to her mum to look.

"Oh, that's Tom. The mystery book guy."

"What's he doing?" Betty asked curiously.

Dotty shrugged her shoulders as they both continued to watch from the window.

Tom swallowed his nerves down before he tapped his knuckles on the window. El didn't move, so Tom reached for the door handle.

As he opened the door, she still didn't move. The rain ran down Tom's soaking wet hair onto his cheeks as he stood outside the car, hoping El would look up at him, but she didn't.

"El?" Tom's voice was soft as he spoke to her.

Slowly, she turned her head to look at him. Her sad, red-rimmed eyes met his. She had lost that sparkle in them, dulling them to look like a misted window.

"Are you alright?"

El swallowed, her bottom lip quivering as more tears threatened to fall down her puffy, tear-stained cheeks.

The rain was pouring down around Tom as he stood, unsure what to do.

"Why are you here?" El asked him. Her voice was hoarse and quiet as she furrowed her brow at him in confusion.

A small smile tugged at the corner of his mouth before it immediately faded. "I bought you another book," Tom quietly said.

He reached into his jacket and pulled out the yellow tissue-wrapped package.

El's eyes followed his hands, but she didn't say anything. She stared at it as he held it out but didn't move to take it from him.

Tom slowly leaned into the car and placed the book on her lap, his head next to her face. His wet hair dripped onto the tissue paper, causing darker circles to appear on it. Tom turned to look at her. She looked broken.

As El sat staring at him, something within Tom sparked. He could have kissed her. He could have grabbed hold of her head right here, right now, slamming his lips to hers. Instead, Tom turned his head, looking down at her hands on either side of her lap as her fingers dug into the fabric of the car seat.

"She's gone."

Her voice ghosted across his cheek as her tears began to fall, adding to the wet patches on the yellow paper.

Tom's eyes watched as they soaked into the tissue-wrapped book. He reached for her hand, slowly placing his over hers. He gently and carefully wrapped his fingers around them, holding her hand. He lightly squeezed her fingers, and to his surprise, El squeezed back.

Tom turned his head to look at her before he quietly spoke. "I know."

6.

The Easter holidays were over, and they were into their final term at Cambridge. There was a lot of nervous excitement in the air around campus. Undergraduates were sitting exams or adding the final touches to their dissertations. Postgraduates were furiously compiling their research and writing papers, hoping they would be good enough for publication.

Tom could feel that nervous energy as he walked through the halls to the library. He was glad that it was all over for him for now. At least by doing his PhD, he could control most of his schedule, apart from the meetings with his supervisor. They had determined his deadlines together, and Tom was well ahead of his original plan.

Sitting in the corner of the library, he looked across to El's favourite spot. She wasn't there. She hadn't been on campus since the term had started a few weeks ago.

El had been secluded in her room for most of the time. Tom had been welcomed into her home by either her mother, father, or sister. They apparently didn't want to leave her alone in the house, and it was evident to Tom why.

After that first night in the car where Tom had stayed with El, he visited her every day. He had sat in the car with her for hours that night until she had fallen asleep. El had leant against his shoulder as Tom held her hand, rubbing soothing circles across her skin. He gently stroked her hair as he rested his head against hers.

Whilst Dotty and Charlie had been in bed together, just making conversation, Dotty had told Charlie about Tom visiting El every day. Charlie had recounted to her how Tom had left their parent's house in a rush once he discovered what had happened to Dotty and El's grandmother. Charlie had found Tom's reaction to this news surprising, but once Dotty had told Charlie about the books, he was a little less shocked about Tom's behaviour.

Tom had always been one to fall quickly for girls, even as a ten-year-old boy. He proclaimed he was in love with a female popstar, decorating his walls with pictures of her and love hearts. He was obsessed with her, and Charlie had used it to his advantage to tease Tom mercilessly about his crush. Charlie even went as far as to show Tom paparazzi snaps in a gossip magazine of her with a man she was seen kissing to tease him more, laughing at Tom as he cried.

Tom had then stormed to his bedroom and torn every poster of her from his wall, ripping them into tiny pieces before trying to flush them down the toilet. He managed to block the waste pipes in an attempt to rid himself of his heartbreak and ended up grounded for a month by their father.

Tom had stood emotionless in their flooded bathroom, staring at their father with a blank expression as he screamed at Tom for being an idiot. Charlie stood behind their father, John, smirking as he watched Tom being told off, revelling in the delight of seeing his younger brother's punishment.

After that, Tom became distant from Charlie and started to keep more and more secrets from him. It was something that Charlie had become accustomed to during their teenage years. So much so that they barely spoke about their personal lives to save arguments and jibes at one another.

Every day, Tom had stood in front of El's bedroom door and gently knocked, hoping she would let him in, but she never answered. He never even heard her move about in her room. Her family were getting increasingly worried, and with the funeral for her grandmother, Enid, coming up, they didn't even know if El would attend.

The grief had utterly broken El, leaving just a shell of her former self behind.

Tom had seen it in her eyes that first night in her father's car and didn't know how to make it right.

As he sat on the chair in the library, his mind began to wander, and he placed his hand into his shirt pocket. Wrapping that small piece of mousey brown hair tied with a bit of yellow ribbon around his fingers, wondering what he should do.

El's family had been very gracious with him. Her mother, Betty, had even bought him tea and snacks as he sat outside her bedroom door.

Tom had filled the quiet void that El's absence had left by mainly speaking about Shakespeare, but that was his favourite subject. It felt good to Tom to fill the emptiness with something, even if it was just his voice. He would talk about his day and research, telling El that he missed seeing her at University and that it wasn't the same without the chance to see her around campus.

At night, whilst Tom was in the security of his own home, he would imagine El lying next to him on his bed as he stared at her pictures in his wardrobe. They would have conversations that turned into passionate arguments about the originality of Shakespeare's work and its satire. He would often imagine the angry make-up sex they would have after their disagreements.

Tom would pound into her, drawing every last moan and gasp from El's mouth as she eventually agreed he was right. He did love it when she called him Professor as her orgasm took hold of her, and she cried out.

Charlie had spoken to Tom and apologised for his behaviour on that Bank holiday Monday. Tom couldn't believe his ears when Charlie said he was sorry and that it was uncalled for about what he had said. The talk with Dotty helped Charlie see that he needed to repair some of his relationship with his brother, and this apology could be the start of that.

Tom sighed as he tried to concentrate on the journal he was reading in front of him but couldn't focus on the words as he sat in the library, thinking about El.

Enid's funeral was tomorrow, and Betty had invited him to attend if he wished. She had hoped he would be able to convince El to go. They would leave at seven in the morning to get to Worthing Crematorium for the service. They would then head to the beach where Enid had wished her ashes to be scattered into the sea.

Tom packed away his things; he had only been in the library for a short time, but what was the point in staring at a page of black ink, hoping that he would absorb the words when all he could think about was El?

Betty had told him that Enid had wished El to play her violin at her funeral. Death was always an open subject in their home, which Tom felt was refreshing.

We were all going to go at some point; what was the point in pussy footing around it? It should be part of everyday conversation, just as any other subject. It shouldn't be some taboo subject that's never spoken about until it's too late and the person you love has gone. If it was talked about more, perhaps people wouldn't be so afraid of it.

Tom was again standing outside of El's bedroom door later that afternoon. Her father, mother, and sister had gone out to collect some things for the next day, leaving him alone in the house with her.

After what had happened that night in the car with Tom comforting El, her family trusted Tom. They trusted him to be alone with her. He thought it ironic that they were placing their trust in a serial killer, but he had no intention of harming El or any of them. Unless, of course, they ever upset her.

Tom tapped his knuckles on her bedroom door, taking a deep breath before he spoke.

"El? I know you can hear me in there... I just... I want to make sure you're ok... so I'm going to open the door."

He had had enough of waiting and not being able to see her in person since that night in the car. This was a perfect opportunity with her family not being there for Tom to fulfil his need to see El.

He paused with his hand on the doorknob, but before he could twist it to see if it was unlocked, he heard the click of the lock undoing and felt the doorknob turn in his hand. Tom automatically let go of it as El opened the door to her room. Little did he know she had been behind the door every time he came.

There she stood. A blank expression across her tired face.

Gone were the puffy red eyes, replaced with deep dark circles under them. El still looked just as vacant as she had when they had first returned from Atherington just a few weeks ago.

El was dressed in loose-fitting grey jogging bottoms hanging low from her hips and a black t-shirt barely clinging to her shoulders. She had lost weight, a lot of it. Perhaps these clothes had once fit her, but now, they barely clung to her petite frame.

Her hair was pulled back from her face into a tight ponytail, but it didn't look like it had been washed in days. A greasy sheen was clearly evident as the light from the afternoon sun streamed in through her window and reflected off it. Her cheeks were hollow and sunken, showing yet more of her weight loss. El's soft, peachy lips were now chapped and sore, making her look dehydrated as if she had been caught in a shipwreck at sea and stranded for weeks out in the harsh elements.

She slowly turned away, walking back towards the window seat in her bedroom, slumping onto it to stare out the window.

Tom hesitated at the threshold of her door, unsure if he should walk in or wait to be invited. But as he stood there, he looked around at the mess that greeted him.

El's books were strewn across the floor, dirty glasses of old milk on her tables, her bed unmade, her music sheets torn into pieces, and her violin smashed on the floor. There was a blatant hole in the wall where she must have hit it against it repeatedly. The sunflowers

Tom had given her with the replacement books were now dead in a vase on her table, sitting in thick green water. The petals were dry and crisp and had fallen onto the wooden top. The only things that weren't a mess were the stack of five new textbooks that still sat perfectly on the edge of her shelf.

Gone was the sweet, pleasant smell of vanilla and jasmine that had wrapped around Tom when he first saw El's room. It was replaced with the sour smell of gone-off milk that made Tom nauseous as he stood in the doorway looking around her room.

El looked up from the window seat at him.

"Well... you can see I'm alive, so... you can go now."

"El..."

"You. Can. Leave." The softness of her voice was gone. She was cold, harsh and unforgiving with her emotionless stare.

Tom swallowed the feeling of nausea down as he stepped into the room.

"I'm not going to leave you, El. Not like this." He started looking about the room and bent over to pick up a book before placing it on her desk.

El just sat there and watched him as Tom took the glasses of spoilt milk downstairs to the kitchen, quickly washing them up before returning.

Book after book, paper after paper, Tom silently tidied her room. He placed everything back where it originally went. Things that were torn were placed in a separate pile to be replaced. The torn pieces of music were collected and put in the rubbish bin. He even stripped off her bed, taking down the dirty linen and placing it in the washing machine with washing powder and fabric softener before turning it on to wash it.

"Do you have any clean bedding?" Tom asked as he entered back into her room.

El turned away from him and looked out the window before Tom approached her and crouched beside her. He placed his hand on her knee, and she froze instantly.

"El? Do you have any clean bedding?" he asked again.

She forcefully pushed his hand off her leg and snapped her head back around to look at him. They now faced each other at eye level as a rage seethed within her.

"Why the fuck are you doing this?" She quickly stood, shoving him away from her.

Tom fell back on his ass. He'd let her push him over.

She now stood over him as her anger took over, and her face turned to rage.

"WHY. THE. FUCK. ARE. YOU. DOING. THIS? WHO AM I TO YOU!?!" she screamed as she balled her fists at her sides.

Slowly, Tom started to stand back up in front of her, causing El to take a step back, tears streaming down her face.

"Why are you coming every day just to sit outside my room? Why are you bothering with me? Why did you even replace the books? You don't know me! You don't owe me anything."

El scoffed loudly as she looked at Tom before she started maniacally laughing. A serious, deathly look graced her features as she went quiet before she shoved him harshly in the chest with both hands.

Tom wavered slightly with the shove, taking a step back before he stepped forward again. He stood there in silence with his hands by his sides as she shoved him repeatedly.

Every time she pushed him, and he stumbled back, he would take that step back towards her as if they were playing a game that he wouldn't let her win.

El's anger spilt out as she took it out on him. He knew she needed this. He had felt that kind of rage too, only he would find someone to take it out on, and Tom wouldn't stop but wouldn't just use his hands. A knife, an axe, a bat, anything he deemed a satisfactory ending to that life and relieve the tension in his body that his rage caused.

El screamed in frustration that he was letting her do it. She took a step back, taking deep breaths. Her eyes were focused on his chest.

Tom's breathing was calm, and even as he stood there as if mocking her. It made her even more furious.

El's eyes travelled up to meet his, and he swallowed as they met.

That anger and frustration were still in her, even more so now as Tom looked into her eyes.

Her nostrils flared, and El swung at his face in rage with her open palm to slap him. Tom caught her wrist before she made contact. He just continued to stare down at her as she seethed at him.

"GET OFF ME!"

"No," Tom calmly said.

"GET THE FUCK OFF ME!" she screamed loudly.

"El..." he kept his voice even as he spoke to her.

"FUCK YOU TOM!" El screeched in his face. She started pulling back, trying to escape his grip, but he held firm. "LET GO!"

"I said NO!" Tom raised his voice to her as if scolding a child.

His heart started racing in his chest, adrenaline coursing through his veins. That rush he felt just before he plunged a knife into someone scratched under the surface. The needs and desires to fill his blood lust were straining to get out, like an itch that needed to be scratched. The tension was building in his body so quickly that it felt like it would tear him apart at any second as she pulled against his grip.

She started hitting him with her other hand before Tom grabbed that too and pushed back against the wall, holding her wrists. Her poster of Beethoven crumpled behind her back as Tom held her arms flat against the wall. He manoeuvred his leg between her thighs to pin her buttocks against the poster. His breathing was ragged as he stared wide-eyed at her, seeing the same look within hers as El kept struggling against his grip.

"STOP IT!" Tom shouted at her as his hands tightened. He could feel his resolve slipping as the tension in his body built. He didn't want to hurt her if he finally snapped and gave in to it.

El drew her head back before spitting in his face in an attempt to get him to let her go.

The frothy white saliva ran down his cheek and dripped onto the floor. Tom let go of one of her wrists and slowly wiped it off with the back of his hand as El stood motionless, debating with herself if she had just made a terrible mistake.

"You shouldn't have done that," he said quietly before he grabbed hold of her throat and lifted her up, pushing her back flat against the wall. The noise of the poster tearing filled the room as El struggled in his tightening grip. She was so lightweight that it was effortless for him as he held her up by her throat in one hand, his other balled in a fist by his side.

El kicked and kicked, banging her arms onto his. Tom's psychotic side had taken over, and he seethed at her. A panicked look flashed across her eyes as she gasped for breath, seeing the change in his eyes and behaviour. He was terrifying. Tom's grip slowly tightened even more, cutting off her air entirely. He seemed to enjoy it, fully wrapped in the feeling of holding her life in his hands as it ebbed away.

Tom loved it. He craved that feeling.

El stopped hitting and kicking him. Something within her knew to stop antagonising his inner demon. She may have thought about ending it all these past few weeks. She may have even planned how she would do it. But every day, she had waited to hear Tom's voice through the door.

Every day, she was consumed by those evil, horrible thoughts of ending everything to not burden her family and that they would be better off without her. But every day, it was his voice that brought her back, his voice that shut them out, his voice that grounded her, making her want to continue to hear him again the next day.

Tom felt her body relax as if she was giving in to him. He saw the change in her eyes as the fight left her, and he instantly dropped her, only now realising what he was doing as he locked his inner demon back away within himself. A horrid thought raced through him that she wanted him to kill her, and he was doing just that.

El slid down the wall, the torn poster sliding with her as her legs crumpled under her from the lack of oxygen to her muscles.

Tom dropped to his knees in front of her, his hands shaking from the adrenaline and fear that he was only seconds from killing her.

"I'm sorry... I'm sorry... I-I-I... I don't know what came over me... Are you ok? Are you hurt? Did I hurt you?" Tom's voice rambled as he started panicking that he'd hurt her.

He didn't touch her again, even though it pained his heart not to. He wanted to comfort her but was frightened of himself and what he was capable of at that moment.

El's head hung down as she took some deep breaths, the oxygen returning to her body. It caused her to have pins and needles across her hands and feet. She started chuckling, leaving Tom utterly confused.

"Are you ok? El? El?" the concern evident in his voice.

She just nodded her head as she looked up at him. El reached out and took his hand, gently squeezing it.

"I'm ok... Just... I hate pins and needles so much. They make me feel like I'm being tickled, and I can't stand to be tickled," she giggled.

It was the most heart-warming laugh Tom had ever heard in his life. From him almost doing the unthinkable to El holding his hand and laughing within a few minutes. He was dumbstruck. It seemed there was so much more to El than he first thought. She seemed to be hiding something darker within her too, and Tom had just started to scratch the surface of what was hidden beneath her sweet exterior. Tom realised that El hadn't stopped fighting to allow him to kill her. She had stopped because she saw something in him that she saw in herself.

"El? Tom?" A sing-song voice echoed from downstairs. El's family were home, and Betty was headed straight up the stairs.

El quickly looked up at Tom as she sat with her back against the wall. She quickly used her free hand to pull her hair out from the tie and shake it loose so it fell around her face and neck, knowing she was hiding the red marks that would undoubtedly be around her throat. El still kept holding his hand as Tom sat back on his heels.

"Hey? Everything all right?" Betty poked her head around the door to see them both sitting on the floor holding hands.

El turned her head to look up at her mother briefly before she looked back at Tom.

"Yeah... Everything's fine, mum."

Her eyes never left Tom's face as she spoke.

7.

Bang on the dot at seven in the morning, El's family left their house. The sun had already crested over the horizon over an hour ago, breaking through the early May morning and chasing the dew away from the grass.

Tom was waiting outside on the driveway, standing by his car parked next to El's father's, ready to follow them to the Worthing crematorium. He was dressed in a formal fitted black suit and tie. His usual mop of curly hair had been slicked back out of his face to make his appearance smarter for this sombre occasion.

El wore a simple, high-collared black dress that sat just above her knee, the sleeves fully covering her arms, her hair loose around her face and for shoes, she wore a pair of black pumps. Dotty and Betty wore similar outfits, while Mark, El's father, wore a black mourning suit with a white dress shirt and black tie.

Mark came out of the house with a suitcase and placed it into the trunk of their car.

"Right, well... will you be all right following us, Tom?" Mark asked as he closed the boot and looked over at Tom as he waited patiently for everyone to be ready to leave.

"Yes, I'll be fine," Tom answered politely as he gave a single nod of his head.

"Do you have a sat nav in case we get separated on the motorway?"

Tom smiled at him briefly, "No... but I'm sure I'll be able to find it."

El stepped past her dad to stand beside Tom before she turned around to face her family.

"I'll go with Tom, Dad. Make sure he doesn't get lost."

Since yesterday, El had been different after what happened in her room with Tom. She joined her family for dinner that night, and they all sat chatting and telling stories about Enid. It was a complete turnaround and something that had happened before with El after a tragic event.

Tom managed to pull El out of the solitude her head had created and bring her back into the world beyond the sanctuary of depression she had made in her bedroom.

El smiled at her dad, who smiled back at them both.

"Ok... Let's get going then," Mark said.

Tom looked down at El to whisper to her, "Honestly, if you want to go with them, I'll be all right." He was conscious of being alone with her again after yesterday.

Once Betty had looked in upon the two of them, Tom quickly exited, saying he needed to get back to studying. Confusion about what had just happened between them made him panic. It felt like that first rush he had after killing someone and not knowing what to do with the residual adrenalin that lingered in his body.

"You will be coming tomorrow, won't you, Tom?" El had called out to him from the garden gate as she rushed out after him.

He stopped at his car and nodded his head as the tug of a small smile pulled at the corner of his mouth, but he didn't look back at her.

Tom quickly jumped in his car and drove down the road as a rush of emotions coursed through him. His feelings changed to something akin to hope. Hope that El was starting to want him near her and perhaps more.

When he stopped at the junction, he looked in the rear-view mirror to see El standing at the gate, watching his car, causing a flutter in his chest.

Tom drove a few roads away and parked before walking back to El's house, unable to stop his temptation. He had stayed hidden away in some bushes near enough to her house that he could see into the windows. Tom watched as El came downstairs to join her family. He saw an immediate change in her. Something had clicked in her when Tom had pinned her against the wall. Tom couldn't work out what it was, but he felt even more connected to her now.

"No... I'm coming with you." El smiled up at him.

Perhaps she was putting on a front for everyone else's sake. Maybe she was about to have a complete mental breakdown during the funeral. Whatever was going on with El puzzled Tom, and like always, Tom did enjoy a puzzle.

"Ok." Tom smiled at her before he went to the passenger side door and opened it for her, expecting her to get in.

El pulled a screwed-up face at him and shook her head. "Sorry, Tom... I-I-I can't sit in the front... Erm..." El took a quick breath as she looked at him apologetically. "I get car sick... Is it ok if I sit in the back?"

Tom furrowed his brow at El before he shut the door slowly and opened the back one instead. He placed his hand on the top of the door and gestured for her to climb in.

Usually, people get car sick sitting in the back, but whatever. He was happy just to have her with him, even if he was a bit apprehensive of being alone again with her.

As El moved past him to clamber into the car, she placed her hand on his, holding the top of the door and lightly squeezed Tom's hand. Tom's eyes were glued to his hand as she did it. El had only touched him briefly, but he could still feel her touch against his hand. It felt like static across his skin, drawing him to her to chase that feeling.

El looked up at him after she secured her seatbelt.

"I think Dad's ready to go." She gestured down the road as Tom blinked a few times and snapped his gaze away from staring at her. He looked over at the other car, waiting patiently at the end of the cul-de-sac.

"Oh shit, yes... Sorry."

Tom quickly closed the door, jumped in the front, and started the car. He adjusted the rear-view mirror so he could see El, and she smiled back at him before Tom focused back on the road.

This would be a good test of Tom's willpower not to constantly look at her in the mirror. He had a terrifying thought that perhaps they might crash because of it, but he put that to the back of his mind.

"Right then... Off we go."

...

El sat looking out the car window, watching the world whizz past her as she got lost in thought. Her mind drifted off to conversations with her grandmother and how much she would miss the sound of her voice and her presence. She was upset with herself for smashing her violin during a violent outburst of grief.

During a family dinner last year, Enid had asked El to play at her funeral during one of the casual family conversations about death and what they would each want. El felt immense guilt for breaking her promise to her Nan and smashing her beloved violin when she couldn't control her temper.

El would need to broach the subject with her mum when they returned home to see if she'd lend her the money for a replacement instrument. El hoped she could travel back down to Atherington and play for her Nan again while she stood on the beach, fulfilling her promise even if it was a little late.

Tom kept checking the rear-view mirror, looking at El as he drove, not realising that he had, in fact, lost El's parent's car on the M25.

"Shit." Tom cursed under his breath as he realised their car wasn't in front anymore and that perhaps he'd missed the junction they needed.

"You ok?" El asked as his voice drew her back from her thoughts, and she turned her attention to him.

"Yeah... Huh... I seem to have lost your parent's car. Erm... do you know what junction we need?"

El turned her head to look out the window for a signpost. Tom was watching her again. Her expressions as she concentrated made him smile, just like they had in the library, as her tongue poked out from between her lips.

"Oh, I don't think you've missed it... It's this one. Quick, quick, the A24 you need," El quickly said.

"Oh fuck!" Tom blurted out as a panicked, stricken look washed over his face as he checked the mirrors.

Tom was in the fast lane and needed to get across the very busy, slower lanes of traffic for their exit. He flicked on the indicator, but no one was letting him in. Lorry after lorry blocked his way until he saw a gap and floored the car to swerve into it before hitting the brakes to slow down, stopping them from ploughing into the back of the slower lorry in front.

"Shit!" he exclaimed as a lump formed in his chest from the surge of adrenaline.

Tom's heart raced as they left the motorway onto the slip road. He loved the rush he had just gotten and could already feel the buzz fizzling out.

El started laughing, causing Tom to look in the mirror again at her. "Well... that was close," she managed to giggle out before her eyes went wide, and she shouted, "FUCK!"

Tom's eyes shot to the road as he slammed the brake pedal down, narrowly missing the stationary car in front of them that was waiting for a space to join the roundabout at the junction.

El's fingers had dug into the seat covers as she braced herself for the impending impact, but it never came.

"Holy fuck, Tom!" El scolded him, slapping his shoulder hard as the tension in her body relaxed slightly. "Perhaps I should drive," El huffed as she sat back in the seat and crossed her arms over her chest.

Tom swallowed down the lump that had formed in his chest and the nauseating feeling in his stomach from their near miss. He was definitely struggling to concentrate with El sitting in the back, just as he had feared.

"Can you drive?" Tom asked El, genuinely contemplating letting her drive the rest of the way as he navigated the roundabout to head down the A24 towards the coast.

"No... But I think I could probably drive better than you." El started giggling. Her fear dissipated immediately as she looked at Tom in the mirror. His eyes focused on the road, and she placed her hands on her lap, relaxing back again.

"Well, I'm glad I could amuse you after nearly killing us both," Tom's tone was irritated as he breathed out a huff. He wasn't annoyed at El; he was upset at himself for getting so distracted. He was the one who was supposed to be in control of the car, and he'd nearly caused El harm by his lack of concentration.

El chuckled at him, unfazed by his annoyed tone, as she looked out the window at the familiar scenery.

"You know it would help me concentrate better if you sat in the front, El."

El's gaze snapped to his as she swallowed nervously. She started to unconsciously rub the scar on her arm that was hidden by the sleeve of her dress as her anxiety built. El hadn't sat in the front passenger seat of a car since the accident nearly two years ago. Her anxiety was starting to peak as she slipped into a flashback. El's heart raced as sweat beaded on her back and soaked into her dress. Tom's driving skills really didn't help the situation.

Tom looked at her in the mirror again as she had gone silent after the suggestion. A vacant look graced her glassy eyes as she continued to rub her scar. She looked deathly pale all of a sudden.

"It's fine, El... I don't want you to feel sick." Tom said, concerned.

El swallowed her fear and tried to concentrate on his voice as it grounded her back into the present. Her voice was quiet as she spoke.

"Tom?"

"Hmm?"

"Talk to me," she told him as she placed her hands on either side of her thighs and leaned slightly forward.

"Talk to you about what?"

"Anything."

8.

The rest of the journey was uneventful, and they actually arrived at the crematorium before El's parents and sister, much to Tom's surprise. El joked about how she would be surprised if he didn't get a speeding ticket as they sat in his car briefly. Tom just rolled his eyes and scoffed at El's comment before smirking at her.

Ever the gentleman, Tom got out of his car and opened the back door for her. He held his hand out for El to take as she twisted her legs around to place her feet flat on the floor. She gladly accepted it as the crunch of gravel sounded below her pumps as he helped her out of the car to stand before him.

There was that awkward silence between them as they looked at each other, their eyes searching for reassurance from one another. A quick beep from El's father's car horn snapped them out of staring at each other, and Tom dropped El's hand, feeling as if he'd been caught doing something more than he actually was. Tom instantly missed the feeling of her skin on his. He felt empty as he rubbed the back of his head with his hand, trying to ease some of his tension.

El's family came to stand with them as they waited patiently for their family's turn to enter the crematorium building.

As they went to walk inside the sombre building, El retook hold of Tom's hand, squeezing it gently. She needed to feel he was there next to her. She needed him to ground her during the service with the reassurance of his touch. He looked down at her and gave her a tight, thin-lipped smile as he squeezed her hand back. He felt a sense of pride as he walked beside El behind the rest of her family for them to take their seat. He had expected to sit away from them at the back during the service, but El was having none of that as she held his hand and manoeuvred them both to sit together on the front pew. Tom sat nearest to the wall with El beside him.

The service went smoothly and was a beautiful tribute to Enid.

El, Dotty and Betty all cried, as did most of the congregation. Tom had silently passed El a tissue as he squeezed her hand comfortingly. He had to suppress the urge to wipe her tears away himself with his thumb, wanting to swipe away the sadness that marred her skin. The grateful but brief smile El gave Tom was enough to quiet the desire to do it, and instead, he rubbed his thumb across the back of her hand.

Afterwards, they all headed to Enid's home for the wake, which was only a twenty-minute drive from the crematorium. The entire house was full of family and friends. There were laughs and more tears as they grieved as a family, recounting fond stories of the family's promiscuous matriarch.

When it came to scattering the ashes, everyone headed to the beach. The weather was beautiful, a gorgeous spring day. The sea was calm, and as Enid's grandchildren took to the water, this was the only time El had left Tom's side since coming out of her house this morning.

El and Dotty stood side by side as their cousins stood beside them. They each took a small handful of ashes from the urn as it was passed along the row and waited for a few moments, gathering their thoughts and love for their grandmother before they simultaneously let her go into the water.

El watched as the ashes mixed with the swirling sea. It lapped around her legs as the grey powder melted into the calm waves of the English channel. No one cared that the bottom of skirts or trousers were getting wet. No one complained about how cold the sea was or the breeze that had started swirling up around them. They all just stood silently, each with fond memories of their beloved, eccentric grandmother.

El and Dotty were the last ones left standing in the water as the rest of their cousins headed back towards Enid's home to warm up. El and Dotty's legs and feet went numb from the cold as they held each other for support, Dotty's arm around El's shoulders and El's arm around her waist.

"Are you coming in, El?" Dotty asked as she caved in, unable to stand the cold anymore.

"Just a few more minutes."

"Ok."

Dotty turned and gave her sister another tight hug before she left her standing alone in the water and walked up the beach.

The sea level got lower on El's legs as the tide started to ebb away, leaving a cold numbing sensation in her bones where the water had been wrapped around, caressing her body.

El rubbed the scar on her wrist unconsciously as she closed her eyes, taking the time she needed to say goodbye. El was the grandchild who had had the closest relationship with their grandmother, and no one batted an eyelid that she would be the one who would be most affected by her death.

Tom had stood at the back of the gathered crowd of friends and relatives the entire time, watching El, his eyes focused on her mousey brown hair as it blew around in the breeze.

As everyone started to head back to the house to warm up, Betty stopped by Tom and placed her hand on his shoulder.

"Thank you for coming today. I don't know what El would have done if you hadn't come into her life when she needed someone," Betty said appreciatively, a noticeable glass sheen to her eyes as she held back her tears. She felt exhausted from the amount of tears she had shed since her mother's death, but she was happy that Tom had come into their lives when they needed him. He had been the one to save El from herself even though the rest of the family had tried; this stranger that had come into their lives had given El what she needed.

Tom was speechless. Betty was so grateful to him; Tom could see it in her eyes. He smiled and bowed his head to Betty before she walked back to the house, wiping at her falling tears that she could no longer hold back.

Dotty came to stand next to Tom.

"Hey, Dotty... Are you ok?" he asked her with genuine concern.

Dotty just nodded as she turned to watch El standing alone in the sea. A few minutes of silence passed as they watched El together before Dotty spoke.

"Thank you, Tom."

"For what?"

"For bringing her back again."

Something in Dotty's voice intrigued him, something she seemed to hint at as he picked up on her final word.

"Again?" he asked curiously as he tilted his head to look at Dotty.

Dotty sighed before she continued speaking as she watched El. "I shouldn't really be telling you this."

"Tell me what?" Tom turned his whole body to face Dotty as she continued to watch El.

"El has done this before... The shutting down... Shutting everyone out."

Tom furrowed his brow as he tilted his head, "What do you mean?"

"El nearly died two years ago. After she woke up in hospital after her operation, she-she just shut down immediately. She wouldn't speak, and she wouldn't eat. We were losing her in front of our eyes, and there was nothing we could do about it. Guilt consumed her."

"What do you mean she nearly died? Was she in an accident?" Tom asked, concerned.

Dotty nodded her head. "Yeah, she was in a car crash. It's why she won't sit in the front of a car."

"Oh my god. What happened?" Tom's heart raced as he turned back to look at El. He had nearly lost her before he had ever even met her, and it tore a hole in his heart at the thought of never having met her.

"You can't tell her I told you. She doesn't ever talk about it. Well... not with us, but she did with Nan. That's why they were so close." Dotty took a calming breath before she continued. "After El had gotten her

A-level results, we went out to celebrate the following week. She had gotten what she needed to get into Cambridge. I was so proud of her that I wanted to treat her on a night out." Dotty paused, remembering that fateful night before she started talking again.

"She used to love going out with friends and partying. She was funny and cute, and she was happy. But that night... my-my boyfriend at the time said he'd drive her home. She was really drunk, and he hadn't been drinking or anything. But his car spun off the road into a tree for some reason. El managed to get out, but Andy he... he didn't. The car caught on fire, and he died in it."

Tom remained silent the entire time as he listened to Dotty while looking at El, his heart pounding with emotions he couldn't place.

"They found El unconscious in the road. She had internal bleeding and cuts all over her arms and chest. They managed to save her, but after... after, we thought she'd be fine, ya know? A bit of counselling, therapy, whatever she needed, but she just retreated away and shut everyone out. It was only when Nan came and insisted that she came to stay with her here that we saw a change in her a few weeks later. El was back. Well, almost... She was quieter. She had lost some of her sparkle, but at least she was talking and talking about her future. That's why when Nan died in front of her, we thought we'd lose her for good this time, but then you..."

Dotty took hold of Tom's hand and turned to face him as Tom mirrored Dotty.

"You brought her back, and I'm so grateful... We're so grateful, Tom. You have no idea what you've done for us, for her. I just thought you should know that." Dotty squeezed his hand before going up on her tiptoes to place a quick peck on his cheek. She smiled gratefully at him and let go of his hand before she turned and walked back towards the house.

Tom stood there on the shingle, his heart pounding in his chest. He was glad that Dotty had trusted him enough to share El's history with him, that her family trusted him with her. But, deep down, he wished that El had been the one to tell him about her past.

El was still standing in the same spot when Tom approached her. The water was barely covering her ankles as the tide went out. Tom took his shoes and socks off, rolling his suit trousers up as best he could before standing next to her in the water. Tom took a few calming breaths to shut out the cold seeping into his feet as he took hold of El's hand and linked fingers with hers. This was the first time their fingers were entwined, and it felt the most intimate thing for Tom as he ran his thumb over the back of her hand reassuringly.

"Thank you for today, Tom." After a few peaceful moments, El turned her head to look up at him. Her cheeks were tear-stained from where she had been crying. Tom turned his body fully to her and lifted his free hand to cup her face.

"Whenever you need me... I'll be there, El." He wiped the remnants of her tears away from her cheek with the pad of his thumb as she leaned her head into his palm. Her eyes were watching his as he looked down at her lips. El's mouth slowly parted as her tongue dipped out to wet them. The intimacy of this moment pulled her towards him as El forgot her sadness for a brief moment and was swept away in his gaze like the sea washing away from her legs as the tide went out.

Tom's breathing was ragged, his pulse thumping in his head as the noise of the sea joined the rush in his ears. He moved closer to her, the edge of his suit jacket brushing against the material of her dress. His eyes never left her mouth as he let go of her hand to place it around her waist, pulling her gently to him as he stepped closer so that the fabric of their clothes moulded together. That static feeling he seemed to get when they touched now raced across his entire body.

El placed her hand over his on her cheek as her other hand went to his bicep. She swallowed down any nerves as butterflies danced around her stomach. El's feelings for Tom started to shift to something more.

Here was the man who had pulled her out of the darkness and back towards the light, towards him as he made her face death at his own hands. And she relished it.

Tom looked into her eyes for the silent permission he was craving. Those unique eyes had drawn him to her in the first place. One blue, one brown staring back up at him like spiralling whirlpools, dragging him further under.

El looked at Tom's lips as he subconsciously licked them. The sound of the sea around them faded to a whisper as she focused solely on him. Her hand slid up his arm and wrapped around the back of his shoulder, pulling him down to her as she tilted her chin up slowly. This was the permission he needed.

Tom lowered his head to hers, his breath ghosting across her lips as they closed the gap between them. El held her breath as she closed her eyes, waiting for the softness of his lips against hers. Tom's fingers moved into the edge of El's hair as his grip tightened on her waist, pulling her even closer so that her hips were now resting against the top of his thighs. He closed his eyes just at the last moment.

"EL!" Mark's voice cut through the air, instantly ruining their intimate moment.

Their lips were so close to touching that only a thin sheet of paper could have passed between them as they both opened their eyes with a look of disappointment.

Tom cursed her father internally as he took a small step back, letting his fingers slip from her hair. He looked over to the top of the beach to see El's father's figure crest over the edge. A wave of frustration coursed through Tom as he looked at El's father.

"El! We need you back at the house. The lawyers are here."

El slumped back, disappointed that her little fantasy moment had been cut short, letting Tom go before she smiled at him nervously. "Back to reality," she sighed, and her eyes dropped away.

For El, that entire moment with Tom felt like a dream she didn't want to wake from. Whether it was because she was merely caught up in the moment with the emotional day taking its toll or that El had actually wanted this to happen with Tom and cross the line of just being friends, she didn't know. But she did know that something had shifted in their dynamic. Tom had felt the same as he watched El leave the water and grab her shoes.

El's father was standing at the top of the crest of shingle with his hands on his hips, gesturing at them to hurry up. "Come on, El... We've been waiting for ages for you. They apparently won't start until everyone is present."

There was an oddness to Mark's voice, which Tom found disconcerting as he looked up the beach towards him. Considering the day's events, Mark's tone showed a hint of frenzied excitement, which gave Tom an ominous feeling in his gut, like something was off.

"Coming," El called back to him as she quickly pulled her shoes back on her frozen feet, seemingly not noticing her father's tone.

Tom followed after her as he crunched up the beach before sitting to put his socks and shoes back on, pushing Mark to the back of his mind.

Tom slipped on the shingle, falling on his ass when he went to stand back up. El's reaction was to burst out laughing as she stood, watching his crumpled, tall form slip again on the shingle as he tried to stand.

"Was it too cold for those giant feet in there? Are they that numb?" she giggled.

"Ha. No. I just slipped on the shingle," Tom huffed. "It's wet."

"Well, you'd think those feet would give you good balance." El continued to snigger as she looked down at Tom.

He tilted his head and looked up at her as she stepped closer. "What are you saying about my feet?"

"Well, you know... Big feet, big... surface area to balance on." El's eyes raked down Tom's body to his crotch, her pupils dilating as she looked down at the sizeable bulge that was covered by the stretched material of his formal black trousers.

Tom tracked her eye movement with his own. He smirked and raised an eyebrow, causing a blush to creep up her cheeks because he had caught her looking. El cleared her throat as she looked away, making Tom chuckle.

Something had undoubtedly changed between Tom and El's relationship since yesterday's events in her bedroom. Even more so now that they had shared an almost kiss.

"Well, if you would assist in helping a gentleman to his feet. We could continue on our journey, darling, as my *big* feet seem so unreliable."

El stuck out her hand and helped Tom to his feet as she tried to hide her giggles.

As Tom held her hand, he quickly pulled her towards him, causing El to bang into his chest and them both to giggle. But as El's eyes tracked up his black tie and their eyes met, a loaded silence crept between them. El placed her free hand against his chest, her thumb gliding over the material of his tie, feeling the shirt buttons beneath it. She could feel his taunt muscles flex under her fingertips as she slowly moved her hand across his chest. Butterflies danced in her stomach as she looked up at Tom and saw the dark look of desire in his eyes.

Tom sucked in a breath as the tension built between them, his hand tightening around hers that was holding her hand by his side. He leaned down next to her ear to whisper the words that were burning in his mind. "Just so you know, El... nothing else that's *big*... is *unreliable*." He stood back up with the most irresistible look of pure smugness and lust across his features as he looked down into her eyes. El's lips parted as she took in his words, and her pupils widened.

"Come on, you two!" Mark called out.

9.

"Mark, wait!" Betty called out to her husband as he slammed the front door and stormed out after another argument. It had been a few weeks since the will had been read at Enid's wake, and El's parents had been arguing almost constantly since.

The lawyers had dropped a bombshell on the entire family, causing the news to disintegrate their relationships. It shattered El's family unit's usual peace and tranquillity like it had only been held together with a glass thread instead of unbreakable silk bonds.

...

"So... There you have it. Ethel will be the sole beneficiary of Enid's estate with the exception of one hundred thousand pounds for each grandchild. This money will be put into a trust with Enid deciding prior to her death at what age each individual would receive it."

El had stood there frozen to the spot as silence echoed around the room. Each family member slowly turned their head to look at her, their eyes boring into her, making her the centre of attention she hated. Some with a look of shock plastered across their faces, whilst others looked at her with jealous contempt.

She squeezed Tom's hand as she tried to absorb what the portly, older lawyer in the dark brown suit had just told her family.

El had inherited the majority of Enid's savings and bonds, totalling over thirty million pounds. In addition to that extortionate amount of wealth, El inherited all of Enid's properties. Some were in London, others in Cambridge, and the house in Atherington they were standing in now. It totalled an additional fifty million pounds, bringing the grand total of El's wealth to over eighty million pounds.

El was now an extremely wealthy young woman and potentially had gained quite a few enemies immediately within her own family through their jealousy.

No one in the family had any clue that Enid was quite that wealthy. She led a simple life. She may have been married several times, each of her four children with a different husband, but they all accepted that it was in her nature. Enid had never liked to be tied to one person for long. She could never feel settled in the company of one man. Her family never did without, but they certainly never lived in the apparent luxury that they could have afforded.

The lawyer also stated that El would only have access to this wealth that had been put into a trust fund once she turned twenty-one. Her twenty-first birthday was in October, less than six months away.

"Tom... I, I need to sit down." El's voice was quiet. She started swaying slightly as the news overwhelmed her, making her light-headed.

He quickly pulled a chair over for El to sit down on as her family swarmed around her. They were like bees buzzing around a honey pot with hidden stings ready to stab her in the back.

El was hit with a barrage of constant questions and noise from all directions as people started tearing into the envelopes they had been given. Her senses were overloaded with the sounds of disbelief. Crumpled-up and torn paper echoed around the room as everyone was pushing over each other to get closer to her.

Before the lawyers left, they handed each family member an envelope with a handwritten letter from Enid. El was clutching onto hers for dear life.

Tom crouched in front of her, trying to block some of it out as he held her free hand, hoping to get her to focus on him. He could see the panic in her eyes as she stared vacantly ahead as though she was looking through him. His touch couldn't break her out of it as he rubbed his thumb across her knuckles, and it seemed she couldn't hear him either as she shut down from becoming too overwhelmed with anxiety and shock.

Someone barged into Tom, knocking him forward and onto El's knees. That was the last straw.

Tom sprung up, letting go of El's hand and spun around to face everyone with rage coursing through his veins. "Everyone needs to SHUT UP! And BACK the FUCK UP!" he shouted at them as his hands balled into fists at his sides.

Instant silence fell across the kitchen they were all squeezed into. Everyone took a step back as Tom stood protectively in front of El, like a lion protecting his lioness from the gathering hyenas. He almost snarled after he had shouted at them, not caring what they thought of his colourful language or conduct. All Tom was concerned about was protecting El from them, not that he had shown them all a glimpse of the monster lurking beneath.

"Can't you see El's in just as much shock as the rest of you? You're meant to be her family, for Christ's sake!"

Betty pushed through the crowd and stood next to Tom.

"Everyone out!" commanded Betty as she gestured towards the kitchen door.

Mark and Dotty lingered around the kitchen, not knowing whether they should leave too, but the look that Betty gave them had both of them gesturing the remaining family out of the room.

Betty was Enid's daughter, and she had a feeling that something like this would happen before the lawyer had even started reading the will out to the gathered family. Betty had had a few conversations with her mother about El's choices in private last year. Enid had briefly spoken about her will to Betty, but Betty didn't realise how wealthy her mother actually was when she talked about leaving everything to El. Betty thought she was joking, as Enid had laughed when she said it.

Looking back now, she realised why her mother had laughed. Enid had known exactly what kind of drama she would be causing their family, having the last laugh.

The news had left a sour taste in Betty's mouth, knowing her and her siblings' struggles over the years. But she also would never go against her mother's wishes. Betty respected her decisions but would speak to her brothers and sister about it later. Betty's concern was for El; she buried the sour taste down to deal with by herself later. Her children always came first, and right now, El needed her.

"Well... That was a bit of a surprise." Betty said as she turned to look down at El and then back up at Tom.

Tom took a deep breath and crouched back down in front of El. "El? Do you need anything?" he asked concerned.

El clutched the envelope as she held it against her chin. She could smell her grandmother's perfume on it, which helped soothe her overworking mind and eased some of her anxiety. El had no clue, not a single inclination, that her grandmother would do this. She felt guilt start consuming her as she sat silently on the kitchen chair.

Tom drove El back to Cambridge soon after, leaving everyone else at the house in disarray. He wanted to get her away from the rest of them. She needed space to absorb this information without the constant barrage of noise or pressure from everyone's expectations that El would share her newfound wealth with them.

El sat silently in the back of his car, still holding the envelope as she stared out the window, watching the leaves of the trees blur into a forest of green haze.

As they arrived at her home, Tom got out and opened the door for her. She took his hand as Tom led El silently towards her house. He opened his free hand for her to pass him her house keys and let them both inside.

"Would you like some water? A cup of tea?" Tom hesitantly asked her as El let go of his hand. They had wandered into the kitchen, Tom thinking a nice cup of tea would help soothe her. She hadn't spoken in the car the entire drive back, and he was deeply concerned that she had slipped back into her depression. The events of today might bring all her dark thoughts back, and he was worried that this would all overwhelm her so much that he might not be able to get her back a second time.

"Err... Tom," El spoke quietly as she took a shallow breath. "I just need a moment alone. I don't want you to go, but..." El's voice drifted off as she sighed, looking down at the floor and chewing on her lip. She wanted him to stay but couldn't bring herself to say the words out loud.

A smile tugged at the corner of Tom's mouth as he reassuringly squeezed her shoulder, causing her to look up at him.

"I know... I'll wait here in the kitchen for you. You just need to call me if you need me to come," Tom said as he gave her a small smile.

She smiled gratefully at him as his hand slipped off her shoulder, and she headed upstairs to her bedroom.

El sat down at her desk and took a deep breath before opening the envelope. It was sealed with a wax seal and embossed with a red rose. El chuckled slightly at her grandmother's creative side and penchant for the dramatic. She carefully peeled the wax seal back and took the paper out, pressing it gently to the table to flatten it out. El reached for her lamp and turned it on to see the writing more clearly on the piece of paper on her desk. She took another deep breath before focusing on the handwritten words.

My dearest El,

You are probably wondering why I chose to keep my intentions hidden from you and the rest of this wretched family. Why I hid my wealth from everyone will become apparent within the next few weeks, months and years. There will be people who will be jealous. People who will try to guilt you into giving them money.

DO NOT LET THEM!

This is solely for you and you alone!

You must be careful who you trust, El. I could not protect some of my children from whom they fell in love with, and I wish I could have. But their choices were their own in the end.

You are the mistress of your destiny, my sweet, and you control who you want to be. You have the means now to do as you wish. To be that person you once dreamt of. To follow your heart and passions. To pursue your talents. I'm just sorry that I won't be there to hear it.

Grip each chance with both hands, and don't regret anything.

There is no point in letting the past rule your life, my sweet, as I have told you many times before. Don't let it hold you back. You cannot change it, but it will shape you.

I will not write here about how much we know of each other because that, my sweet girl, is our secret to treasure and not commit to paper.

You will be the centre of someone's world, just as you should always be. Take a chance at love, El, and never settle for second best.

You are in control.

You have always been in control. You just need to follow your dreams and make them a reality. Show the world that inner fire that is buried inside. The fire you showed that night. Show them who you are, El, that no one but you can influence your choices.

I love you for eternity, my sweet, sweet El.

I'm just sad I won't be there to see you conquer the world.

X

El sat back in the chair, taking in what was written on the paper. Tears ran down her cheeks as she sniffed, trying to compose herself.

After a few minutes, she carefully folded it, placing it back into the envelope. She removed the wax seal and put it on the table before she got up and lifted the corner of her mattress, placing the envelope underneath.

"Tom?" El called out to him, and he instantly appeared in the doorway, having silently crept upstairs to wait outside her room, knowing she would call him.

He walked straight in and put his hand on the back of her head, pulling her into his chest as she started to sob, her tears soaking into the fabric of his white dress shirt as she clung to him.

...

"Mum? Are you alright?" El asked as she came downstairs to find her mother crying at the kitchen table. She had been listening to music with her headphones on and hadn't heard the latest argument between her mother and father.

She was sick of the arguing. With trying to study for her end-of-year exams this week, one of them being tomorrow, she needed to drown out the noise.

Betty quickly wiped her face, forcing a smile.

"Yeah, I'm fine, love... Nothing for you to worry about."

El frowned at her mum. She didn't believe a word she said and could see how upset Betty was.

Mark had distanced himself from everyone, especially El, and Betty hated it. What had happened wasn't El's fault, and every time Betty said something about his behaviour, it just turned into an argument.

"What did you want for tea, love?" Betty asked as she forced a smile to form.

"Oh, erm..." El paused as she sucked her cheeks in against her teeth.

Betty smiled at El and her hesitation to answer.

Betty suddenly remembered, "Oh, sorry, love. I forgot. Tom's taking you out for dinner, isn't he?"

"I can cancel, Mum," El said quickly.

El was worried about her mum, and Dotty was never in the house anymore. She hated the arguments, too, and got very upset about them. Dotty told El she couldn't be around it and was staying with friends most of the time, especially as Dotty also had her end-of-year exams. It was Dotty's final year of her undergraduate politics degree, and she had wanted to stay on for her Master's, meaning she needed to get at least a two, one.

"No, no... You go have fun. You've been studying so hard recently. You deserve a break." Betty gave her a tight smile.

There was not a chance El was going to leave her like this, even if it pained her not to see Tom. El had started to crave his presence constantly, especially after they had spent more time together over the past few weeks. She smiled back at her mum and went upstairs, grabbing her phone from her back pocket as she walked. She dialled the first number in her call history.

"Hey, El. Is everything okay?" Tom answered on the second ring, and when he didn't get a cheerful hello back, he knew something was wrong immediately.

"Erm..." El hesitated before she swallowed it down. "I'm sorry, Tom... but I'm going to have to cancel dinner," El apologised.

Tom pulled the phone away from his ear, placing his thumb over the speaker as he sighed heavily, clenching his jaw and gritting his teeth. His other hand gripped his leg tightly, digging his nails into his thigh as he sat on his bed. He took a deep breath and shook his head before bringing the phone back to his ear. "What's happened?" Tom asked. He wasn't annoyed at her, not one bit. El had told him how her father was being, which angered him. It frustrated him that he couldn't really do anything about it. Well... nothing good anyway. He had to restrain himself from storming around to her house and driving a knife straight into Mark's neck, slicing it open and spraying his own face in Mark's blood. Tom had even dreamt about it, but his hand wasn't holding the knife. It was El's.

"I just don't want to leave mum at the moment. I'm sorry," El said sadly.

Tom smiled to himself at her apology. She wasn't the one who needed to say sorry.

"What food does your mum like?" he asked as an idea flashed in his head.

"Erm... Thai is her favourite. Why?"

"I'll be round at six to pick you both up," Tom stated.

"What?" El asked, confused.

"Tell your mum not to cook. I'm taking you both out. My treat."

"But Tom," El whined.

"No buts, El... My treat."

10.

Sitting in the Thai restaurant with Betty and El, Tom couldn't contain his smile as he watched El with her mum.

She looked so happy as she laughed with her mother. Betty was recounting stories to Tom about El getting up to all sorts of mischief when she was a little girl.

"I couldn't believe she had done that."

"Mum! Stop!" El laughed as her mum continued on with her story.

Betty was laughing. "I told her not to try tasting raw flour, but she wouldn't listen. She was a stubborn little thing and still is," Betty chuckled as she nudged El before continuing her story. "She inhaled the flour from the spoon, coughing it everywhere. She looked like a little steam engine, all red-faced and mad because the flour didn't taste like the cake I had promised her."

El's face was bright red from both embarrassment and laughter.

"That's one of my first memories," El giggled. "I must have been about three, I think?"

"Yes. You were three when that particular little incident happened."

Tom smiled and placed his hand over El's on the table. She warmed his heart with her laughter and smile. It was so good to see her smiling and happy. Tom was now on a personal mission to bring lightness into her life whenever he could. It made him feel good about himself just seeing her like this, even though he wasn't the cause. He enjoyed basking in her light.

"Well, I'm sure my mother could tell you plenty of embarrassing stories about me, too," Tom chuckled.

"Oh, we must meet your parents, Tom," Betty said.

El looked at her mother wide-eyed. "Mum!"

Betty just shrugged as she ate another piece of her Pad Thai, ignoring El's displeasure at the suggestion.

"Friends don't meet each other's parents, mum."

Betty frowned as she swallowed her mouthful. "Of course they do," she said as she tapped El's arm. "At any rate. You two are obviously more than just friends."

"MUM!" El scolded. Her plan of distracting her mum from the arguments with her dad had spectacularly backfired into Betty embarrassing El in front of Tom, making her cheeks heat.

Tom smirked and looked down at his plate of food, pretending to be very interested in his curry suddenly as he poked his fork around in the red-curry-stained rice.

El and Tom had gotten closer over the past few weeks since Enid's funeral. Tom had taken El out for coffee and cinema trips, anything to take her mind off what had happened recently with her grandmother and the revelations that Enid's will had brought. He had even been helping her study for her exams, trying to give her an unperceived advantage with his knowledge of the previous English Literature exams that he had taken at University.

Tom had subtly steered conversations to topics that he knew may come up in the exam. It wasn't cheating. It was simply helping El with her studies. It was also another excuse to spend time alone with her, even if nothing more had happened between them other than subtle touches and looks. Tom was content at the moment to just be around her. His fantasies about El and him together were thoughts that he kept to himself for his nighttime activities.

Tom hadn't acted on any urges to kill anyone in the recent weeks as all of his energy was spent making sure that El was okay. He just hadn't had the time to give in to his murderous tendencies. El was far more important than satisfying that itch. Plus, he couldn't really murder her father, Mark, even though, with what El had been telling him about her father's increasingly distant behaviour during their last cafe trip together, he had wanted to.

El had grown so fond of Tom and started to rely on him for comfort, but she didn't know how to take it further. She'd never had a friend like him before and didn't want to ruin what they had developed by crossing that invisible friend's line, even though she had sometimes wanted to. He was there for her. She didn't want to push him away because of selfish desires.

After they had finished their meals, Tom paid the bill and drove them all back to El and Betty's home. Betty recounted more stories as she sat in the front passenger seat with El grimacing in the back. Tom couldn't help but keep looking in the rearview mirror to watch El burying her embarrassed face in her hands. It was an endearing sight. Her cheeks flushed in a pinky hue. Seeing the corners of her mouth pulled up with laughter made Tom smile and warm his heart.

"That was fabulous. I haven't laughed like that in a while." Betty chuckled as she opened the front door to the house, letting both El and Tom in.

"It was my pleasure, Betty. I'm glad you enjoyed yourself," Tom smiled at her.

"Thank you, Tom. I needed that," said Betty as she stepped into her home.

El smiled at him as they walked in behind her into the house, hand in hand.

"Would you like a cup of..." Betty was cut off by her husband as she stilled just inside the kitchen as El nearly crashed into the back of her.

"You... Yyyou're finally back then, I see." Mark sat at the kitchen table, slurring his words. A large bottle of whiskey, which was nearly empty, was sitting in front of him on the table. An abandoned crystal tumbler glass sat next to it, the last remnants of the amber liquid in the bottom. Mark reached for the glass and brought the remaining liquid to his lips. He tipped it back quickly, finishing the contents before he slammed it back down on the table, making El jump, and her hand tighten around Tom's.

"Jesus Christ, Mark!" Betty rushed over to him as he stood up from the table and nearly fell over. She grabbed his arm just in time to stop him from crashing to the floor, holding him up as his weight sagged against her.

"Take yyyou out, did he? Huh? Trying to ggget in your knickers too, huh?" Mark stuttered as his unfocused eyes looked at Betty.

Tom immediately tensed. He could smell the stench of vomit and cheap whiskey on Mark's breath from across the room. He let go of El's hand and stepped to her side.

El put her hand on Tom's forearm to stop him from rushing forward as he went to take a step forward. She could feel the rage radiate off him, just like it had in her bedroom all those weeks ago. El looked up at Tom as his eyes narrowed with a laser focus on Mark.

He had that look in his eyes again, like he wanted to murder someone, as the subtle clinch of his jaw tightened, giving away that he was clenching his teeth together.

El quickly turned her body in front of him, blocking his way. "It's probably best you go." Her eyes were already starting to fill with tears as they threatened to spill down her cheeks. She forced herself to take a deep breath and steady herself to try and calm Tom down.

"No... I think I should stay." Tom's voice was low and authoritative as he watched Mark's every movement over El's shoulder like a predator ready to protect his mate.

"YYYOU! You think you're some bbbig shot, don't you! Sssome clever posh ppprick!" Mark swayed more as he pointed his index finger accusingly towards Tom.

"Mark, stop it! You're drunk!" Betty wrapped her arm under his to try and lead him away.

"GET OFF ME!" Mark shouted as he pushed her back, causing her to slip over in the vomit on the laminate floor where Mark had emptied the contents of his stomach earlier.

A loud thump echoed through the room as Betty fell backwards, hitting her head on the kitchen counter and knocking herself out.

El spun around from blocking Tom's way at the sudden noise as she had a flashback of her grandmother laying on the floor. A terrifying sinking feeling wracked through her that it was happening all over again.

"MUM!"

El's whole body tensed with shock as she looked at her mum, slumped down against the kitchen cupboard, not moving. Her eyes zeroed in on her mother's body, watching for the slightest sign of movement. Relief washed over her as El saw her mum's chest rise and fall as she took a laboured breath. Her eyes were then drawn to the cause of it all. Her father.

El now stood between Tom, who was radiating rage behind her and her drunk, swaying father in front.

Mark stumbled his way around the table towards them, ignoring Betty on the floor as his anger focused on the pair.

El tried to move towards her mum, but Tom grabbed her arm, pulling her back as Mark grabbed the bottle from the table.

"Dad! Dad, you need to stop! Mum's hurt!" Tears ran down El's cheek as she watched her father adjust the grip on the bottleneck. He pointed it threateningly at both her and Tom as he held it out in front of him, simmering with irrational anger.

"Hhhe's only after your mmmoney. Mmmoney, that should be mmmine. I NEED IT!" Mark yelled at El.

"I suggest you sit the FUCK DOWN, MARK! Before I make you!" Tom seethed at him as he pulled El back away from her dad, who was now approaching them. Tom's fingers splayed across El's abdomen as he held her back, not wanting her to get hurt.

Tom purposefully put himself between El and her father in a protective stance, his feet wide apart and ready to move if needed. There was no way that Mark was getting anywhere near El with Tom there.

Betty started to groan on the floor before she began to sit up, shifting her legs from out under her to lay them flat on the floor. She rubbed the back of her head with her hand as she leaned back against the kitchen cabinet with her eyes closed. Her features tightened as her hand passed over a sore bit on her head, and she winced with pain.

"WHO! WHO THE FUCK DO YOU THINK YOU ARE! TTTTELLING ME WHAT TO DO IN MY HOUSE!" Mark shouted at Tom with a frightening rage that El had never seen in her father before. He swung the bottle at Tom's head, missing entirely as Tom leaned quickly back and out of reach.

Tom backed up, pushing El backwards through the kitchen door with his hand on her stomach as Mark approached them with a furious look in his drunken eyes.

Mark swung again, smashing the bottle against the door frame. The glass scattered across the laminate floor of the kitchen, spreading out onto the hallway's wooden parquet. It left Mark holding a jagged, sharp bottleneck as his feet crunched through the broken glass. Mark thrust the glass in his hand towards Tom and El as he moved forward as if he were stalking them. His eyes looked filled with purpose as he took small, threatening steps.

"You need to stop, Mark... before I make you." Tom's voice was deathly calm as his eyes focused on Mark's slightest movement. He gently pushed El back, readying himself for whatever Mark was about to do as Tom dropped both his hands by his sides.

Tom watched as the muscles in Mark's neck and arms tensed before he was going to make a move again. He lunged forward at Tom, screaming incoherently. The sharp shards of the bottle in his hand pointed straight at Tom's face.

El screamed as she quickly backed away from her raging father into the hall wall. Her eyes were filled with terror at what was happening. Their night of laughter had descended into chaos at the flix of a switch.

Tom sidestepped Mark's thrust and grabbed his forearm as he did, spinning Mark around so that his back was now to Tom's chest. Mark was tall but not as tall as Tom, giving Tom the easy advantage. Tom now held Mark's body flush to his. Tom shifted his grip to tighten around Mark's hand as he bent it towards Mark's own throat. The broken sharp edges of the bottleneck now pushed against Mark's neck, threateningly close to his pulsing jugular. Tom's other arm was up under Mark's free arm, across his chest, gripping the side of Mark's jaw with his large hand. Tom twisted Mark's head to the side, exposing more of the delicate skin of Mark's neck to him, laying his life bare before Tom's eyes.

El's eyes widened in panic as she saw the look on Tom's face. It was terrifying as a serenity washed over it. Tom closed his eyes, almost as though he was savouring the moment, the calm before the storm. The air of the hallway suddenly felt suffocating, making it hard to focus on anything else apart from Tom.

Tom breathed in deeply as his murderous rage coursed through his veins, filling his body with adrenaline. He was quickly reaching boiling point as his fingers subtly flexed around Mark's body, tightening slowly, preparing to strike.

Mark struggled against Tom, but it was useless. His free hand flew in the air uselessly like he was trying to grasp something to prise himself away from Tom.

It didn't help that Mark was drunk, but Tom would still have been able to overpower him even if Mark had been entirely sober. Tom was surprisingly strong for his lean build. The years of kidnapping and murdering people had built Tom into an explosive machine capable of tackling men much bigger than himself. He had learnt to use their size against them with the help of some self-defence videos on YouTube, putting himself at a considerable advantage.

Tom opened his eyes and slowly tightened his grip on Mark's hand, pushing the bottle into Mark's neck. It was just starting to break the skin, a fraction at a time, with every tension of Mark's sternocleidomastoid muscle. A small drop of blood began to form under the broken edge of the glass bottle as Tom pushed the glass further and harder against Mark's pulsing skin.

Tom's deep breaths slid across Mark's face as he held him firmly in his grasp like a Venus fly trap, closing in around its prey. A genuinely evil smirk developed on Tom's face at the thought of Mark's impending demise at his hands. He had held onto this urge to kill El's father for so long because of how Mark had treated El that he was now temptingly close to satisfying it; the compulsion for murder buzzed through Tom's body. All Tom had to do was push just that little bit more.

"TOM!" El shouted as she stood before him, trying to get Tom to focus on her. His pupils were so dark they were almost entirely black, as if he had slipped into some sort of void, completely losing himself to the monster within.

Tom's fingers dug into Mark's hand and jaw as he sneered, tightening his grip even more, not hearing El's plea. He was consumed with the thought of spilling Mark's blood and taking his life.

Mark whimpered under Tom's painful grip as the bottle dug into the skin of his neck another fraction of a millimetre, causing more blood to start to trickle down Mark's neck.

The alcohol had thinned Mark's blood, making it flow even faster than it usually would have. The blood glinted in the light of the hallway light above Tom's head, dancing like fireflies in the night sky as the trickle of blood started to soak into the collar of Mark's top.

El stepped closer to Tom, her eyes softening as she tried to calm his inner demons and reach inside the dark void to pull him back out.

"Tom," her voice was soft as she stepped closer. Her hand was outstretched towards Tom's face as she slowly approached him. El's fingers reached for him, trembling with her need for him to focus on her.

Mark struggled again as panic started to take hold of him. The effects of the alcohol were wearing off, sobering him up exceptionally quickly. But all it did was push the sharp edge further into his neck.

Tom adjusted his grip, holding Mark tightly as his eyes focused on Mark's blown pupils, filled with fear and terror. Mark looked back up at Tom with eyes begging for his life. He wanted to say something, to plead with Tom not to do this in front of El, but with Tom holding his jaw so tightly, he couldn't move it to speak.

"Tom... Look at me."

Tom blinked a few times as he heard El's voice call to him in the dark. El was so close to them now that she could feel her father's panicked breaths fan across her face.

Tom felt as though he was standing in a dark room, alone with Mark, holding Mark's life in his hands. He couldn't see anything but the images of dark blood pouring across his hand.

"Tom."

El's voice cut through the darkness, like the sun cresting over the horizon, chasing the night away. She was breaking through his murderous haze.

Tom blinked again, his eyes shifting to El's as she tried desperately to pull him out of whatever place he had gone to.

His bloodlust boiled beneath the surface, scratching to be satisfied as it clawed at him, trying to pull him back down into darkness. The voice in Tom's head told him to do it, urging him to push just that little bit more. It wouldn't take much for the bottle to pierce into Mark's jugular. The voice urged him to see how beautiful El would look, painted in blood. She'd look so pretty in red. It would match her contrasting eyes for sure.

"Tom..." El touched Tom's face, skimming her fingertips along his cheek as she stepped closer. His clenched jaw muscles instantly relaxed as he met her gaze.

The voice in Tom's head disappeared as if he had woken from a dream he couldn't quite remember as the images of El covered in blood faded away to leave her standing in the hallway before him, looking up at him with beseeching eyes.

Tom pulled Mark's hand back away from his neck and twisted it, making him drop the bottleneck. It shattered against the floor as it splintered into sharp fragments, spreading across the floor like a rippling wave. The sudden noise cut through the thick, tense air, momentarily drawing El's attention to it before her gaze landed back on her father. Tom forcefully pushed Mark away from him and El, causing him to slip and fall onto his chest, dangerously close to the splintered sharp shards that littered the hallway.

El spun around to see her father slip across the wooden laminate from the force Tom had used. El's rage seethed within her now; her eyes turned black with a vengeance for what Mark had done to Betty. She couldn't stop herself as she stormed up to her crumpled father's body, crunching through the broken glass on the floor and grabbed the vase from the hall console table without thinking about what she was doing.

Tom stood watching as if stuck in quicksand, unable to move as he watched El lift the vase above her head with both hands.

It all seemed to happen in slow motion as El screamed at her father, causing him to lift his body up onto all fours and turn his head to her before she slammed the vase down across the side of his head, knocking him out cold.

Tom's breath caught in his throat as he watched El hit her father with such force that she might actually have killed him had the vase been something solid and not hollow. His cock twitched in response at the thought of El murdering someone right in front of him without any hesitation. It was the most erotic thing Tom had ever seen and something which he knew he would be thinking about for weeks to come as he fantasised about El taking someone's life with her bare hands.

11.

El hadn't managed to kill Mark, much to Tom's disappointment, but she had given him a severe concussion.

The nosey neighbour had called the police after hearing the unusual commotion and shouting late at night from next door. After they arrived, the police called an ambulance for Betty and Mark. They tried to question El in detail whilst the paramedics attended to her parents. But Tom stepped in and told them to stop. Couldn't they see she was in shock from what just happened? The officers agreed but said they would be back.

El went in the ambulance with her mum whilst Tom followed behind in his car. Mark was taken to hospital with a police escort after they arrested him for assault. This made it much more uncomfortable for El, knowing they were all going to the same hospital. She wanted her mum to feel safe and not worry about potentially seeing Mark there. But thankfully, the police officers and hospital staff kept him well out of sight in a separate room.

Betty got the all-clear from the doctors, and Tom brought them both back home. Luckily, she had only suffered a mild concussion and a small cut to the back of her head that only needed glueing. With a small brown paper pharmacy bag filled with a single packet of paracetamol, the A&E doctor discharged Betty.

El and her mum didn't even ask how Mark was at the hospital. Betty didn't want to know, and El couldn't bring herself to ask, not when she had been the cause of his concussion.

Once home, Betty headed straight upstairs to bed, telling a worried-looking El and Tom that she just needed to rest. Betty wanted a moment alone to process what had happened and how far her relationship had descended into chaos. Considering that she had been with Mark for over twenty years, she felt as though tonight had been her breaking point. An unrepairable crack that had been growing over the past few weeks since her mother's death had now shattered what remained between them with Mark's behaviour. Tonight was the last straw, and Betty saw no coming back from that. Her mother had been right along.

El phoned Dotty to let her know what had happened before Tom helped her clean up the mess in the kitchen and the hallway. They worked together to rid the house of any trace of what had happened. El swept the glass into a dustpan whilst Tom cleaned the blood and vomit, telling El that he didn't mind doing it as he crouched on his hands and knees with a pair of marigolds to protect his skin. He didn't even scrunch his nose up as El watched him meticulously clean the kitchen floor of the contents of Mark's stomach.

Within twenty minutes, Dotty was back home checking El over, looking her up and down before examining her hands. Dotty pulled El into a tight embrace. She felt guilty for not being at home, but she just couldn't stand the arguments. But, yet again, she was so grateful to Tom for being there to save the day.

"Thank you."

Dotty whispered against his ear as she hugged him before she headed upstairs and climbed into bed with her mum to ensure she was all right.

El checked in on them about half an hour later to make sure they were both okay.

Slowly, she cracked her mum's bedroom door open as quietly as she could, as though she was checking on a sleeping child before heading to bed herself. A small smile tugged at the corners of her mouth as she saw Dotty curled up next to their mother with a protective arm across her as they slept.

El's emotions overwhelmed her. She felt contrasting waves of guilt and relief as she looked at her mum and sister.

Was this all her fault?

If she would have given her father some money, perhaps this would never have happened.

Her Nan's voice echoed in her head, repeating the words in the letter she had left her. El was not to trust anyone. People would try and guilt her into giving them money. But did that apply to her own father as well?

El could hear Enid's voice as the words from the page bounced across in front of her eyes.

I could not protect some of my children from whom they fell in love with.

Was Enid talking about Mark? Had she known all along that Betty had fallen in love with someone that she should need protecting from?

El had so many questions that she needed answers to, but her Nan wasn't here to answer them. It made El's heart ache with loss.

As she closed the door softly, her tears started to fall. She quickly turned away and rushed downstairs, needing to feel the comforting warmth that she knew Tom would give her. She craved the smell of his clean peppermint scent that was constantly surrounding him.

Tom was immediately at the bottom of the stairs after hearing El's sobs, holding his arms open to her, inviting her in. She rushed into him, wrapping her arms tightly around his middle as he stroked her hair and pulled her close. Tom closed his eyes as he breathed in her vanilla and jasmine scent, wishing he could do more to ease her burden.

Yet again, something had threatened El's life, and if it weren't for her stepping in, Mark would have been Tom's eleventh victim. Tom knew, deep down, that he wouldn't have been able to stop himself from craving out Mark's throat if El hadn't been there to pull him out of his blood lust. It had sunk its claws in deep into Tom and it almost shocked him that El had managed to pull them out, considering the claws were often barbed. His own conscious that screamed at him to stop and show mercy had never been able to remove those hooks, but it seemed that El could with just a touch and her sweet voice.

Tom comforted her as she sobbed into his chest, her tears soaking into his top. If only Tom could, he would absorb all those sad and guilty emotions she was feeling. He wanted to take the burden on himself if he could because he knew he could absorb the guilt as if it were nothing. He had already done it for ten lives. A little more wouldn't hurt.

El wanted to forget everything that had happened, and Tom suggested they watch TV for a bit to help clear her mind. As they sat on the sofa, Tom's arm around El's shoulders, holding her close to him, her head resting against his shoulder, El looked up at him.

"Thank you, Tom, for being here." Her voice was quiet as she spoke.

Tom looked down and smiled briefly at her as he twisted the end of her chestnut hair around his fingertips. He leaned down and placed a delicate kiss on her forehead.

"I wouldn't be anywhere else, El." He closed his eyes as he whispered against her skin, savouring the contact that made him feel warm and tingly inside.

It wasn't long before they both fell asleep as the TV continued to play trash TV at four in the morning.

Thumping noises woke them both as Betty dragged two suitcases downstairs. She had stuffed all of Mark's clothes into them and threw them outside in the front garden. Betty didn't want him in the house. She didn't want him near her.

Dotty stayed with their tired-looking mum whilst El and Tom left for university that morning. Dotty wouldn't let their father in the house if he showed up, and Tom told her to call him immediately if Mark did try to get in. Dotty had already arranged for a locksmith to come and change the locks on the front and back doors for security. She assured Tom and El that she wouldn't let anything happen if Mark did show up.

As they walked through Cambridge, Tom told El that if she didn't want to sit her exam now, he would go with her to her tutor to explain the situation. Even though she was exhausted and emotionally drained from last night, she refused. She only needed to get a pass in year one to get into her second year, and that was all she was aiming for.

With access to her inheritance in a few short months, El still hadn't decided whether she wanted to continue with university. Her Nan's letter had hinted at her following her passion for music. Her inheritance would mean she had the financial security to do just that now.

She wanted to talk with her mum about not continuing her course but had yet to find the courage to broach the subject.

The events of last night had put those thoughts to the back of her head. But perhaps she could talk to Tom about it instead at some point. It was too late to turn back now anyway, she needed to sit this exam. El's stubborn nature kicked in with wanting to prove something to herself, that she could do this. All her hard work since her nan's funeral would be in vain otherwise.

Tom walked with El to the examination hall. As they stood outside it in the corridor, waiting with the other students to be allowed in, Tom bent down and placed a lingering kiss on El's cheek. The doors opened, and students started to file inside, the nervous chatter dying down as the corridor emptied. As Tom and El broke apart, she smiled up at him as he wished her good luck before entering the hall with the last few students. El briefly looked back at him, butterflies dancing around her stomach with the tiniest hint of a shy smile pulling at the corner of her mouth. Whether the butterflies were because of her nerves for the exam or because of the loving look that Tom had in her eyes, she didn't know.

Once El had finished, Tom was still sitting outside the building on a bench waiting for her. He was worried about what they were going to tell the police. He had been thinking about it since El had left him in the corridor. It made him feel strange and uneasy as the police were bound to want a statement soon from them.

He had never been close to getting caught for any murder he had committed. He had never once been seriously questioned by the police about anything, even after the first time when he had been the only witness. But if he had made a mistake, if he had slipped up after being so careful with a previous murder without realising, and they asked him for a DNA sample now, would they catch him? Would they be able to piece two and two together?

The thrill of getting caught had excited him in the past, but now it was different. He never had any strong thoughts about being apprehended or the implications of that. It was always in the background, like a little extra thrill. An afterthought that would excite him for the following few days and weeks. Of course, there was always the jeopardy of losing and that feeling of not being smart enough to outwit the police, which niggled from time to time but never truly stuck. But now that he had El, Tom didn't want to be caught. He didn't want to be taken away from her. He couldn't lose her.

El had already thought about what she would say to the police, and when Tom broached the subject on the walk home after her exam, her brain immediately defended Tom by leaving his part entirely out of it. Her father probably wouldn't remember what he'd done anyway, as he was so drunk. No one would believe Mark that Tom would have threatened him with the broken bottle pushed to his neck.

It was two against one, potentially three if El's mother agreed with El's version of events. Betty was unconscious when it all happened anyway, and El was convinced she could persuade her mum that her story was the truth.

El didn't want to lie to her mum, but the feeling of protecting Tom outweighed the small amount of guilt she felt if she did need to lie to her.

"He slipped on the floor and fell... He wasn't pushed... I saw an opportunity and grabbed the vase, hitting him over the head with it."

"But El..."

"But nothing, Tom... That's what happened. He slipped, and I hit him. End of story."

12.

El fidgeted nervously with the hem of her yellow shirt as she stood queuing at the reception desk at Cambridge Police Station. She had received a phone call the morning after her exam, asking her to come to the police station to have a voluntary interview the next day.

Betty had stayed home to pack more of Mark's things into boxes. She had wanted him out of the house completely, and putting his stuff into boxes was cathartic for her. The police had already taken a victim statement from Betty whilst she was at the hospital. Perhaps her having a head injury meant they couldn't rely on her statement very much if this case went to court and she hadn't been asked for any more information. At least not yet.

El had all the confidence in the world during her walk home with Tom after her exam when she told him she would leave his involvement entirely out of it. Tom had only witnessed what had happened and didn't do anything other than watch in horror as the events unfolded.

Now that she had slept on it, doubts had started to creep into her head. Even after speaking with her mum about what had happened, her mind wasn't entirely at ease. It did matter that Betty had told El she couldn't really remember anything until the paramedics arrived, meaning she hadn't seen what Tom had done to Mark. Betty told El what she had said to the police. She hadn't seen anything, or at least, she couldn't remember anything after being knocked out.

El had replayed the whole incident over and over in her mind, wondering how she could explain the cut to her father's neck that Tom had made with the sharp bottleneck.

"Miss?"

El's eyes snapped up as the police officer behind the reception desk looked at her expectantly. She swallowed the nervous lump in her throat as Tom gently pushed her forward with his hand on the small of her back. El stepped forward to the wooden reception desk, placing her hands on the edge to ground herself and look more confident. She could do this. She had to. Having Tom with her made her realise how much she needed to protect him from getting into trouble, even if that meant lying to the police and taking full responsibility.

She had lied to the police before easily enough. She could do it again.

"Hi," she smiled at the middle-aged officer as she removed her tinted glasses, letting him see her contrasting, unique eyes. "I had a phone call yesterday about coming here for a voluntary interview?"

Why she had made it sound like a question, she didn't know, but the reaction she received from behind the desk put her a little at ease as the man's lips parted slightly, taking her in. He blinked a few times before clearing his throat and smiled reassuringly at her as his eyes flitted between her and Tom's.

"What's your name, Miss?"

"Ethel Fletcher."

The officer shifted his gaze to the computer screen to his right and clicked the mouse as he searched through what El could only assume was an appointment list. He smiled brightly and turned his head back to face El. "If you'd like to take a seat, Miss Fletcher, an officer will be out with you shortly."

El smiled curtly at the man before turning to find a seat on the small number of chairs that lined the reception area, finding only two left empty. Luckily, they were next to each other so that Tom and El could sit next to one another.

She knew that using her eyes was against her usual morals, but today called for an advantage, one she knew her eyes would give her by capturing the attention of the police officers she was going to be speaking to and hopefully distract them enough to allow her lies to seep past their natural inquisitive, sceptical judgements.

She sat down, and Tom sat next to her, immediately taking hold of El's hand as if it was an instinctive thing for him to do.

"You, okay?" Tom asked as he rubbed his thumb gently along the back of her knuckles, trying to reassure her. He knew she would be nervous about talking to the police, especially as she was about to lie to them about his involvement and take full responsibility.

El took a short breath before slipping her hand out from under Tom's. She had thought through this extensively. She and Tom were friends. It would look like they were a couple if the officers interviewing her saw them holding hands beforehand. That could put Tom in jeopardy.

Tom's eyebrows furrowed at El's hand moving from his. He didn't understand why she was pulling away. Was she cross at him for insisting he came with her? He only wanted to make sure she was alright. But when she smiled at him reassuringly as he looked from her hands to her face, he felt the heavy weight of doubt lift.

She leaned closer to him to whisper against his ear so that no one would hear her. "I don't want them to question what I'm about to say if they think we're more than just friends, Tom." El quickly squeezed over the top of his forearm to reassure him. He understood her actions now and nodded his approval.

After a few minutes of silence, as they waited, an officer appeared from behind a coded door and called out El's name as he looked up from an open manila folder in his hand.

El raised her hand as if she was answering a registration call at school and made her way to stand. She turned her head to give Tom a comforting smile as he remained sat down, looking up at her.

He didn't look nervous. In fact, he almost had a face of indifference as he looked up at El. If it weren't for the slight crinkle of fine lines at the corners of his mouth and the twitch of his eyelid, she would have thought he didn't care. But to El's well-trained eye, his tiny reactions were the confidence boost she needed. He trusted her, and the faintest indication of a smile proved it.

They clarified their story with each other yesterday during their walk back to El's home.

Mark knocked Betty over in the kitchen and then came after Tom. Tom backed up into the hallway as Mark threatened him with the smashed bottleneck, but Mark slipped on the broken glass. El panicked and grabbed the vase, hitting her father over the head with it. Mark must have cut his neck on the glass as he lay on the hallway floor.

The only lie was how Mark had cut his neck.

There was little for the police to probe, limiting their chances of sniffing out a lie.

El was admitting to hitting her father with the vase and was going to use her fear of what could have happened to her friend if she didn't. Mark had threatened Tom, so there was no lie there. They were just going to keep Tom almost slicing into Mark's jugular out of it.

Tom did like that El was taking the blame because Mark could press charges against her for hitting him, but El didn't care. She knew she was taking a risk if Mark retaliated but hoped he wouldn't. He was still her father.

El followed after the policeman and down a corridor lined with various doors and rooms, past a few other people dressed in suits or uniforms. She focused on the back of his head as he spoke animatedly.

"I'm Officer Hughes. I'm leading this investigation."
"Oh? Okay."
"You're here to give your version of events, yes?"
"Yes. I had a phone call yesterday about coming here this morning."

The officer paused in front of a door with the words, interview room 3, written in bold letters on a laminated piece of A4 paper that looked like it had been blu-tacked to the door.

Police budgets really were being cut, El thought to herself.

After unlocking and opening the door, Hughes gestured for El to step inside and followed behind her.

El's eyes quickly scanned the small magnolia-coloured room with no windows and only a bright fluorescent light above their heads. There was a wooden topped table with metal legs against the wall with audio recording equipment on, four plastic chairs with two on either side of the small table and a camera in the corner of the ceiling pointed towards the table. It all looked like something out of a police drama series and somewhat intimidating.

"Please take a seat, Miss Fletcher. Another officer will be in shortly."

El nodded and took a seat at the table facing the door as Hughes took a seat opposite her. He briefly looked at El and smiled reassuringly at her before his eyes drifted back to the pages of the manila folder in his hands.

Hughes was probably in his early thirties but had the frown lines of a man who had dealt with a lot of stress in his life, making him look older.

El's eyes scanned his face as she wondered if the deep-set lines between his brows were from the horrors he'd no doubt seen or the night shifts he had endured that had left him looking like he had a permanent scowl.

He was tall with broad shoulders that filled out his police uniform nicely, showing the hints of large, muscled shoulders and the chest of a man well accustomed to the gym. His light blue eyes were a stark contrast to his dark brown hair, giving him a piercing gaze that was currently trained on the writing he was focusing on. He carried himself with confidence and authority, making it clear he was someone in a position of authority as his jaw clenched and unclenched whilst scanning the pages between his large, veiny hands.

He was handsome with a rugged sort of look as the first signs of stubble started to grow through, giving him a five o'clock shadow across his chin. But he wasn't El's type. Not that she couldn't appreciate an attractive man, but something felt off as she looked at him. She wasn't feeling the usual signs of attraction that would make her shift in her seat, needing to squeeze her thighs together.

Maybe it was because Tom was the only man she could think about lately. Had he corrupted her mind to think only about tall, lean men with messy auburn curls and dark blue eyes that held a dangerous darkness behind them? A darkness she wanted to explore and shine a light on as she allowed it to wrap around her, consuming her.

El watched Hughes's movements as her fingers twitched nervously under the table, hidden from his sight. Taking in his appearance was a distraction from overthinking what she was about to do. His hands stilled before he looked back at her and double-took as his gaze drifted straight to El's eyes.

El saw the subtly drop in his shoulders as a breath escaped quickly from his parted lips. As he swallowed, the bob of his Adam's apple was a clear indication that she had caught more than just his attention.

Her plan was working perfectly so far as she feigned an aura of innocence, slowly tucking her hair behind her ear.

The door to the room opened, and Hughes had to drag his eyes away from El to look at the new police officer who entered the room behind him.

The female officer smiled brightly at El before she closed the door and nodded at Hughes in a friendly work-colleague sort of way.

She had blonde hair tied back into a low bun and grey-coloured eyes that showed a kindness held within them. But her demeanour oozed that she wasn't someone to be trifled with as she walked confidently into the room.

Her police uniform pinched in at the waist, giving the hint of an hourglass figure hidden underneath the authoritative look she carried. Her face was bare of makeup except for a bit of mascara that accentuated her eyes, giving them an almost cat-like look. El could almost picture her lounging around one minute, wanting belly rubs before she switched into a fearsome hunter, focused and stalking her prey.

"Hello, Miss Fletcher. My name is Officer Larkin."

"Hello, officer," El smiled back at her.

Hughes trained his gaze back onto El's as Larkin sat next to him and placed the notepad in her hands on the desk. Larkin took a pen from her top pocket before whispering something to Hughes that El couldn't make out. It made El a little more nervous as her fingers moved up under her sleeve to start rubbing the scar on her arm. Larkin straightened out in her seat before removing the lid from her pen, preparing to write on the paper and take notes.

El's eyes flitted between the two officers as they sat opposite her, waiting for them to start asking her questions. She wasn't sure how this all worked.

"So..." Hughes began after clearing his throat. "Miss Fletcher, we'll be recording our conversation on audio tape for evidence."

El's face paled slightly as he mentioned that this was getting recorded as evidence, but she quickly composed herself.

"Am I under arrest?"

"No," Larkin shook her head and gave El a reassuring smile. "This is just a formality, so we have the evidence if you were to be charged, Miss Fletcher."

Hughes and Larkin proceeded to start recording the conversation. They told El her rights and that if she wanted a lawyer present with her, she was entitled to have one. This all suddenly felt a lot more serious than El had first thought. But asking for a lawyer felt like she might be judged more by the police. To El, it could be construed as her wanting to cover up something, so she declined to have any legal representation present.

"And you understand that this is a voluntary interview?"

El nodded. "Yes. I understand."

"Do you have any questions before we begin, Miss Fletcher?" Hughes asked her.

El shook her head, "No. No questions yet." She sounded confident as she looked back at Hughes and stopped rubbing her fingers against her scar.

"Miss Fletcher, can you run us through your version of the events that happened on the night of the twenty-fifth of May?"

El swallowed down the nervous lump that had formed in her throat and nodded her head. "Yes. Of course." She didn't want to go into too much detail. El thought if she did, they might be able to start picking apart her story. Giving as little information as possible and answering their questions directly was the best way to approach this. At least, that's what she hoped.

El went through what had happened when she got home with Tom and her mum, keeping to the facts and trying not to speculate about any emotions that may have been going through anyone else's head that was involved. El knew she needed to be concise as the officers started asking her about the events. But as she began to speak and answer their questions, she couldn't help the nagging feeling that she needed to show more emotion about what had happened.

"So, your father slipped on the broken glass of the whiskey bottle in the hallway?"

"Yes. He was so drunk and slurring his words. His balance wasn't great. That's why my mum had tried to help him to stand when he hit her."

"I see... And you say you just picked up the vase and hit your father with it on instinct?" Hughes frowned at El as he spoke, probably trying to picture how such a sweet-looking young woman would turn to violence without a second thought.

El took a deep breath and lowered her head, chewing on her bottom lip. She knew she needed to change her tactics. She wanted to make it seem like she regretted doing such a horrid thing to someone she loved. She even managed to produce tears in her eyes as she looked back up at the two officers.

"I didn't mean to do it. I don't know why I did. I was scared. Scared for my mum, for Tom and myself. I didn't want anyone else to get hurt."

Larkin passed El a tissue from the box on the table.

"Thank you," El sniffed as she looked at Larkin before dropping her eyes away and dabbing at her tear-stained cheeks. "I just wanted him to stop," she said quietly. El hoped her remorseful act was working, and from the concerned look on Larkin's face, she could tell she was at least convincing her.

Hughes cleared his throat and shifted in his seat to sit back and observe El as he asked his next question. "Why didn't you or Tom call the police?"

El sighed and looked directly into Hughes's eyes. "It all happened so fast. I just didn't think." She sniffed again as she forced more tears to well in her eyes. "He was just so angry. I've never seen him that angry before."

"Has your father ever shown any aggression or anger towards you?" Larkin asked.

El shook her head and swallowed before she answered. "Not like that… Of course, I've been told off as a kid. But he's never been violent if that's what you're asking…"

Larkin hummed as she wrote down some notes on her pad and then looked at Hughes. They shared a look between them that El picked apart mentally. Larkin was convinced El was telling the truth, but Hughes seemed to want more information. He turned his head to look back at El. "Do you know how your father sustained the injury to his neck?"

El furrowed her brow and tilted her head as if she didn't know what he was talking about. "Injury? I don't understand. I only hit my father over the head with the vase."

"Your father suffered a laceration to his neck as well as bruising around his jaw."

The lines in El's brow deepened as she gave a confused look. "I have no idea how he got those," she paused as she gathered her thoughts. "I mean, he did fall onto the glass in the hallway," she shrugged and sniffed again, wiping her nose with the tissue before balling it in her hand.

"You said that Tom Hendricks is your friend, correct?"

"Yes. Tom's been there for me since my grandmother passed away." El felt a swell of genuine emotion wash over her as she thought about her Nan.

"So, he's just your friend. Nothing more?" Hughes pressed.

El gave a humourless scoff as she glared at Hughes. "Our relationship is entirely platonic. Not that it's any of your business," her tone was sharp as she almost snapped at him. El took a breath before she softened her voice and continued, "Tom is my best friend, and I don't like what you're insinuating," she took another deep, frustrated breath. "He's the kindest person I know." El cut herself from saying any more. She knew if she said, 'he protects me', 'he makes me feel safe', she could open herself up to a whole world of further questions about why he didn't intervene.

Hughes's eye twitched before he cleared his throat.

It made El feel as if she just made a big mistake by getting so defensive about a simple question. Her eyes flitted between Hughes and Larkin as she waited for one of them to speak, trying to tell if they would press further about her relationship with Tom. El needed to shift the conversation back towards her father, so she gave up more information about why her father may have acted as he had.

"My father's behaviour changed once my Nan's will was read."

Larkin tilted her head as she listened to El, intrigued by this new information, "Go on…"

"When he found out that I was the sole beneficiary of her estate, he started distancing himself from me. He and Mum would argue almost constantly about things."

Hughes shifted in his seat and leaned forward as he asked, "What sort of things did they argue about?"

"Money mainly… and the business."

Larkin took further notes as Hughes hummed as El divulged more information about her father's behaviour towards her and Betty after she inherited her grandmother's money.

"It's all in a trust fund, though, so I don't have access to it until I turn twenty-one."

"I see," Hughes said before he looked at Larkin and gave a single nod to her before looking back at El. "Well, I think that's all, Miss Fletcher, unless there is anything else you wish to ask?"

El pursed her lips and then asked the question she didn't really want or need the answer to. "Is my Dad okay? We haven't spoken yet. My mum is still quite distraught about the whole thing and doesn't want me to talk to him." She knew she was taking a risk by doing this but thought that Hughes needed a little more convincing about her remorse.

Hughes nodded. "He's alright. But perhaps you should be asking him yourself, hmm?"

El nodded and sniffed, trying to show a little more emotion about missing her father as Larkin ended the interview and stopped the recording tape.

"Thank you for coming in, Miss Fletcher. We'll be in touch if there's anything else we need." Larkin stood and gestured for El to do the same as Hughes stood and moved to open the door. El nodded at Hughes as she walked past him and gave him a tight-lipped smile before following Larkin back down the corridor towards the reception area.

Tom was sitting in the same spot, reading a magazine, as El entered back into the reception area. He immediately placed the magazine on the small table beside his chair and stood to greet her, opening his arms wide to invite her in.

Larkin watched the interaction with interest as Hughes came to stand next to her in the doorway.

El walked over to Tom and wrapped her arms around his middle, giving him a quick squeeze as he bent his head down to rest his chin on her shoulder.

"She's watching us... isn't she?" El whispered against Tom's ear.

"Mmhmm..." Tom mumbled quietly as he kept the officers in his peripheral vision.

Tom let go of El and looked down at her with a friendly smile whilst keeping the officers in his sights. "Are you okay?" he asked loud enough in a warm tone to make sure that they heard him as Tom slipped his arm around El's shoulders to guide her towards the exit.

El nodded and leaned into his side as they walked past the officers and out of the building. Tom looked briefly over his shoulder to see the coded door closing where the two officers had stood as he and El passed through the exit door and outside.

El waited until they were a reasonable distance down the road before she let out a long breath that she didn't realise she had been holding. The whole thing had been so stressful, but she was happy with her performance and keeping herself in check for the most part.

Tom gave her a reassuring squeeze around her shoulders as he looked down at the side of her face. "Was everything okay?"

El pushed her tongue into the side of her cheek and swirled it around her mouth before she spoke. "I think so. I think they believed me."

"Did they ask about your Dad's neck?"

"Yeah. But I told them I had no idea how he had done it. I just told them he slipped over on the glass."

Tom nodded his head before he kissed the top of El's head. He closed his eyes briefly and took a deep breath as he took in the scent of her shampoo and whispered against her hair, "Good girl."

13.

"Two lattes, please," Tom smiled politely as he gave the barista his and El's order at the counter whilst El sat patiently at a corner table in their regular coffee shop.

It was near the university campus and a frequent haunt of the students and faculty alike. It was cheaper than the leading branded coffee shops and tasted just as good, if not better.

It was a quaint place with about fifteen tables inside and another six outside that lined the side of the building and along the pavement. There were old and modern black-and-white photos of Cambridge adorning the pastel blue walls with a fresh, small arrangement of flowers on each table. Today, the vases held sweet pea blooms of lilac, pink and red flowers that sat proudly in their little white vases. Their scent cut through the rich smells of coffee that floated through the café with the fragrance of orange blossoms and hyacinth, alleviating the aromatic caffeine tones with some much-needed sweetness.

It had been a couple of weeks since El had given her statement to the police, and she hadn't heard anything more from them.

Her mother was still going to press charges against Mark. Betty was determined that he wasn't going to get away with assaulting her and wanted him to feel the full extent of the law.

Tom had been asked to give a witness statement at the police station the following day after El, which he was obliged to do. He only told them the version of events he and El had discussed, leaving his involvement out entirely.

It didn't sit well with Tom as he recounted El hitting her father over the head with the vase, making it sound like she was to blame for the entire thing.

But he kept his composure and defended El in the best way he could by telling the police that El immediately regretted her actions and hoped that Mark could forgive her. Suppressing the urge to clench his hands into fists as he thought about strangling Mark's throat was the most challenging part of the entire process for Tom as he replayed it in his head.

"Here we are," Tom smiled brightly at El as he placed her coffee in front of her on the table and sat opposite her. His long legs couldn't quite fit under the table, so his knees rested against the edge as he angled his body to fit in the space. He placed his cup down and smiled back at El as she blew lightly over her steaming cup before taking a sip of coffee. El smiled contentedly as she sat back in her comfy seat, relishing in the warmth that spread down her throat and soothed the nervous ache in her stomach.

"So... How does it feel to have finished your exams now?" Tom asked her.

El held her cup as she rested her elbows on the chair's armrests, looking through the rising steam at the swirling caramel-coloured liquid.

"Odd."

Tom tilted his head as he watched her with curiosity. "Odd? That's an odd choice of word," he chuckled softly before his chuckle fizzled out, seeing the serious look on El's face as she raised her gaze to meet his. "Is something wrong?"

El sighed and placed her cup on the table, ensuring she did not spill a drop of precious caffeine. She leant forward towards him as she chewed on her bottom lip and rubbed the scar on her arm. She was nervous about what she wanted to talk to Tom about. It was the reason she had asked him to meet her here after he had finished some research in the library. She hadn't spoken to her mum about it and wanted to talk to Tom first anyway. He was her best friend, and she sought his opinion, valuing it above anyone else's.

"Nothing's wrong, Tom. I just wanted to get your opinion on something."

He raised his eyebrows as he studied her face, wondering what it was that was obviously bothering her. "Go on."

"What do you think if I didn't continue with University? I mean, if I quit now?"

Tom's heart immediately plummeted, and he had to fight the urge to reach forward and grab El's hand, almost as if to stop this ridiculous decision. He swallowed down the lump that had formed in his throat as his eyes flickered between hers, searching for the reason as to why she was making such a rash decision.

Tom cleared his throat before he asked the question that was burning a hole in his brain, "Why? Why would you quit?"

El sat back in her chair at Tom's sharp tone. She dropped her hand away from the scar on her arm as she looked down at her lap, feeling almost ashamed from the confused glare Tom was giving her.

She paused before she reached forward to take hold of her cup but thought better of it as she lifted her head and looked at Tom's now panic-stricken face. Her fingertips traced the edge of the cup handle as she watched Tom's increasingly distraught reaction bloom across his features. He suddenly looked as if the colour was draining from his face as he absorbed this information. El cleared her throat before she gave her reason.

"Because it's only a few months, and I'll have access to my inheritance. I don't need to go to University. Hell, I don't even need to work for the rest of my life if I manage this right. I can do whatever I want then."

Tom couldn't stop his hand from reaching across the table for hers. His long fingers skimmed across the back of El's hand as he searched her eyes. He was worried she wanted to leave University so suddenly because of him.

Was he coming on too strong?

Was he too much for her?

Was her inheritance just an excuse to get away from him?

But El was here with him now. She'd asked him to come. She always seemed happy whenever Tom turned up at her home, especially after what had happened with her father. He was always there, often coming for dinner or staying late.

Tom had taken her out for dinner and trips to the cinema to break up El's revision. They'd even joked that Tom was giving her little rewards for all her studying efforts.

He was doing anything to make her happy, even if it was just spending time with her while she read, and he studied for his PhD so that she wasn't alone. They were content with their companionable silence as they spent hours together, and Tom didn't want to lose that.

Doubts raced through Tom's mind like a tornado, throwing everything in the air. His thoughts were compelling him to want to cling onto her now as his fingers wrapped around her hand, prising her fingers away from her cup and into his familiar security.

"You can't just quit, El," his grip on her hand tightened as he beseeched her. "You can't. It would be a mistake."

El's eyes flashed from his hand gripping hers to his eyes and back again. His hold on her was tightening with every pulse of the vein in his neck as his heart beat faster with every passing second of her silence. It wasn't a bruising hold, but it was undoubtedly possessive.

El placed her free hand over his, rubbing her thumb across the back of his hand to calm him. She could see his panic as clear as day.

"Tom... We'll still see each other. I'm not going anywhere. I don't plan on leaving Cambridge."

"But El..." Tom paused as everything he wanted to say rushed through his head. He didn't want her to quit University. Not now. He had plans. Tom was going to teach her next term. He had already started making arrangements to ensure he would be her lecturer. They'd have more time together. He couldn't let her quit. He needed to change her mind about this and change it quickly. "Why give up now? You've worked so hard to get here," Tom relaxed his grip on her hand and traced the inside of her palm with his index finger. "What's another two years?" he shrugged. "You've got your whole life ahead of you to go off and do whatever you want."

El sighed, feeling his reassuring, calming touch as Tom traced the space between the lines of her palm. He was already making her question whether this was a rash decision. It had only been a fleeting thought as she had thought about the contents of her Nan's letter.

Enid had mentioned in that letter that El should follow her passions.

Did she mean becoming the professional violinist El had always dreamt of? That's what El had assumed her grandmother had meant. Enid knew of El's desire to one day become a professional musician. This inherited wealth would be the answer for her dreams to flourish and take the leap without the constraints of financial burdens.

El had thought about it before her first exam. She had been stressed by what had happened with her father, and it had only been her stubborn nature that had caused her to take that exam.

Over the past few weeks since that first thought about quitting, she had thought about it more as she looked through the music sheets in her bedroom when she was alone. After smashing up her old one, El still needed to purchase a new violin. But she had been looking through various websites to try and find her perfect match. She wondered whether to hold off until her inheritance had come through to buy a top-class violin. She would then be able to afford whatever she wanted.

El had still taken the other three exams, putting in even more effort with her revision as Tom helped her study, insisting that he wanted to help her. Tom had even spent late nights at the library and El's home helping her revise. He had stayed several times at El's home, sprawling out across the sofa downstairs to sleep as his long legs flopped over the armrest.

On those occasions when he had spent the night, Tom had taken the opportunity to sneak upstairs to watch El once everyone else was asleep.

She looked so peaceful and innocent; her face relaxed, and lips parted slightly as she snored softly, bringing a smile to his lips. Her eyelids would flutter as she dreamt, leaving Tom to hope her dreams were about him.

Tom had recorded El a few times as she slept, using the moonlight streaming through her window as the lighting for his midnight videos.

El looked like a fallen angel. Her soft, worriless features and chestnut hair cast dark shadows across her skin as the moon illuminated the curve of her brow and slant of her button nose before highlighting the cupid's bow of her lips.

Tom had gently tucked her hair behind her ear numerous times as El slept, wanting to help the moonlight bathe her in more light. He loved how the corner of her eye would crinkle as she felt the sensation of his fingertips lingering on her cheek. He desperately wanted to do it again while she was awake like he had on Atherington Beach. Tom wanted to see her pupils dilate as he touched her face. He'd watched the videos of her sleeping on playback whilst he lay on his own bed, her face playing next to his on his pillow. His fingers had played with the piece of El's hair he had cut from her head as he fell asleep, dreaming of holding her as they fell asleep together.

But he kept those thoughts hidden while watching her in the coffee shop.

Giving a tight-lipped smile, El took a deep breath through her nose before her gaze dropped away to the milky brown liquid in her coffee cup on the table.

Could she give up her degree now that she had already put a whole year's work into it?

"El. Don't make a rash decision about this," Tom squeezed her hand reassuringly, drawing her gaze back to his. "I know you've had a tough few months with everything that's happened. But you've come out the other side and fought so hard to get here. Don't waste it, El."

Tom looked down at their joined hands, rubbing his thumb across her knuckles as El did the same to his.

"I'll help you with your studies."

"You've already been helping me, Tom. I can't ask you to keep helping me when you have your own work to do."

Tom tsk at El's response to his offer of help.

"El… You know I don't mind helping you. I wouldn't do it if I didn't. Plus, you help me too."

"I know," El sighed and smiled at him. "But you can tell me to piss off if ever I'm asking too much of you."

"Pfft…" Tom scoffed. "Yeah, right. Like that's ever going to happen. I like you too much." Tom immediately gawped at his own words and cleared his throat. "I mean your company… I like your company too much," he stated as he tried to cover up his mistake, but the pinky hue creeping up his cheeks gave him away.

El sucked her bottom lip into her mouth and looked down at her coffee cup before sliding her hand out from Tom's and picking it up. She brought it to her lips and took a small sip of the creamy coffee as her eyes drifted across the blush on his cheeks to his eyes. She studied his face as his eyes darted everywhere around the table before they settled on hers. His face softened as he looked at her, watching him.

Tom should have felt nervous for letting that thought slip from his mind and out of his mouth. But as he looked at El, he felt anything but anxious as she smiled softly at him behind her cup.

Whilst El moved her right leg to cross it over her left, her foot accidentally brushed against Tom's calf. His pupils widened just a fraction as the sole of her shoe rested against his jean-clad leg. Whether she knew she was touching his leg or not, Tom didn't know. But he did know that El had yet to move it away.

El smiled to herself behind her coffee cup as she absorbed his words.

Their flirting had increased since they had nearly kissed at her grandmother's funeral. They were still very much in the friend zone they had created, but spending more and more time together had allowed them to become more and more relaxed when in each other's company.

Hand-holding had become a regular occurrence between them. The subtle nudges and smiles at one another as they walked anywhere were now a natural part of their friendship.

They always greeted each other with a hug and a kiss on the cheek. Sometimes, the kiss on the cheek lingered, especially if Tom was staying the night at El's house.

To anyone on the outside, they would think that they were dating because they would share secret jokes, which no one else seemed to be in on. The smiles they shared as they spoke about anything and everything and how Tom and El would gravitate towards one another when they didn't realise they were doing it.

It all just proved one thing.

Something was growing between them. The only problem was they didn't know how to cross the line, even though they both wanted to.

Tom cleared his throat before he rested his hand on his knee. "So... Erm..." he chuckled nervously as he didn't know what to say, his fingers drumming rhythmically on his kneecap. "Don't quit, El. I think you'll regret it if you do," he said earnestly.

El placed her cup back on the table and fiddled with the sleeve of her yellow cardigan as she mulled it over.

"It would be a shame to give up now, considering I always wanted to study at Cambridge. It was kind of a life goal."

Tom clapped his hand against his knee.

"Exactly. Why give up now? Plenty of people would kill for your place."

El giggled. "It is something to brag about," she smiled. "I studied at Cambridge," El purposefully accentuated a posh accent as she drawled out her words and gestured with her hands. She half shut her eyes as she dropped her lips to form a smarmy upper-class look.

Tom chuckled and started copying her as he straightened his posture and looked down his nose at her. "One can only imagine the eloquence of studying English Literature at the prestigious Cambridge University." He gestured around his hand as if reciting Shakespeare. "And you, my dear, Miss Ethel Fletcher, would be wasting your exceeding adept intelligence."

El giggled and blushed at Tom's antics as he took a chance and said what was burning in his mind.

"And dare I say it, Miss Fletcher... I'd miss your exquisite, beautiful features if I could not lay my eyes upon you daily. To bathe in your light is my purest form of joy."

The blossoming colour on El's cheeks only intensified at Tom's compliments.

His hand sank down from his knee as he leaned forward and let his fingertips brush against the inside of El's bare ankle.

Her lips parted as she felt his gentle touch against her skin, letting butterflies flourish in her stomach for a moment as she felt the prickle of goosebumps rise up her leg.

The pair sat staring at one another as the chatter of the café fizzled out around them, leaving them with the feeling of being the only two people, surrounded by the perfumed scent of sweet peas and the sharpness of bitter coffee.

The smashing sound of a teacup breaking behind the counter had them instantly pulling apart from one another as the bubble of building romance burst, plunging them back into the chaos of everyday life.

Tom cleared his throat and sat back up straight, letting go of El's ankle and raising his cup in a toast.

"To my best friend... El... May she continue her educational journey with me at her side to annoy her on a daily basis."

14.

El sighed as she lay in the garden, reading her book whilst sunbathing under the baking hot rays of early August. She was taking a well-earned break after passing her first-year exams and being accepted into her second year of university.

Two months had passed since the incident with her father, and she hadn't seen or heard from him.

Besides removing his things from the front garden, Mark had yet to return home. Well, not that El knew of, and her mum didn't want to talk any more about it. El had spoken further to her mum about what she could remember that night, wondering if any memories had started to come back. But her mum said she couldn't remember anything else, putting El's mind at ease. She was thankful she didn't need to lie to her mum about Tom's involvement. El was worried about what her mum might think of Tom if she did know what happened that night.

Lying to the police was one thing, but lying to her mother was a whole other disintegration of trust. El was putting her conscience at ease by not bringing it up. Therefore, there was no need to lie about it. She just pushed it to the back of her mind. El didn't want to think about how Tom changed in that situation, the calmness in his eyes that hid the devil behind them. She didn't want to dwell on the monster that called to her from within. The one that clawed at her in her nightmares.

Both El and Dotty had asked their mum what was going to happen between her and their father but she also didn't want to talk about that either, keeping it to herself and busying herself with household chores and gardening. Betty didn't want to worry her girls about what was happening, thinking she could handle it herself.

In private conversations between the sisters, they were convinced that their mum was going to file for divorce at some point. They were just unsure as to when she would finally tell them.

Betty did, however, end up changing her mobile number. She claimed she was sick of the nuisance of cold calls, which was why she wanted to change it. But El and Dotty didn't believe her for a moment. They had a feeling it had to do with their father pestering her, as they had both seen their mum roll her eyes whenever her phone rang during the first week after what had happened. It wasn't long after that she had gotten herself a new phone.

"Hey," Tom called out as he came through the garden gate. A large box wrapped in yellow tissue paper in one hand, tied with a yellow bow and a large bouquet of sunflowers in the other.

El lifted her head from her book, putting her bookmark in to save her page for later reading. She moved her sunglasses down the bridge of her nose as she rested her elbows on the cushion to scan over Tom. Her eyes travelled up his body, taking in every inch of him as he walked towards her in the hot sun.

Black trainers covered his size thirteen feet. His perfect, lean, muscular calves and thighs flexed as he walked like a hypnotising metronome, drawing El's eyes further upwards.

The black running shorts he wore sat about two inches above his knees, swishing against his skin as he moved towards her with a big smile plastered across his face.

The sway of the bulge at his crotch flitted from side to side with the beat of each purposeful step he took as he approached El. Tom was obviously commando, as everything was so loose, making El automatically clench her thighs together at the tempting sight.

Tom's black t-shirt was tight enough to show off the faint hint of his v-line, which directed El's gaze downwards again for a moment before she caught herself from staring. El blinked furiously, hoping he wouldn't notice her looking at his groin before her eyes continued their journey up Tom's body. There was a hint of muscular abs and pecks below his t-shirt, which clung to his body in the hot sun.

El salivated as her lips parted, and her eyes travelled further up his form, shamelessly taking in every detail. She just couldn't help herself from wondering what her best friend would look like in all his naked glory.

Tom's arms and neck glistened in the sunlight from the thin sheen of what El hoped was sweat but was probably just sunscreen. She thought about what he'd taste like as she licked across his Adam's apple and up that bulging vein in his neck, causing her to swallow the glob of saliva which had built in her mouth.

She wondered if his veins bulged anywhere else too, as her tongue unconsciously dipped out and wet her lips as she thought about it.

What would his long, thick, veiny cock feel like as she slipped down onto it?

Would it fill her entirely with painful pleasure?

El was sure her pussy would clench around every inch of it as she slowly lowered herself down onto it, bottoming out until her clit rested on his pubic bone. Her fingernails would dig into his chest, leaving crescent shapes in their wake as she rode him.

Tom would be tied down to a bed, obviously. His long arms stretched above his head, his wrists shackled to the bed frame, and his dark blue eyes focused solely on her. His eyes would take on a midnight blue colour. His pupils would be blown wide with desire as he watched her take everything from him, groaning with pleasure.

El's recent porn searches may be the cause of those ideas, she thought to herself as she replayed the most recent one in her head, imagining it was Tom and her.

El had insisted that Tom went home one night after falling asleep during a film they were watching at her house. He had spent the last few nights staying at her home, sleeping on the sofa downstairs. It can't have been comfortable for his long frame to sleep on, and Tom must have been so tired. He never fell asleep when they were together, and El was worried about him.

After some persuasion, El convinced Tom to go home to sleep in his bed and get some much-needed rest, promising she'd call him in the morning.

Once Tom had left, El made the very conscious decision to watch porn after she couldn't keep her eyes off Tom as he slept next to her on the sofa.

Her hands had been tantalising close to giving in to her fantasies as she moved her fingertips along the steady pulse in his neck downwards towards the neckline of his t-shirt. El wanted to run her hand down his sternum, breathing in the scent from his neck as she leaned closer. It was getting harder and harder to ignore the urge to touch him whilst he slept next to her. It was almost lucky that El's feather-light touches had stirred Tom awake, causing her to flinch back, pretending there must have been a midge or something flying around them as she waved her hand around.

El wasn't "overly experienced" in the area of BDSM kinkiness. It was only what she had watched during her quest for the perfect porn to suit her needs that she'd found something that piqued her interest. A man tied to a bed with a woman dominating him.

The man had groaned and moaned as the woman had ridden him, throwing her head back as she bounced on his cock.

El was no virgin, but she kept having thoughts about what she wanted to do to Tom. Her thoughts were explicitly pornographic, and she didn't understand why. She'd never had those thoughts before about anyone, especially a friend. But she did know if Tom wanted it, she'd do anything he wanted her to.

"Errr... Earth to El? Come in, please?"

El blinked, not realising Tom had been talking to her as the images of her fantasies flashed away in the blink of an eye. El cleared her throat and shifted her legs slightly as she lay on her front, straining her neck back to look up at Tom.

Tom was now standing over her, looking down at her with a confused look. He chuckled and asked her, "Have you been lying out here all morning?"

"Perhaps... Why?" She rolled over onto her back to lean back on her elbows. Her body stretched out on the lounger as she got comfortable. El pushed her sunglasses back up her nose to protect her eyes from the sun's glare as she looked up at Tom from a much more comfortable position.

Tom took his sunglasses off his face, looking down to tuck them into the neckline of his t-shirt.

"I think the sun has frazzled yo-"

His voice trailed off when he lifted his head back up, and his gaze landed upon her body.

El chuckled at him as he now was the one gawking at her.

Tom's eyes took in the yellow bikini top she was wearing that just about covered her breasts, but due to the position she was now lying in, they were almost spilling out over the top as her new position forced her chest forward. The swell of her budding nipples was clear to see under the thin material, causing Tom's lips to part slightly as his eyes bugged.

Tom swallowed as his eyes travelled down her exposed midriff.

El's toned, sun-kissed stomach dipped in at her hips, drawing Tom's eye. It was a shame that she still had a sarong covering her lower half. Tom might not have been able to hold himself back if he had caught sight of her backside in only her yellow bikini briefs.

It was a miracle that he had managed to starve off the temptation to touch her body, content with just watching over her sleeping form at night when he had stayed over. El always wore her full-length pyjamas, which covered everything, only giving a glimpse of her shapely peachy ass that Tom wanted to sink his teeth into.

But now, it was Tom's turn to fantasise about El as she lay there in the hot sun.

His mouth salivated as he thought about what lay beneath that tiny amount of clothing she was wearing. How he would worship El's body with his. He was committing every inch of El's skin, every freckle, every scar to memory as his eyes roamed over her.

She was perfect in his mind.

As El watched him looking at her, she suddenly started to feel anxious. She swallowed the lump of nervous energy that had lodged in her throat. Her mind went to the dark doubts about her body with Tom staring at her. The thoughts that plagued her self-confidence about her scars tore through her head. The marks reminded her of what had happened whenever she looked down at herself, wishing she could erase them as easily as a rubber to pencil marks on paper.

El quickly sat up and grabbed her green t-shirt next to her, slipped it over her head, and pulled it down quickly to cover herself, hiding the bumps and white lines.

She hadn't spoken to Tom about her accident, and this was the first time he would have seen the scars across her ribs and stomach, as she always made sure to cover up. It made her terrified about what he might think had happened to her.

Would he ask her what happened?

Would he pity her that her body was permanently marked if she told him what happened?

Would he think she wasn't beautiful because of them? That she was hideous.

Would he not be attracted to her now that he had seen them?

Was he only staring at her because of the scars?

El didn't know if she was ready to tell anyone outside her family yet, even though Tom and she had grown so close in recent months. Really close. Best friends even.

It made her feel guilty that she had kept this part of her secret from Tom. But she wasn't ready to face it yet, especially as it would be the second anniversary in less than two weeks. She didn't even know how she would tell him what had happened.

Tom cleared his throat and quickly moved the yellow package in his hand to cover the growing package in his shorts as he looked away. He thought El had put her top on because he was ogling her. He didn't even think it was because she was worried about what he'd think about the multiple scars across her body.

"Ehehe..." he chuckled nervously before he swallowed, trying to compose himself. "Erm... These are for you," Tom blurted out as he looked back to El.

He thrust the sunflowers towards her to try and distract her from the current situation growing in his shorts. He would need to go and deal with it soon, or he might end up taking her there and then in the garden. He wanted to kiss, touch, and tell her he wanted to be more than friends. It made his palms itch with the need to vent his true feelings for her. To admit to her how obsessed he was with her.

But El didn't take the flowers from his hand. She looked anywhere but at Tom as her eyes darted around the garden.

Tom's hand dropped slightly, confused at her reaction as she didn't meet his gaze.

El slowly moved her legs to sit with her knees up to her chest, her arms wrapped around them as she pulled the sarong down to cover her knees and hugged herself.

"El... I..." Tom's voice again drifted off. He didn't know what to say. It was pretty obvious El was now very uncomfortable with the situation.

They had been flirting a lot, holding hands a lot. The subtle touches, the glances at each other, and the awkward laughs they shared when they caught the other watching them. But nothing more had happened since Enid's wake and their "almost" kiss, even though there was obviously sexual tension between them that had been building for weeks.

Neither one knew how to push past the friend zone they seemed to find themselves in when confronted with the reality of each other and not the fantasy of their relationship in their head.

They both stalled whenever an opportunity arose to take it further. Neither knew whether that was because of what had happened with Mark and if it was because of them lying to the police. Neither knew how to broach the subject of being more than friends with the other.

It was a stalemate between them, a game of chess that neither seemed to want to win or surrender.

"Tom... I didn't know you were here." Betty's voice sang out across the garden. She smiled at him as she came out of the house with a tray packed with sandwiches.

"Oh, erm... I just popped by to give El a present for passing her exams." Tom thrust the package towards El.

She looked at his hands and gently took the yellow-wrapped parcel from him. Their fingertips just brushed each other as El's eyes moved to his. That static feeling rushed across Tom's fingers and up his arm from the slightest of touches from her. She briefly smiled, but it didn't reach her eyes before she broke eye contact and looked at the package.

Tom knew that smile wasn't genuine and couldn't work out what he'd done wrong.

The package was heavier than El expected as she placed it in front of her on the lounger.

"Oh, Tom, those are gorgeous. Shall I put them in water for you, El?" Betty asked as she placed the tray laden with food on the glass garden tabletop before standing back up, her eyes drifting between Tom and El. Something seemed off between them.

Tom handed El's mum the flowers as she gave him a questioning look, slyly gesturing towards El so she wouldn't notice. Tom shrugged his shoulders in response to Betty's subtle question, not knowing what he had done wrong.

"Would you like to stay for some lunch, Tom? There's plenty." Betty asked him as she walked into the kitchen to sort out the flowers.

"Erm... If it's all right with El?" Tom looked at El expectantly. He was apparently in the doghouse for some reason and didn't know why.

El didn't look up at him. She swallowed down her sudden nerves as she focused on the package and adjusted her sarong across her knees for the tenth time.

She hadn't felt nervous around Tom in a long time, but after he had seen her mutilated, scared body, she was very anxious about what he would think of her, and her anxiety soared through the roof, pushing her back within herself.

Betty came back out of the house with some drinks on another tray.

"Oh, of course, it's all right, isn't it, El," Betty stated.

El didn't say anything but suddenly got up and walked away into the house, pulling her t-shirt down as she walked. Her flight instinct had fully kicked into gear as she hurried inside and up to her room.

"El? El?" Tom called out to her before he sighed, defeated, as he watched her walk away.

Betty clicked her tongue to the roof of her mouth. She knew what was coming up, and El had been quieter when Tom wasn't around, drifting off into thoughts. Betty cleared her throat.

"Just a bit of advice, Tom... If she walks away quietly... Go after her," Betty pointed towards the house, gesturing to him. He hesitated as he looked back and forth between Betty and the door.

"Now..." she told him.

"Oh... Yes, right, of course."

Tom started to walk away but stopped mid-step as he heard Betty call out.

"Tom... Don't forget the present."

"Right... Of course."

He spun on his heel, walked back and grabbed it off the lounger before heading inside.

Betty chuckled at Tom. He may have been an intelligent young man, but he was still pretty clueless about some things.

15.

El was sitting on her bed, the envelope containing her grandmother's handwritten letter in her hands. She knew the written words by heart now and could see them in her mind when she closed her eyes. The curly script of the handwritten letter was seared into her memory so much that she could probably forge Enid's signature by now. Whenever she had doubts about herself, she held it in her hands, giving her the little confidence boost she needed with the words swirling repeatedly in her head...

'You are in control'

"Hi... May I come in?" Tom asked hesitantly as he stood in the doorway holding the large box wrapped in yellow tissue paper.

El quickly stuffed the envelope under her pillow before sitting back up and looking down at the space beside her on her bed.

"Sure," El's voice was quiet as she spoke before her gaze was drawn to Tom. She looked at his mouth as he smiled at her, that tight-lipped smile he did when he was nervous.

"May I?" He gestured to the bed, asking permission to sit next to her.

El nodded her head and smiled softly at him. Tom sighed as he sat down and placed the present on the bed between them, creating a space between them as his fingers rhythmically drummed on the package. He was nervous that he had done something wrong to make her angry and felt compelled to keep a distance between them to not upset her further.

Tom's fingers stilled before he spoke, "Have I done something wrong? You suddenly went very distant and quiet outside."

El took a deep breath. She didn't know if she was ready to tell him or not.

"Tom..." She turned to face him, lifting her legs up to cross them in front of her on the bed. It was almost a barrier that she was putting up between them, furthering the distance between them.

Tom turned his head to look at her and shifted his knee onto the bed to sit more comfortably, angling his body to face her as he rested his hands on his lap.

El took another deep breath before she started talking.

"The reason I... Fuck..." El paused to gather her thoughts before she started again. "Look, Tom... The reason I..."

"If you're going to say it's me, not you, then..."

"No... No, that's not what I was going to say. God, that's such a cliché line..." she chuckled softly. "But anyway... What I was going to say is that I left because..." El paused again, taking a deep breath to build courage before admitting anything. "Because I didn't want you to see my scars and ask me what happened."

Tom's brow creased with confusion, then relaxed almost instantly with realisation.

El didn't know that he knew already how she had gotten her scars after Dotty had spoken to him at Enid's funeral.

"I don't know if I'm quite ready to tell you and..." El sat, picking at her nails absentmindedly as Tom's mind began racing.

Should he come clean and tell her he already knew and didn't care about her scars... Well, he did care. He cared greatly that she nearly died and wasn't there for her, to protect her if he could have. Tom could have lost her before he found her; if she wanted her scars to disappear, he would do anything to help her. Tom wished he had the means to take them away, not because they were ugly or unsightly, but because they were a reminder of what had happened to her and that he didn't want her to have that following her around constantly every time she looked at her body. That feeling of guilt that she must have been carrying because she lived whilst someone else died. Tom wished he could take that away. He was already used to that burden, and it didn't faze him in the slightest.

Or should he lie?

Was he even technically lying if he said nothing?

Dotty had said she probably shouldn't tell him. It wasn't her story to tell. What if it was a secret between him and Dotty that she'd trusted him with? After all, he had plenty of secrets he didn't want El to know about. Not yet, at least. But if he did say he knew, would El want to know how and who told him and-

"Tom? Are you even listening to me?" El asked, breaking Tom from his daze of consuming thoughts that had made him drift off.

"I know," Tom blurted out as he reached across the package towards her.

"What?"

He didn't want to lie to her. Well, not about this, but killing people wasn't what they were currently talking about.

"You know?" El didn't sound pissed, maybe a little surprised, but not angry. That was positive, Tom thought, but her voice was suddenly oddly calm as she spoke.

Tom's hands rested on the box between them as El's hand stilled from picking at her nails.

"Who told you? Was it mum?" El furrowed her brow as she focused on Tom's pupils, looking for a reaction when she said each name. "Was it Dotty?" she asked as she leaned forward slightly.

El knew the slight pulse in Tom's pupils was a giveaway. His tell was the most negligible expansion of that black dot in the centre of his eyes. She could already read him like a book from all the times he had tried to tell her he was fine watching 'Love Actual' again because it was El's favourite film, even when he couldn't stand that love-sickening-inducing movie. Or when he told her that her cooking was excellent and tasted fantastic, even though El had somehow managed to burn the pasta. She had seen through every white lie he had told her, calling him out on it.

"It was Dotty," she sighed loudly as she leaned back and started to rub the scar on her arm.

"El... She was worried about you. She wanted me to know that the last time you shut everyone out, your nan..."

"Don't, Tom!" El snapped back at him as her nostrils flared. "It wasn't her story to tell. Dotty should know I would have told you when I was ready."

"El... She cares about you. She cares deeply about you. Dotty's your sister. She just wants you to be happy."

"Huh... Happy?" El scoffed. "You mean she wants the attention that she craves. Her sister nearly dying is the most interesting thing about her."

"Woah... El..." Tom sounded so shocked as his brow furrowed at her vicious tone.

That fiery rage in El smouldered under her skin. It made her fingertips tingle. The nasty, spiteful side was starting to rear its head as El's anger at Dotty for revealing her secret to Tom without her permission ate away at her once pleasant demeanour. El's shell cracked under the pressure like a damaged egg in boiling water, leaking out the white from inside to solidify.

Tom placed his hand on her knee to try and calm her down. He could almost see the flames of rage in El's eyes, dancing around her irises, clawing to be let out in an explosive fury of remorseless words.

As soon as his hand touched El's knee, she froze.

Her pupils blew wide in fear. She still couldn't stand anyone touching her there, even Tom.

Instinctively, she flinched, and Tom immediately withdrew his hand, resting them on the present between them. She had done that before when he touched her knee. He usually refrained from doing it, but now, with El's anger, it was instinctive for him to try anything to calm her, but her constant reaction to him touching her knee made his curiosity peak.

"Why do you flinch when I touch your knee, El?" Tom was trying to deflect her anger at Dotty by distracting her and also wanting to quench his inquisitiveness.

El looked straight into his eyes. Her nostrils flared again like a bull ready to charge. Was she going to try and slap him again like she had all those months ago before Tom broke her from her depressive cycle?

"Dotty doesn't know everything, and I'm not ready to tell anyone else." Her voice was full of venom as she snapped back at Tom.

Tom's heart ached with her words, causing his own cracks to form in his delicate false facade.

Was he just classed as anyone else to her?

His temper started to rise like a simmering pot of water on the stove just before it hit boiling point and spilt over the sides.

"So, I'm just anyone else then?" he scoffed as his face turned sinister.

"What?" El asked, confused as her eyes narrowed at him.

"You just said... you aren't ready to tell anyone else, El... Am I classed in that? Am I classed as just a random person to you?" Tom seethed.

El balled her fists and bit the inside of her cheeks between her molars. She wanted to wallop him right now to knock some sense into him. How could he not see he was anything but just some random person to her? He was everything.

El gritted her teeth, verging on splitting her cheeks as they ground against the soft skin of her mouth. Her breathing was ragged as her adrenaline surged through her blood, fuelling every organ for her to fight or run.

She needed him to know what he meant to her. In a moment of brief panic at his crushing words and her own overpowering emotions of anger, she grabbed the front of his t-shirt and pulled him to her, slamming her lips to his.

It was a shock to them both that El had actually done it.

They both still had their eyes wide open, staring into each other's eyes as their lips touched for the first time.

El's thumbnails dug into Tom's chest as she pulled him closer. She wanted him to close his eyes, to give in to her, but he wasn't.

Tom felt the same way as his hands gripped the yellow wrapping paper of the present, tearing it slightly. He was unsure whether to grab her back and wrap his arms around her.

They were locked in a weird stalemate, staring into one another's eyes with a look of dominance, wishing the other would give in.

After a few moments, El's grip on Tom's t-shirt slipped away as she let him go, her heart thrashing wildly from fear and rejection. All those doubts flooded her mind again.

Tom's seen your scars, and he doesn't want you.
You're ugly.
No one will ever want you.

She pulled her head back, breaking the kiss and looked away, saddened that he hadn't given in to her.

El started apologising, thinking she had made a terrible mistake and somehow ruined their friendship.

"I'm sorry, I shouldn't..."

Tom cut her off, taking his opportunity to show her exactly what she meant to him. One hand cupped her face with his thumb brushing against her cheekbone, turning her head back to face him. The other was around the back of her neck, his fingers tangling in her hairline, holding her there. Tom leaned in and shut his eyes as soon as his lips touched hers.

El melted against him as a small moan escaped from her lips after she too closed her eyes, them both giving in to each other.

The static feeling completely consumed their bodies as they shared a gentle kiss full of unspoken emotions. Their lips moved in sync together as the kiss started to build rapidly. Months of tension snapped like a rubber pulled too taunt as they deepened the kiss.

El needed to be closer to him, she wanted to feel his body against hers. Her hand fumbled around to find the yellow package between them on her bed. When her hand touched the soft texture of the tissue paper, she pushed the box off the bed and uncrossed her legs. She pulled at the sarong that was wrapped around her waist as she moved, opening it up to give her the freedom to place her leg over Tom's lap and straddle him. The sheer material covering her legs fell and pooled on the floor at Tom's feet.

Tom wasted no time as his emotions took over, driving his actions of needing to finally touch El as he had always craved to do so. His hands travelled down the back of the t-shirt that concealed her body from him to her waist, pulling her closer to him.

His cock was already starting to harden as El rolled her hips against him, edging her core closer to his crotch with a desperate need to feel him against her. Tom's fingertips just skirted under the hem of her t-shirt, along the waistline of her bikini bottoms, as she moaned against his lips.

El licked along the edge of Tom's bottom lip as their mouths moved against one another passionately, asking him to let her in, which he willingly obliged, parting his mouth.

His tongue swirled with hers as he ground his straining cock up against her clothed mound. El could easily feel his prominent hard length against her, making the wetness that built between her legs soak into the material of her bikini bottoms. It threatened to seep further into his shorts as El ground against him more, seeking out that delicious thrill of friction against her bundle of nerves, craving to be touched.

El's hands had found their way into his hair, and she glided her nails across the back of Tom's scalp, earning a delicious, rumbling growl from his throat as their tongues danced together.

She could feel the ridge of a scar on the back of Tom's head as her fingertips slid along the edge of it but she was too lost in their kiss to ask about it now.

The boundaries of friendship they had created over the past few months were shattering like glass around them as they gave into their desire for one another and crossed that imaginary line letting their true feelings for one another flow.

Tom was ecstatic that this was finally happening, and El was too.

Tom suddenly lost all control of himself and stood up with her, her legs still wrapped around his waist. His hands glided down over her hips to hold her ass cheeks. Tom's fingertips went under the material of her bikini bottoms and dug into her skin, causing her to moan into his mouth. He spun El around and laid her down on the bed. Tom was now on top of her, taking charge, never breaking the kiss as he kept the majority of his weight off her.

Tom was kneeling between El's legs, which still had a vice-like grip around his waist. His hands roamed her body as he broke away from her lips to kiss along her jaw to her neck, wanting to feel her pulse against his lips. He needed to know this was really and not just another fantasy in his head.

As soon as he found her sweet spot on her skin, just above her jugular, she arched her back up into him, practically purring as her hands clawed at his hair and shoulders. Her legs tightened as her clit rubbed along his length, spreading the wetness along her slit, causing El to moan at the friction. Her head tilted back as she closed her eyes, savouring the feeling of Tom's hands and mouth finally roaming over her body.

Tom's hands ended up with one under her t-shirt, groping her right breast. He kneaded it in his hand as his fingers pushed the material of the bikini top out of the way to gain access to her hardened nipple. His other hand was now around her throat. Not squeezing it, just holding her there, as he started to suck her skin, feeling her pulse thrash against his tongue. His thumb traced the outline of her windpipe as his fingertips wrapped around the hair behind her ear.

They didn't hear the phone ringing downstairs. They didn't hear El's name being called or the creak of the stairs as Betty ascended upstairs.

"El! You've got a phon-" Betty nearly dropped the phone as she walked into El's bedroom. "Oh shit... Sorry, sorry," Betty stuttered, embarrassed, before quickly backing out as she saw the two of them.

The door was wide open, so Betty assumed they were just talking, not that she would walk in to find Tom between El's legs. His head buried into her neck as El's feet pushed his shorts down, exposing the top of his bum. Betty could see Tom's hand, obviously groping El's breasts as she moaned, her head tipped back against the bed.

As Betty left the room, she closed the door softly behind her, still mumbling apologies as she kept her eyes firmly on the carpeted floor.

Tom clambered off El, pulling his shorts back up over the top of his ass. He looked down at her as he stood next to the bed. His breathing was ragged, his heart hammering in his chest, and his cock straining to get out of the confines of his shorts. His desire was still evident in his eyes as his pupils were almost totally consumed, his irises turning to the midnight blue that El had imagined.

El was in just as much of a state as him. She was lying on her back. Her hair was a mess around her shoulders. Her stiff nipples were visible under her t-shirt, and a pronounced darker yellow area was between her legs, where her arousal had soaked into the material.

She quickly sat up, pulling her bikini top back down to cover her breasts and adjusted her t-shirt. El bent over and grabbed the sarong from the floor. As she raised her head, she was now eye level with Tom's still raging hard cock as she stayed bent over, looking at the impressive tent.

Tom's mouth hung open as he caught his breath and ran his hand through his hair to smooth out where El had had her hands running through it.

He looked down at the top of El's head, noticing that she was staring at his crotch. Tom moved his hand slowly into her hair, wrapping around the roots to tilt her head and make her look up at him.

El met his intense gaze with a smouldering look of her own as she licked her bottom lip before her teeth sunk into it, biting it softly.

"Jesus fuck, El... Don't do that." His voice was low and husky as he looked down at her mouth.

"Do what?" she raised her eyebrow teasingly, "This?"

She bit her lip again, and a shuddering breath left Tom's parted lips as he moved his free hand to run his thumb across her bottom lip.

Suddenly, the front door slammed downstairs, and they could hear Dotty crying loudly as both their heads snapped to El's bedroom door. El shot an apologetic look to Tom before she clambered off her bed and stood up, wrapping the sarong around her lower body and opened the door. El was met with a hysterical Dotty, almost bumping into her.

Tom spun around, drawn to the commotion as Dotty wailed loudly.

"He's cheating... He fucking cheated on me."

16.

"I can't wait to finish what we started," Tom whispered against El's ear before he licked along the edge of it, lightly nipping at her lobe and keeping his actions out of sight of Dotty. El giggled quietly under her breath and watched him leave her bedroom with a longing in her eyes.

Dotty's wailing and intrusion into El's bedroom had put a stop to El and Tom's amorous activities before they could start again after Betty's prior interruption.

Tom hurriedly left El's house, eager to get back to her once he found out what happened between Dotty and his brother. Tom looked like a boy caught with his hand in the cookie jar when Betty called out to him from the kitchen as she made some fresh tea, causing Tom to pause at the front door and turn to look at her.

"The apology went well then, I take it?" Betty smirked as she leaned against the kitchen door frame.

Tom smiled shyly, his eyes glinting with mischief before he said goodbye to Betty and left to head to Charlie's flat. Betty asked him if he wanted to stay for lunch, but Tom declined; he needed to go and find out what had happened. Tom said he would pop back later this evening, though.

Betty really did like Tom, and he was the perfect fit for El. She had witnessed him protecting and comforting her so many times already. Betty was ecstatic that they were finally doing something about their obvious attraction to each other. She just hoped he didn't break her heart.

...

Dotty was sitting on El's bed, eating from a tub of ice cream, wallowing in self-pity as she waited for her sister to get out of the shower. Dotty thought El was taking ages as she had been in the bathroom for at least thirty minutes, much to Dotty's annoyance. El should have been sitting with her, helping her to deal with her breakup, not preening herself in the bathroom.

El had to compose herself with a cold shower after her earlier making-out session with Tom and the promise of what would come later when he returned.

But the cold water still hadn't quenched the heat between her legs; it had simply made her body shiver, the chill reaching deep into her bones. When El stood wrapped in a warm fluffy towel to try and bring some warmth back into her body, she looked in the mirror to sort her hair out. The dark scarlet mark of a hickey on her neck that Tom had given her stood out like a beacon. The deep red mark was starting to turn purple where her blood had been sucked to the surface of her skin, breaking the capillaries underneath, leaving it to bruise.

El gently traced the mark with her fingertips as she thought about Tom's mouth there. She hadn't realised how hard he must have been sucking on her skin, too lost in the intimacy of the moment to notice, but she wanted more. El had never wanted someone to mark her body before, to put their claim on her so obviously for the world to see, but she did with Tom. She wanted everyone to know that she was his.

El also couldn't help thinking about marking him and covering his body in bruises of ownership.

Would he let her?

Would he want her to stamp him as hers for everyone to see?

Her other hand travelled down her body over the soft bath towel she had wrapped around herself as she thought about it, following the valley between her breasts.

Just thinking about his hands roaming over her and the memory of his touch made her ache with anticipation and a feeling of emptiness that needed to be filled. El had to drag herself back from just giving in to pleasuring herself when she heard Dotty whine her name loudly, interrupting her.

El let out an irritated huff before she quickly dropped the towel and threw some clothes on. She came out of the bathroom to see Dotty had managed to eat almost the entire tub of Ben and Jerry's cookie dough ice cream by herself. El plopped beside her sister on the bed, tutting into the empty space of the bedroom before Dotty placed the near-empty pot on El's bedside table.

"I am sorry, El, that I told Tom. I know you don't like to talk about the accident, but I thought he needed a little nudge to tell you how he feels about you. Obviously, he's in love with you, and if he knew, he might understand why what he did for you was so important."

"He's not *in love* with me, Dotty, and as for telling him... I am still pissed at you for that... But... I suppose it saved me from getting super anxious about doing it."

El just had to think of a way to tell Tom the rest of what had happened. The parts that only her nan knew about. She wanted him to know everything about what had happened that night. But she worried he wouldn't want to be with her if she told him the whole truth of what had happened that night.

Would he look at her differently, perhaps not even want to be with her? Would he be scared of her if she exposed what she had done?

Dotty furrowed her brow at El as she questioned if Tom loved her.

"If any guy looked at me the way he looks at you, I would think that I had died and gone to heaven. He's definitely in love with you, El... even if he hasn't said it yet. He will. I know it," Dotty paused as she studied her sister's features, wanting to see the truth in her eyes. "Do you love him, El? You obviously like him?"

El paused as she mulled over the question. She didn't know what love felt like. She had never felt it before, so she just didn't know if these feelings she had were love. El knew she liked him that way; she was attracted to him, always had been, even if there was initial hesitancy on her part. Their friendship had grown into something more than just being close friends. El wanted more than just friends with benefits. She wanted to be with Tom constantly. He grounded her when she started to lose control.

El wanted to do more than just kiss him, although that was the most fantastic make-out session she'd ever had. Filled with passion and the promise of more. She had even wanted to get down on her knees for him, letting him use her mouth however he wanted.

Blowjobs were something she had never really enjoyed, but she wanted to do everything with him. She missed Tom when he wasn't there. She longed to hear his voice and feel his touch upon her skin. Even the scent of him she craved. His presence brought comfort to her and made her feel more at ease. Even that dark edge to him she yearned to be around. It excited her, causing heat to pool in her core as she thought about that look he got in his eyes when he pushed that broken glass to her father's neck, but at the same time, it frightened the living hell out of her.

Dotty could see El's brain processing her feelings. El had that far-off stare she got when she was thinking things over.

"I think you love him, El... you just have to tell him..." Dotty smiled at El as she rubbed her shoulder before something caught her eye. "What's this?" Dotty asked as she picked up the yellow package from the floor, interrupting El's thoughts and passing it to El.

El placed it on the bed beside her, tracing her fingers along the tear in the yellow tissue paper. She had forgotten all about the present she had shoved out of the way to get closer to Tom as they kissed.

"It's from Tom."

"Another present? He loves to spoil you. Why couldn't his brother be the same?" Dotty sniffed. "The only thing he's ever given me is chlamydia."

El's eyes snapped to Dotty, a look of disbelief washing over her face as she wasn't sure she had heard clearly what Dotty had said.

"WHAT!?!" El looked at her, shocked by the information she had just heard fall from her sister's lips.

Dotty shrugged, her head drooping down sadly before she started crying again.

"That's how I know he's cheating... I get checked regularly, and I was clean before... before..." Dotty trailed off, unable to finish the sentence.

"Oh, Dotty," El grabbed her sister and wrapped her arms around her. "That dirty fucking bastard. He doesn't deserve you, Dotty."

Dotty sniffed as she reciprocated El's comforting hug.

"It's my own fault. I should never have started sleeping with Charlie. It was a stupid mistake."

El stroked Dotty's hair, trying to soothe her. "Don't blame yourself because he can't keep it in his pants. You're worth more than that. So much more."

Dotty sat back and met El's eyes. "You sound like nan."

She smiled a little at El before they started crying and hugged each other again.

It was the first time that Dotty had told El that she had reminded her of their nan. They were similar in so many ways, not just in their appearance but also in their actions. The kindness that they both possessed. The fierceness when someone within their family was threatened. Dotty knew that El would grow into the matriarch and protector of their family when she was older.

Dotty had been envious of El's relationship with their grandmother when they were younger, but now she could see that it was something that couldn't be helped. Anyone could see those two were like two peas in a pod, destined to be close and able to know what the other was thinking without words.

After a few moments, Dotty and El let go of each other and sat back, looking at the present.

"Well... Are you going to open it?" Dotty asked, wiping her nose across her sleeve with her free hand.

El looked behind her at the package and smiled. How had Tom known her favourite colour was yellow without her telling him?

"I think I'll wait to open it with him," El said.

Dotty smiled at her and placed her hand over hers. "You two suit each other... You know that, right?"

El smiled shyly at her sister before they heard the phone ringing downstairs, followed by their mum answering and calling out to El.

El came downstairs to see her mum with her thumb over the speaker, holding the phone out for El to take as Dotty followed her.

"It's the property management company again. They want to talk to you," Betty told her.

In the paperwork that El had received in the post the following week after Enid's wake, there was a bound leather folder from a property management firm in London, 'Bespoke Property Management'. They apparently ran all of Enid's properties and had done so for several years. Inside was a portfolio of all the properties that El now owned.

She didn't even look through it. She just put the folder with her other personal paperwork in her wardrobe and forgot about it. She didn't want to think about any of it at the moment. It was still too raw to deal with.

El took the phone from her mum, holding it to her ear to speak.

"Hello? Ethel Fletcher speaking."

"Good afternoon, Miss Fletcher. My name is Matthew Johnson from Bespoke Property Management. I'm your new account manager."

"Oh? Good afternoon, Mr Johnson," El replied formally. She had slipped into her telephone voice, causing a smirk on Dotty's face as she listened.

"Oh, please... call me Matthew."

"Okay... Matthew... May I ask why you are calling?"

"Well, it's nice to get a hold of you finally. You're a hard woman to track down, Miss Fletcher. I did call earlier, but you were indisposed, I was informed?"

El had to stifle a snort. She had definitely been "indisposed" when he called earlier. She cleared her throat to compose herself after being reminded of her earlier activities with Tom.

"Oh? Yes... Sorry."

Matthew sounded very upper-class with his posh London accent. His voice was low, gravelly, and full of confidence and authority, even though he sounded pretty young.

"I did also send a large envelope. There was a letter within it, with your portfolio, requesting a meeting with you at your earliest convenience. As I didn't get a response, I tried calling the contact number, but it seems that has been changed?"

"Oh? Who was the contact number?" El asked. She could hear a rustling noise down the phone as he flicked through the paperwork on his desk.

"A Mrs Betty Fletcher, Ms Enid's daughter."

"My mum. Erm, yes. She changed her phone number a little while ago."

"Oh, okay… Well, can I arrange a meeting with you, Miss Fletcher? I didn't just want to turn up at your home, but I was getting close to that." He chuckled down the phone before clearing his throat and continuing, "We need to discuss your plans with your properties as you are the new account holder."

"Oh? Erm..." El shrugged her shoulders at her mum with a slight look of panic. "Erm... Can't you just do what my nan did with them?"

He chuckled again. It verged on being condescending and caused El to clench her jaw before she took a deep breath and sighed.

"I'm sorry, but I don't really know what I'm doing and-"

"Miss Fletcher. Your grandmother met with us once a year to discuss her plans for her properties, and that annual meeting is well overdue now. I know the circumstances have changed, but we are responsible for ensuring your investments are taken care of."

"Oh. I didn't know about any meetings. I'm sorry. It's just that I have a lot going on at the moment."

"Well... Can we book a meeting for in a month's time? It would give you time to look through your portfolio and see what you own now and what you wish to do with it?"

Now that... That tone he used with her was definitely condescending.

"Yes, well..." El said, flustered as she rubbed the scar on her arm as Matthew pushed her for an answer.

"Shall we say September fifteenth at eleven?"

"Well, I suppose..."

Matthew immediately interrupted her. "That's fabulous. Everything is booked for you, Miss Fletcher. I will send the car for you."

"I'm sorry, what car?" El asked, confused.

He chuckled again. The posh prick, El thought. She already didn't like him.

"Our company car will pick you up from home at nine-thirty to bring you to the office for our meeting at eleven."

El hesitated as she mentally tried to take this all in.

"It's our courtesy service for our larger accounts, Miss Fletcher. I look forward to meeting you on the fifteenth in London. Have a pleasant afternoon."

El went to say goodbye, but Matthew had already hung up, cutting off the line. She pulled the phone away from her ear as the annoying tone of a dead phone line rang through her ear. El looked down at the phone, puzzled.

"So..." Betty raised her eyebrow at El, wondering what was happening.

"Err... I've got a meeting in London on September fifteenth at eleven, but they're sending a car to get me at nine-thirty. Apparently." El just looked totally confused and flustered.

"A meeting with who?" Dotty asked.

...

Tom went to Charlie's flat to see if Charlie was there. He rang the bell for flat 1 on the console keypad outside the front door.

After a few minutes, the buzzer crackled to life, letting Tom in through the main door and into the black and white chequered hallway.

Tom walked along the corridor to Charlie's flat and knocked on the door. When Charlie opened the door, Tom could smell the alcohol on his breath as he stepped past his brother into his flat.

"I suppose you heard... Come to tell me off, brother?" Charlie asked as he closed his front door and followed Tom. "Come to tell me what a disgusting pig of a human being I am?" Charlie asked sarcastically.

Tom walked silently into Charlie's kitchen to make coffee to sober his brother up.

"I'm guessing Dot told El then? And she's told you?" Charlie asked as he followed Tom into the kitchen.

Tom looked up from filling the kettle with fresh water.

"Actually, no..." Tom said as he turned the tap off and closed the kettle lid. "Dotty technically told me you'd cheated when she barged into El's bedroom."

"Oh? I thought she might... Hang on... El's bedroom?" Charlie may have been drunk, but he wasn't that drunk that he didn't hear Tom say he was in El's bedroom with a bitter tone. "Are you and El?" Charlie made an obscene gesture with his hands, causing Tom to tut at him as he turned the kettle on.

"No... Unfortunately, we were interrupted before it got that far," Tom sighed as he reached up for the coffee mugs on the shelf.

"Oh? Oh... Shit... Sorry..." Charlie put his hands up in surrender as Tom turned around to face him and leaned his backside against the counter.

"Yes, well... Here I am to check on my stupid brother and question his choices as El looks after Dotty."

Charlie pulled a barstool from under the kitchen countertop and sat gingerly on it. Tom immediately noticed him wince as he sat awkwardly.

"Everything all right?" Tom asked curiously as he gestured at his brother's waist with his hand.

"Turns out Dot has quite the strong knee," Charlie replied as he shifted on the seat, trying to get comfortable.

Tom chuckled and shook his head. "Well, that might teach you for dipping your wick in anything willing."

"Urgh... Tom, please don't start. Can't you see I'm an injured man? I've had enough punishment for one day."

"What would mum say?"

Charlie groaned and rolled his eyes.

"Oh, please don't give me the whole 'what would mum say' treatment. I've had enough of being berated today, let alone from you."

Tom sighed and clicked his tongue against the roof of his mouth. He was glad that Dotty had given Charlie some sort of punishment. If that had been Tom, he would undoubtedly have done more than just knee Charlie in his crown jewels. Charlie wouldn't have had any crown jewels left attached. Tom would have stuffed them down his throat to watch him choke on them.

17.

That very one-sided conversation with Matthew completely ruined El's mood. She had enough to contemplate, let alone prepare for a property management meeting. She had absolutely no clue what was involved with property management or what she was meant to do. She could have been slightly more prepared if only her nan had simply said something to her.

El had spent the rest of her afternoon worrying about what she was meant to do. She didn't want to spend the next month trying to figure out how to manage properties. It wasn't something she ever needed to think about before.

Plus, with the anniversary of her accident coming up, El's mind kept flashing back to memories of it as the stress got to her.

Last year, she spent the entire summer at her Nans' home in Atherington and only went back to Cambridge because of starting at University.

Now, all El could think about was getting as far away from Cambridge as possible. She hoped Tom might go with her and stay in Atherington, but she didn't know how to ask him.

At least he knew about the accident now, which saved her from working out how to start that awkward conversation with him.

El also needed to figure out how to broach what had happened earlier between them in her bedroom.

Was it just an in-the-moment thing where they had gotten carried away, or did he really like her like that?

She didn't want this to be a quick thing he would regret later if something more happened between them. El certainly didn't want it to ruin their friendship because they acted impulsively and took things too far.

She needed reassurance that this was what Tom wanted as well.

El was sitting, poking around at her dinner; she hadn't eaten much today and just didn't feel like it as her mind swirled with a thousand different things.

Betty was watching her like a hawk. She knew what was coming up and was already worried about El's state of mind. Betty was unsure how El would cope without having her grandmother around to comfort her like Enid had last year.

Enid had told Betty in confidence the previous year how El had started having flashbacks and nightmares when the anniversary was approaching. El could wake the dead with her screams caused by her nightmares. She could be violent, and Enid found it difficult to wake her up when the nightmares took hold of El as El thrashed on the bed, tying herself in the bed sheets.

Betty was increasingly concerned with El and how she would drift into her memories when Tom wasn't around. The vacant look would wash over her face as if she was looking straight through you.

Betty was also worried about Mark. After she had changed her mobile number, he had then started harassing her via email, begging her to take him back. He wrote about how sorry he was about everything and wanted to make it up to her and El. Nothing was mentioned about Dotty in his rambling words to her, though. Not that it concerned Betty, as Mark had never seemed to have a problem with Dotty. Dotty wasn't the one to inherit the majority of Enid's fortune. El was.

Betty was determined to go ahead and press charges against her husband. If there was one thing Betty had learned from her mother, it was never to let a man get away with hurting you or your children. It didn't matter if it was physical or emotional torment; that sort of behaviour wasn't to be tolerated by any person.

There was a knock at the door, and Betty got up to answer it.

"Hi, Tom... Come in," she said brightly, relieved that Tom was back.

Tom smiled at Betty as she stepped out of the way for him to come in.

He was excited to see El again and hoped to continue what they had started early in her bedroom when they were alone. In fact, he couldn't fully concentrate at Charlie's. All he kept thinking about was El. That little taste he had had was driving him to distraction, more so than ever.

"How's Dotty?" Tom asked as he made conversation with Betty.

"Upset still. She just needs a bit of time and some antibiotics."

"Antibiotics?" Tom furrowed his brow in confusion.

Betty tutted. "Oh... Me and my big mouth... I thought Charlie might have told you, as he's your brother."

"Hmmm... Something he seems to have forgotten to mention," Tom huffed, annoyed. He would deal with Charlie later.

"Yes, well... El's at the table, and just to warn you, she's pretty distracted."

Tom walked immediately into the kitchen. Suddenly, his needs disappeared, and he just wanted to ensure El was okay. He wasn't used to caring about another's feelings so much, but it was completely different with her. Her happiness was his sole focus.

El's eyes immediately lit up when she saw him before they softened again, and she looked down at her plate. Her worries quickly invaded her mind as she thought about the meeting and the anniversary.

"Hi, Dotty... Hi, El..." Tom said.

"Hey, Tom," Dotty answered, but El didn't as she poked at her food with her fork absentmindedly.

Tom smiled at El as he walked to the table and stood beside her, leaning his hands on top of the back of the empty chair next to her. He looked down at her hardly-touched plate of food and chewed on the inside of his lip.

He had noticed that she hadn't been eating much recently and resorted to buying the occasional snacks to keep her energy up.

"Would you like something to eat, Tom?" Betty's cheerful voice always brought an air of comfort to a room as she broke through the awkward silence between Tom and El.

"Yes, please. I'm famished." Tom smiled over at Betty as she busied herself, dishing up a serving of pasta for him while he pulled out the chair next to El and sat down.

As Betty placed it in front of him, she raised her eyebrow whilst looking at El, who was still poking about at a piece of tomato.

"El? Why don't you tell Tom about your phone call today?" suggested Betty, trying to get El to focus on something and break out of her distant gaze.

"Phone call?" Tom asked curiously as he turned to El and popped a piece of pasta into his mouth.

"Errr, yeah," El answered. "The property management company called to arrange a meeting with me."

"Oh? A property management firm? When for?" asked Tom.

"Yeah. Erm... September fifteenth," El sighed.

"Do you need to go to their office?"

"Yeah, they're sending a car to take me to London," El said as she looked at Tom briefly before going back to poking at her food.

"London? Hmmm..."

Tom didn't like this one bit. El was going to be in London, on her own, with some random stranger Tom hadn't met. His brain quickly ran forward through his upcoming schedule of introductions back at University. He would be in meetings he couldn't get out of that day.

Tom gritted his teeth and clenched his jaw as he realised she would have to go without him. He couldn't stand it and swallowed the lump of disapproval in his throat.

El noticed the change in Tom's demeanour. His pupils dilated slightly as he was thinking, the muscles tensing in his cheeks as he grits his teeth, the grip on his fork tightening to show the whites of his knuckles.

She placed her hand on his arm and gave him a tight smile as she squeezed it gently. His body instantly relaxed into her touch, easing his conflict.

El had managed to eat a few mouthfuls of pasta before she and Tom went upstairs to her room after dinner. The yellow-wrapped present still sat on her bed where she had left it.

"Oh? You didn't open it?" Tom asked as he walked into her room and saw the present still there. He stood beside her bed, looking down at it with his head tilted slightly, a small smile tugging at his lips.

Knowing Dotty's curiosity, he had half expected her to open it herself if El had left her alone in her room. Dotty might have even been able to influence El into opening it without him, but he was also glad that she hadn't.

"No, I wanted to wait for you." She smirked at him and pushed her bedroom door shut with a reassuring click as she turned the lock, not wanting to be disturbed this time.

Tom's ears pricked up at the sound of the click, and he looked over his shoulder at her. He watched as El slowly turned and walked towards him, biting her bottom lip.

El was now the predator stalking him.

Her pupils dilated a millimetre more with every step she took closer to him. He could clearly see the pulse in her neck pumping. He could almost feel the air around him pulsing in that same rhythm.

"Perhaps... I should open this first? I mean... You have given it to me twice already today," El's voice was sultry as she bent over, on purpose, next to Tom as her hand slid across her duvet towards the package.

Tom leaned back slightly to get a better look at her. His eyes followed over the curve of her backside as he stood by El's bed, and she picked up the package.

He cleared his throat as he watched her and adjusted himself as subtly as possible, hoping she wouldn't notice how excited he already was.

He could already feel the blood rushing to his cock, hardening it quickly now that they were alone in El's locked bedroom.

El slowly turned and sat on her bed, patting the space next to her, with a slight smile tugging at her lips as she looked up at him. She knew exactly what she was doing as she pulled the ribbon off gently and laid it across her knee before peeling the paper back.

Tom smiled down at her before he took his place next to her on her bed and watched her delicate fingers undo the package.

Inside was a cardboard box sealed with tape. El scratched at the edge, lifting it to peel it back with a satisfying rip.

Tom's heart was pounding in his chest with nervous energy. He didn't know if he'd done the right thing buying this for her.

As little as Tom knew about musicians, he assumed they might prefer to purchase their own instruments, and he could only hope that he had made the right choice when he had been researching a replacement for El's violin.

As El opened the cardboard box, it was stuffed with those styrofoam cylinder things that tended to get everywhere. She carefully moved them over to avoid spilling them out of the box and onto the floor as she peeked inside.

Tom's excited, nervous energy was hard to contain as he watched her look into the box and push the packing out of the way. He knew she would know exactly what it was as she saw the black leather case.

El's fingers glided over the violin case as she carefully lifted it out. Her breath caught in her throat at the gift Tom had given her.

Tom removed the cardboard box from her lap and carefully placed it on the floor before looking back at her, his heart pounding in his chest from anticipating her reaction.

He slowly took hold of the yellow ribbon and dragged it across her thigh, watching El's pupils dilate. Still, she didn't flinch like she usually would when he touched her there, and he made a mental note of that for later before placing the ribbon in the pocket of his shorts.

El looked shocked as she placed the leather violin case back on her lap. Her fingers traced over the latches one at a time, popping them open. She swallowed before lifting the lid to reveal the stunning, amber-coloured violin.

"Oh, my god."

Her voice was barely a whisper as her fingertips ran over the mixtures of Italian spruce and maple wood of the violin's body. She lightly touched its neck as though she was touching a newborn baby for the first time, being extra careful and delicate with something so precious.

It wasn't strung yet, but that was how El liked it. She loved restringing her old violin. The time she took to tune it was almost pleasurable.

El was enthralled by the gift and Tom's thoughtful idea to buy her this. A huge smile spread across her face as tears ran down her cheeks.

She carefully detached the bow from the case lid and examined it as she turned it over.

"Tom... Tom, this is too much," she gushed.

"Nothing is too much for you. You deserve the best." Tom's heart blossomed at her reaction. He couldn't stop her infectious smile from spreading to him as he watched her.

"Is this a D Z Strad 509?" El asked as she looked at him and saw him slowly nod.

This was one of the highest-rated professional violins in the world and was very expensive. Tom had even bought her two new sets of strings, including for the bow.

"Lift it out, El. See how it feels." Tom was itching for her to take it out.

El carefully placed the bow back before her eyes focused on the neck of the violin. She carefully wrapped her fingers around it and lifted it with one hand whilst her other supported the body. Her hands automatically felt at home as she held the gorgeous instrument. Her heart jolted with pleasure at the beautiful gift Tom had given her.

Something inside the case caught her eye as she held the violin in her hands.

Tom nervously held his breath, waiting for her to see the surprise he had left at the bottom of the case for her.

El refocused her attention on the photograph that was framed inside. Her breathing became ragged as she took in the image, and her mouth dropped open.

There, staring back at her, was a picture of her and her grandmother holding hands and looking out to sea on Boxing Day, the year it snowed. The crisp white flakes swirled around them as their hair whipped up in the wind. They were laughing as they stood, clutching their towels around their freezing bodies with their free hands.

El didn't know what to say as her heart lurched with the conflicting emotions of joy and sadness at the happy memory. She couldn't say anything as the tears rolled down her face.

18.

A minute passed, then two, then three, before El pulled her eyes away from the picture of her grandmother and her on the beach. She carefully placed the violin back in the case, fastening everything down, before she closed the lid, stood up and walked over to the corner of her room. El gently placed it on the floor by her music stand and took a deep breath. Her shoulders rose and fell as she gathered her thoughts. She didn't say a word the entire time, and neither had Tom as he sat watching, entranced by her.

Tom stood up as El lingered by her music stand for a few moments before hesitating to take a step towards her, unsure if he had done the right thing with choosing that picture to place inside the case.

El spun around and rushed at him, jumping onto him and wrapping her arms around his neck as she kissed him. Tears were still running down her cheeks, turning the taste of her lips salty.

Tom's hands had found their way around under her thighs to hold her against him as he kissed her back. The salt of her tears mixed with the taste of the sweet, sharp tang of the tomatoes in the pasta sauce as their lips parted and tongues swirled together.

El's hands were in his hair as Tom stumbled backwards till the back of his legs hit her bed, and he sat back down with her straddling his lap.

El broke the kiss, quickly leaning back to take her top off over her head. Immediately, Tom's mouth attached to her neck, finding her sweet spot from earlier where he had marked it. His hands ran up the smoothness of her back to unclasp her bra. Tom licked his way across her collarbone as El's hands went up under the back of his top, tracing every outline of his muscles as he flexed.

They were both lost in a swirl of emotions as lust overtook them both, and they gave in to their desire for one another without speaking a word.

Tom glided his fingers over her shoulders, slowly moving the bra straps down her arms until she pulled her arms out and dropped her bra to the carpet.

He kissed, licked and sucked his way down each breast in turn, wrapping his mouth around each nipple and sucking them into stiff peaks.

El moaned each time, her head tilting back as the pleasurable feeling spread down her body and pooled in her core as she clung to his hair. Her fingertips almost turned white with the force she used to hold onto him.

Tom's cock was straining to get out of his shorts as El clawed at his back. He leaned back to look at her, his eyes following every dip and curve of her body before he cupped her face and stared into her eyes.

"You are the most beautiful thing I have ever seen, El."

She smiled shyly at him as a slither of trepidation crept into her mind.

Tom was looking at her scarred body again, but his words reassured her and gave her the confidence to ignore that feeling of inadequacy that her scars created in her mind, that her body wasn't perfect.

But with him here looking at her with nothing but lust and perhaps something more, she ignored her doubts and followed her desires that led her to him and this moment.

Tom leaned in and kissed her lips again, running his tongue across them to gain access. Their tongues danced as they deepened the kiss, moaning into each other.

El's hands moved back down his back to grasp the hem of his shirt and hastily pull it over his head. She needed to feel his bare skin against hers. She sought the warmth and comfort from it that his touch brought her.

Tom broke the kiss for a moment to get his top off and chuck it to the side.

Gripping El's back, Tom turned them both over and effortlessly lifted her up the bed underneath him so her head rested on the pillow. His mouth quickly found hers again, kissing her passionately before travelling down her body to seek out more of her skin.

Tom slowed his pace as he started to worship El's body.

There was no need to hurry as he kissed every scar, taking his time. Tom wanted to shower her with the attention and love she deserved and not get lost in the frenzy they had started. He needed to appreciate every inch of her now that he had her. He wanted to make her his in every sense of the word.

Some of El's scars were from cuts she sustained during the accident, and others were from the multiple surgeries she had endured to repair her organs. They were the deepest ones and tingled when Tom touched them with his tongue as a numb sensation washed over her skin in those areas from where her nerves had been cut through. She giggled slightly, which was the most endearing music to his ears as he continued to move down her body as El watched him.

As Tom got lower to her shorts, hooking his fingers underneath the waistband, he paused, looking up at her as he rested on his elbows.

"El? Are you sure you want this?" he asked with an air of foreboding. "Because once I start, I don't think I will be able to stop," he took a sharp breath as he looked up at her through his lashes. "I'll never be able to let you go," Tom admitted as his pinkie fingers traced the waistband of her shorts, gliding against the skin of her hips.

Deep down, Tom already knew he couldn't let her go; his obsession was all-consuming. El took up every thought of his in some way. Even if it had nothing to do with her directly, she would always be considered. But he needed to tell her that before she agreed. He needed to hear her say it to make his desires a reality.

El bit her lip as he looked at her, the sincerity clearly evident in his eyes as well as his lust.

"I'm sure... I'm sure I never want you to stop. I never want you to let me go, Tom... because I'll never let you go either," El said as her eyes softened.

Tom's heart skipped a beat as she said those words, just like El's, as she smiled lovingly down at him and ran her fingers through his hair.

He slid her shorts down and off, taking her knickers with them simultaneously as he kissed every inch of newly exposed skin.

El was now bare before him as he knelt in front of her between her legs on the bed, but she didn't feel exposed. She felt cherished by how he looked at her, as if she was the most beautiful thing his eyes had ever seen.

El bit her bottom lip as she smirked at him with a wicked glint in her eyes.

"You still have far too many clothes on, Thomas."

Her tone was full of playfulness and confidence as she sat up and pushed his shorts down over his ass.

El's fingernails scraped across the curve of his skin, earning her a delicious groan from him as his hard cock sprung free, almost hitting her abdomen as it recoiled back into its ready position. She held back a giggle as she noticed immediately that he didn't have any boxers on, but she didn't say anything. El was glad there wasn't another layer of clothes between them.

El leaned back slightly to let her eyes feast on his bare form for the first time. She couldn't help the slight shuddering intake of breath as her eyes lingered on his cock, pointing straight up at her.

El knew he was bigger than any other guy she'd been with before. She had felt his hard length press against her when they had been making out before Betty interrupted them as she shamelessly ground her core against it. But the mere sight of it out in the open with nothing covering it made her slick and throb with anticipation as her saliva pooled in her mouth.

She kept her eyes on her hands as she ran her fingers around Tom's waist, down the fronts of his thighs and back up. One hand glided to cup and squeeze his firm testicles as the other wrapped around to grip his girthy shaft at the base.

Tom let out a breathy moan as El slowly leaned forward to let a dribble of saliva run out from her bottom lip onto his slit, where a bead of precum had already gathered.

"Jesus Christ, El... That's so fucking hot," his voice was hoarse as he moaned out again.

El glided her hand up his shaft, her thumb swirled around the head to gather the combination of her spit and his precum to then rub it down the underside of his cock.

She lifted her hand to her mouth and licked across her palm and fingers, locking her gaze with his before wrapping them around the head of his length. Slowly, she lowered her hand back down to spread the mixture of her saliva and his own lubricant across his taunt skin. She could feel every bump of his large veins as his cock twitched in her hand, begging for her to quicken her pace.

Tom soon realised that El was in no way inexperienced. He was taken aback by her explicit behaviour as she focused on his eyes, watching the pleasure she gave him rise in them as they darkened.

She adored the sensual groans that were escaping his throat. It made her even wetter. El couldn't stop herself as she continued pumping his cock with one hand and moved her other one to start touching herself between her parted legs.

El moaned as she rubbed against her clit in slow circles, keeping pace with the thrusts of Tom's hips as he began to grind into her hand.

He leaned forward and captured her chin with one hand, forcefully pulling her to him as his other hand found its way down her body to glide over hers as she continued to touch herself.

Tom didn't push her fingers out of the way as El might have expected him to; he just rested his own against hers for a moment, feeling how she moved against herself, learning exactly what she liked.

Leaning forward, Tom rested his forehead against hers as they watched one another, their breath mixing in the air between them as they continued to move at the same pace.

El sunk her teeth into her bottom lip as Tom moved his finger further back along her slit, running the tip of his middle finger around her slick entrance. She ached to feel him there where she felt empty without something to fill it.

She moaned loudly as he eased his finger slowly inside her, quenching that ache, her head tipping back at the feeling of him finally there where she needed him as she continued to pump his shaft.

Tom's thumb traced her jaw as he watched her take the pleasure he was giving her, unable to remove his eyes from her beautiful face and neck that was flushed with arousal.

He pumped his finger slowly in and out of her, matching the same rhythm as her hand on his cock, before adding his ring finger inside her.

Instantly, he could feel her walls clench around his digits as he moved them through her wet core, quickening his pace as her hands sped up, pushing him deeper and harder, chasing both their release.

El's fingers continued to circle her clit, gliding against that bundle of nerves, helping that delicious knot to tighten in her lower stomach. It felt like it might snap any moment the longer the pressure built to a blinding darkness that would consume her.

Tom could feel her pussy clenching and spasming around his fingers, her walls swelling as she was nearly on the cusp of euphoria.

El dropped her head to look back at him, his eyes full of lust as she moaned loudly again, feeling his cock swelling more in her hand as it twitched.

She needed more inside her. This wasn't quite enough. She wanted to feel the stretch of Tom's length inside her; it was the only thing she could think of that would appease that feeling in her cunt. It was all she could think about as she continued to pump him, bringing him nearer to his release.

"Fuck...Tom... I need you..." El moaned. "I need to feel your cock stretch me. I need to feel you inside me."

El let go of his length and laid back on her bed, lifting her hips to pull away from his soaking fingers. He watched as she drew his hand towards her mouth and brought his fingers that had been inside her cunt to her mouth. El licked them clean with the most sinful look in her eyes.

It was the most erotic thing he had ever seen in his life, and it made his cock twitch in the air, seeking out a warm wet place to release in.

Tom could have cum there and then just from watching that. But El had asked him to use his cock, so he held back as she popped his fingers out of her mouth and smirked at him.

He moved up her body, kissing her skin as he went to rest on his elbows that he placed on either side of her arms on the bed.

El wrapped her arms around his neck and spread her legs wider, planting her heels around the junction of his thighs and backside, pulling him down against her entrance.

Tom hissed between his clenched teeth as the tip of his cock pushed against her warmth. It was so easy for him to slip inside her tight dripping pussy as her welcoming walls guided him deeper, drawing him in.

El's back arched from the bed with every inch of him until her body was curved underneath him, pushing their chests flush together. Her nipples rubbed against his chest as he bottomed out inside her.

Tom stilled for a few moments to allow her to adjust before she rolled her hips impatiently, pushing her heels into his arse cheeks, indicating that she was ready for him to move.

Tom moved one of his hands around underneath her waist to hold El above her ass as he slowly started to roll his hips. He wanted to savour every feeling of her as he pulled back, just until only the head of his cock remained inside her, before slowly pushing back into her with a deep rumbling groan.

El's fingers tightened around his shoulders as she moaned, "Fuck, Tom," into his shoulder as her impending orgasm slowly threatened to take hold and wash over her.

Tom's lips found that sweet spot on her neck as he buried his head against her shoulder, and he sucked again, matching the rhythm he was now doing with his hips as his tongue rolled against her skin. His hips undulated as he pushed into her before pulling back out, stretching her inside and causing her walls to clench around him tightly, milking him for everything he had.

"You feel so good, El. So, fucking good." He moaned against her skin. Tom was starting to get lost in the feeling of her as his breathing became ragged as he tried to hold back from pounding into her. He was attempting to be slow and gentle with her. He didn't want to rush this. But the feeling of finally being inside El, of having her wrapped around his cock was driving him crazy.

"Fuck me harder, Tom. Make me still feel you tomorrow."

Tom moved his face from her shoulder to look into her eyes. He needed to check that he hadn't just imagined those words.

He looked down at her as he continued to move slowly and connected with her pleading eyes, seeing the slight nod of her head as her fingers tightened on his back. That was the permission he desperately sought from her.

Tom started to lose himself in her completely.

His pace picked up rapidly as her body jolted up the bed with every deep thrust as his fingers tightened bruisingly around her hip, trying to keep her in place. His other hand moved quickly and slammed against the headboard to give him more leverage as he pounded into her. His knuckles on both hands turned white as his grip tightened even more like they would when he was strangling someone. The ridges of veins popped on the backs of his hands and forearms as blood and adrenaline surged through him.

"Yes! Oh, fuck yes!" El moaned as her head tipped back into the softness of the pillows.

El also couldn't control herself as her body arched, her legs wrapping tightly around him, pushing her heels into the top of his ass cheeks as he lifted her hips from the bed, putting her at a forty-five-degree angle.

He was hitting the exact spot inside that she needed as his cock punishingly drove against her g-spot relentlessly, causing white spots in her vision to burst like moths hitting a flame with every thrust.

Her fingernails dug into the skin of his shoulder blades as she gripped onto him, creating crescent shapes in his skin. El knew she was clawing his back and that he would be covered in scratches, which excited her more to know that she was marking him.

"Right there... Oh, fuck right there, Tom... Don't stop."

Tom's hand moved from underneath El's body to her throat as her legs clamped around him, holding her to him. Her walls clamped around his cock, squeezing it as his fingers did the same around her throat. His other hand gripped tightly onto the headboard. He had to have some control; instead of gripping El's throat so hard that he'd crush her windpipe, he put the force into the wood, making it creek under his grip.

El's orgasm hit like a bolt of lightning, tearing through every nerve ending as she rode that euphoric high.

As she gasped for air, the lack of oxygen only added to that feeling. The white spots in her vision turned to stars as she closed her eyes, allowing herself to be consumed by darkness. The stars danced around the inside of her shut eyelids, turning into fireworks that went off in the night sky with every pulse of pleasure.

El's head tilted further into the pillow, burying it into the bedding as her back arched from the bed, pushing her chest more into his. Her pussy flooded with wetness, coating Tom's cock as it leaked out of her and onto the bed as she came.

Tom's thrusts became sloppy and jerky as his cock twitched, swelling inside her, giving her everything he had. His stuttering breath matched the thrum of El's pulse in her neck as he felt it thumping against his hand.

Tom's own orgasm surged as El's pussy fluttered and squeezed around his cock, milking it even more than she already had.

His prostate tightened with his balls, the pulsing wave of pleasure rising up his cock and coating her walls inside as he ejaculated inside her, sending him to his own high of ecstasy. His eyes rolled in his head as he groaned with gratification, clenching his teeth together so that he didn't sink his teeth into her.

Tom let go of her throat, collapsing on top of her as El gasped. The oxygen returned to her body caused a tingling sensation to spread through her nerve endings, and pins and needles spread up her toes and calves, making her giggle.

The giggling made El's body jiggle, pushing Tom's softening cock out of her, followed by the slow trickle of his cum that ran down her folds and through the valley of her bum cheeks to mix with her juices on the bed below them.

Tom rolled onto his side and gently moved her hair from her sweaty face as he perched his head on the palm of his hand and rested on his elbow. El turned her head to the side to look at him.

At that moment, the deal was sealed in Tom's mind. He would never let her go, and anyone who tried to take her away from him, including himself, would face the rage of an unforgiving serial killer.

'She's mine.' Those were the only words that echoed in his head as he looked into her satiated eyes.

19.

Tom lay next to El, brushing his fingertips over her arm as she lay facing him, her fingers drawing small swirls across his slightly sweaty, sparse covering of auburn chest hair.

She hummed in satisfaction, bathing in her post-orgasm glow as a contented smile graced her features.

"Are you all right, El? I didn't hurt you, did I?" Tom asked with a concerned tone as he looked at the red mark around her throat where he had held her tightly.

He had lost himself for a few moments during their intimate encounter and was worried when El hadn't said anything after he had collapsed next to her, utterly spent.

El frowned at Tom with a gentle smirk.

He had such a cute look in his eyes as he raised his eyebrow and moved his head slightly towards hers along her pillow to get closer to her. His fingers moved from her hair down her bare upper arm as he caressed her gently.

She cupped his cheek as she spoke softly.

"No... I promise," she smiled at him as he smiled back.

She traced the line of his cheekbone with her thumb, and a relief washed over him at her reassuring words.

Tom leant forward and gently placed his lips to hers before pulling her closer as his hand moved around the back of her shoulder. El's fingertips wrapped around his hair behind his ear as she deepened the kiss, opening her mouth to welcome him in.

Tom loved the feeling of her fingers tangled in his hair. He loved the feeling of her touching him, causing that static energy he felt coursing through his body, drawing him to her and sealing their connection with the contact of their bodies.

As El shifted her hips closer, wanting to be nearer to him, she felt the trickle of sticky liquid between her legs. She slowly pulled out of the kiss before she pecked his lips once more and rolled over to swing her legs off her bed.

"Hey? Where do you think you're going?" he asked curiously as he reached for her arm, but El had already stood up.

She looked over her shoulder at him. "To the bathroom."

"Oh? Ohhh... Okay."

Tom rolled onto his back and propped himself up against the headboard, his hands resting behind his head as he watched her scurry to her bathroom with her legs clamped firmly together, making her waddle like a penguin. Tom had to stifle his chuckle as he watched her with the biggest grin plastered across as El tried not to let any of his cum drip onto the carpet.

El turned to look at him as she peeked from behind the door, closing it slowly, her eyes glittering with mischief as she met his gaze.

Tom smiled back at her.

He could tell she was smiling as she had faint lines around the corners of her eyes.

Tom suddenly thought that perhaps he should have been more of a gentleman and gotten her a warm, damp cloth to clean her up, but selfishly, Tom wanted her to stay with him on the bed and cuddle. He secretly wanted her to be covered in his essence, marking her as his. El leaving the sanctuary of her bed to clean herself up made him want to do it all over again.

El quickly went to the loo, feeling Tom's cum dripping from her swollen lips as she sat down. She was on the pill, but perhaps they should have talked about that before having unprotected sex, but she was too caught up in the moment. It was awkward to pause what was happening to ask someone if they had been regularly checked before doing anything bare.

El knew she was clean. She got tested after the last time eight months ago after some random hookup. Even though they used condoms, she wanted to make sure.

Before that, she hadn't had sex for over a year and just had a little blowout around the Christmas and New Year's break before she met Tom. After that, she hadn't thought about anyone else and only realised that now as she sat on the toilet trying to remember the last time she had sex.

Tom had invaded every part of her mind immediately when they met, wrapping around her with his constant gifts and attention.

Once she was finished, she flushed the loo and quickly washed her hands, face, and between her shaky legs. El then brushed her hair and cleaned her teeth, making herself look as presentable as possible.

It was deliciously sore between her legs. El knew she would still feel the ghost of Tom's cock tomorrow morning after what they had just done. The red marks around her neck that she saw in the mirror as she brushed her teeth made her want to do it all again as liquid arousal pooled in her core at the thought.

She liked being marked by him. She wanted the world to know they were more than friends now.

At least, she hoped that's what they were.

El slowly opened the bathroom door to see Tom lying in the same position she had left him. He smiled at her as she walked out, his eyes roaming over her body as she returned to the bed.

El was never shy when it came to sex and nudity, but after the accident, she hadn't taken her clothes off fully in front of another person. El had only had sex in a dark room, under the covers, or still partially dressed to hide her scars from her hookup. She didn't want to face the questions that their curiosity might bring.

With Tom, it was different.

El didn't feel like she needed to hide her scars from him. He gave her confidence in the way he looked at her. His eyes had a hunger that she'd never seen in anyone else, especially whenever he pinned her by her throat, and his eyes were swallowed in darkness. But she still felt they needed to talk openly about what had just happened.

As El walked around the bed, the yellow ribbon from the package was sticking out of Tom's shorts pocket, and it caught her attention.

"Is it all right if I use your bathroom?" Tom asked her.

"Of course it is... You don't need to ask Tom."

Tom jumped up off the bed and headed into the vacant room.

"Erm..." El hesitated. "I just kind of had an awkward question to ask you before you go."

"Okay?" Tom turned around to face her, raising a questioning eyebrow.

"Do you get checked? Ya'know... for things?" she gestured to his crotch as he stared back at her.

He looked down briefly and chuckled at her awkwardness before nodding, lifting his head back up to answer. "Yes... And yes, I am all clear. I haven't had sex since my last check, and that was about seven months ago."

"Oh?" El was surprised by his answer, "me too..." she smiled back at him. Tom mentioning seven months ticked over in El's head. That was about the time they met.

Had he not had sex with anyone since then?

Tom smiled at her before entering the bathroom and closing the door behind him.

Whilst he was gone, El reached over the side of her bed and pulled the ribbon from Tom's shorts pocket, threading it through her fingers as she lay back on her bed. The softness of the silk glided against her skin as she watched the ribbon's path through her fingers, weaving like an eyelash viper through the rainforest canopy.

El didn't notice that the lock of her hair, tied in the same ribbon now wrapped around her fingers, had fallen out of Tom's pocket and onto the carpet under her bed.

The lock of El's hair was from when she had fallen asleep on his shoulder in the car outside her home after her family had come back from Atherington after Enid had died. Tom had secretly cut it whilst El was asleep on his shoulder as a keepsake to always have her close to him.

El heard the toilet flush and the tap running before it stopped threading the ribbon through her fingers. She sat up slightly and placed the ribbon next to her on the pillow.

Tom opened the bathroom door and grinned at her as he stepped out, his eyes raking over her naked form.

There she was, utterly perfect, as she rested her head on the headboard, laying on top of her bedspread, completely bare, just for him. He mentally shut his eyes as if clicking the shutter on a camera to capture the moment.

El was stunning and stole his breath away, making his heart stutter for lack of oxygen. She made his whole body buzz with desire as he looked at her.

The late evening sun was starting to set, and it bathed her in an amber-pinkish glow as it streamed through her half-closed blinds.

It set her eyes on fire, bringing out their colours even more as she stared back at Tom. Her mousey brown hair, with its natural waves, was fanned out around her shoulders, reaching halfway down between her collarbone and nipples.

There would be a full moon tonight, and he couldn't wait to see her naked body illuminated by its light like some sort of offering to the gods.

Tom strode towards her, and El's mouth salivated at the sight.

His muscles rippled across his legs as he walked. The subtle flex of his pecs and abs as he lightly swung his arms made her heart flutter.

But the sight that made the wetness flood between her folds wasn't the sight of his cock swishing side to side against his thighs; it was the pure look of desire in his eyes that left her pussy soaking.

He only seemed to get that hungry look when he looked at her.

Tom could feel it, that crushing addiction of needing her. An all-encompassing need to consume her very being. It was more than predatory. It was almost as if he was looking at a physical representation of heaven before him that fuelled his obsession to want more.

Having El was better than the feeling he got when he murdered someone.

Better than the feeling of holding someone's life in his hands.

It was better than the adrenaline rush he would get as he bashed someone's brains in or sliced a knife across their throat, bathing himself in their blood.

And he craved more of it. More of her.

Tom stood at the end of her bed, looking down at El. He felt he needed to tell her, to express to her how much she meant to him, but he just couldn't think of the right words.

He may have been a literature student, continuously studying words, sonnets, poems, and the most beautiful phrases in the known world for the past seven years, but he couldn't for the life of him describe what she made him feel. Having her felt like an all-encompassing need that drove him to madness, wanting more and quenching it simultaneously.

"El..."

"Tom..."

She bit her lip as they continued to stare at each other.

At this moment, they didn't need words to describe how they felt for each other. Just those looks they were sharing, the looks only for each other's eyes.

Tom knelt on the bed, gently taking one of her feet and lifting it to his lips. He kissed her heel as he rubbed the arch of her foot, making El sigh contentedly under his touch.

It felt amazing.

El had never had anyone touching her feet so sensually.

Tom moved his hand around her ankle as his tongue ran up the underside of her arch to her toes. His lips kissed each individually before he went back and sucked on each one, slowly swirling his tongue around and between them.

El's back arched in response as a breathy moan escaped her throat at the feelings he was evoking between her thighs.

Tom's eyes were glued to her face, watching every twitch of her muscles to see what she liked more and how he could pleasure her more.

El's free foot ran up the inside of Tom's thigh, gently grazing against his skin before she used the top of her foot to push up into his scrotum. She held it there as his balls rested against the back of her foot, feeling their heavy weight against her skin.

El was watching for Tom's reactions, too.

The muscles in his neck tensed as she pushed her foot slightly higher, her toes grazing against his perineum.

Tom ran his hand up the underside of her leg, his fingers following the curve of her calf muscles. He used his other hand to move her foot to his cock. EL swirled her big toe around the head of his now stiff shaft, spreading the bead of precum around it.

El's left knee flopped to the side as her foot continued to work his length, pushing it back onto his stomach as she used the arch of her foot to stroke him slowly.

Her dripping wet pussy was now entirely exposed for Tom, and his pupils blew at the sight of it as excitement rushed through his veins. Her glistening juices now ran slightly along the crack of her bum cheeks, highlighting how aroused she was.

He lifted her right leg higher as his mouth joined his hand at the back of her knee. The skin was so sensitive there that she immediately gasped as he stuck his tongue out and licked across the thin skin behind her knee, causing him to chuckle darkly as she squirmed a little under his hold.

Tom slowly pushed her leg back towards her body to access the back of her thigh. He had to shift his body backwards so his mouth could travel further down her leg.

El whined when she could no longer feel his cock beneath her foot. He was getting fairly close to release with what he was seeing, as well as El's foot rubbing against his cock, and he wanted this to last. He didn't want to rush this. He wanted to worship every part of El's body again and not get lost in chasing his own release.

Tom's mouth was now attached to the back of El's right leg as it was pushed back against her body. He sucked on her skin, causing a hickey to form above the crease of her bum cheek, marking her again as his.

El's hands found their way into Tom's hair again, and he purred against her skin as she ran her nails across his scalp.

Tom now had complete access to her pussy, and El realised it just as his mouth connected to her labia, sucking her flesh into his mouth. She moaned loudly at the sensation and rolled her hips against his lips, pulling him tighter to her by his hair.

Tom pulled his head back and looked up at her as her tight grip slipped from his hair.

"You don't get to move yet, darling," he growled.

She furrowed her brow at him before he shifted onto his knees and hooked his right arm under her left leg, lifting that as well, before pulling her down the bed towards him. He bent her legs at the knees and pinned them back against the bed with his hands. Spreading her legs wide and raising her ass in the air.

"Grab a pillow, El," Tom said as he gestured with his head.

El lifted her arms, grabbing one and passing it to him.

Tom smiled at her. "Thank you, my love."

El's eyes widened at the term of endearment.

Was it just that, or had Tom let slip that he was in love with her?

She giggled quietly as he stuffed the pillow under her raised ass before lowering her onto the soft cushion, keeping her in position.

He pushed his hands slowly onto the back of her thighs and looked down at her, his eyes gleaming with excitement. Her hands were resting above her head on her other pillows. A wicked idea filled Tom's head as he noticed the yellow ribbon beside her pillow, and a devilish smirk spread across his face.

"I want you to keep your hands there, El... And if you move... You will be punished... Do you understand?" he said, his voice taking on a sultry, serious tone.

A grin spread across El's mouth, and she nodded without thinking.

El jolted, her eyes widening as Tom's hand smacked the back of her right thigh. It stung more than actually hurting, and she giggled as the feeling spread across her body.

"You moved, El," Tom growled at her, a deep throaty rumble emanating from his mouth as a domineering look washed over his face.

El had done very little of this kind of thing, the odd sexual encounter handcuffed, but she had read about BDSM in detail as well as watched some porn covering the basics. She was curious about how her body would react to it in real life.

At this moment, her body was hungering for more as her walls clenched around nothing, leaving her feeling incredibly empty after Tom had spanked her thigh.

"Do I need a safe word, Tom?" El asked curiously, her voice raspier than she had ever heard come out of her mouth before.

"Do you think you need one?"

She nodded her head slowly as she bit her bottom lip.

Slap.

The sound reverberated around the room as the stinging sensation travelled across the handprint Tom had just left on her skin.

El's eyes widened with how that felt.

She liked it.

She could feel her wetness building in her core as her pussy clenched in excitement.

"Perhaps you should have a safe word as you are being such a naughty girl."

"Yellow," El didn't even need to think about it before she blurted it out.

"Have you done this before, El?" Tom's eyes narrowed as he looked down at her, his mouth slightly open as his curiosity peaked.

"No... Not like this."

Tom raised an eyebrow. He obviously knew El was no virgin from how she had been acting, but he suddenly worried he was perhaps taking this too far too quickly. His brain then also switched to thinking about what she had done previously, that she'd been with others before him. El had given herself to others before him, and his jealousy surged through his body in envy and possessiveness, making his palm itch with the need to punish her.

She was his.

A sneer appeared across his face as his eyes darkened.

"How many people have you let fuck you, El?"

"What?"

SLAP.

Another smack across the crease of El's bum cheek on the right side. It was firmer than the last, but that delicious sting made her cunt throb.

"Don't question me, El... Answer me... How many people have fucked you?" He sneered down at her as he leaned into her thighs.

El's heart raced as her adrenaline coursed through her blood, electrifying her senses.

"Ten," El quickly stated.

Tom's brain went into overdrive. She'd been with ten people, the same amount of people he had killed.

Had she found the same euphoric feeling when having sex as he had when he killed?

Had she found someone she loved before him?

"Did you love any of them?" Tom asked bitterly.

"No."

Tom leaned further over her legs, pushing her knees into the bed more as he looked into her eyes. He would interrogate her, and he didn't care what she thought about it as the green-eyed monster within spurred him on.

"How many did you let tie you up?"

"One."

"Did you like it?"

"Yes."

"Do you want me to tie you up?"

"Yes."

Tom's eyes went straight to the yellow ribbon before he reached for it, grabbing it from the pillow above her head.

His fingers glided over the skin of her wrists as he effortlessly tied them together. He didn't even need to think about it. It was pure muscle memory for him now that he had done this so many times before, although it was usually much more challenging as people tended to struggle when he was binding their wrists. At least this was consensual.

El let out a breathy moan as he touched the inside of her wrists. He had bound them tightly in a crisscross fashion, from the base of her hands down to her elbows, so her hands were back-to-back, her outer forearms twisted inwards towards each other.

Tom's cock twitched at the sight before him.

El's arms were stretched up above her head, her body bent and open for him to do with as he pleased.

Tom savoured every bump of folded skin where a scar was as he ran his hands down over El's torso. He adored every lump and crease on her body, making her even more unique.

"You must say your safe word if it gets too much, El. Do you understand me?"

"Yes."

"What is your safe word, my love?" Tom asked, needing to make sure she understood where this was going.

"Yellow."

El was now dripping with anticipation; the throb from the surge of blood between her legs was already too much, and Tom could hear the desire in the gravelly tone of her voice.

"Good girl," he purred as the words rolled off his tongue.

He loved her reaction to the praise. El's pupils dilated, her pussy clenching before him as her juices ran out of her entrance, coating her puckering anus.

Tom lowered his head and gently kissed the red handprints he had left on her skin. He could hear El exhale gasping moans as he kissed each of them.

His mouth travelled down each leg, almost to her pussy, exactly where she wanted him, but he stopped before making contact.

El whined out in protest, almost like a puppy seeking comfort, as a begging-like whimper left her closed, pouting lips, imploring for him to travel lower.

"Such a needy girl, aren't you?" Tom said against her skin as he ran his tongue teasingly along the edge of her labia, not quite touching it. "Is this what you want?"

"Mmhmm," El moaned out as her hips moved of their own accord, seeking out more of his tongue.

"You want me to lick you here?" he whispered against her skin before he couldn't resist the temptation any longer.

The tip of Tom's tongue glided between her folds from her puckered ass hole slowly up the front. His tongue gathered her wetness, spreading it across her before swooping across her clit.

"Fuck!" El gasped as she shuddered in delight and closed her eyes, savouring the feeling of his tongue against her sex.

Tom's hand quickly slapped down against her pussy, causing El to squeal at the pulsing sensation that went directly to her core, and her eyes flew open. It felt incredible as the buzzy tingling feel went straight to her clit.

"Bad girl. You moved," Tom scorned playfully.

El hadn't even realised she arched her back, tilting her head against the bed. She was so lost in him, in the pleasure he was giving her.

Tom's mouth attached to her clit as he switched between sucking and swirling his tongue around it. Their eyes were now locked on one another. He could feel El's body tensing under his palms that were holding her thighs down as her orgasm neared and her moaning grew louder.

Just at the point he felt her throbbing beneath his tongue, he pulled back and looked up at her, smirking.

"I'm going to stop ten times before I let you cum. I'm going to teach you that no one else, no other person, has ever made you feel this good. That no one but me owns the right to make you cum. Is that understood, El?"

El's eyes widened at the thought of what he was about to do.

Could she handle that?

Could he bring her to the edge and not let her fall into that bliss that many times?

She swallowed down her nerves.

"Yes," she shakily breathed out.

"I will make sure you remember whose pussy this belongs to now. Who owns you. Whose tongue will be the last to fuck you, to ever touch you again. Whose body will bring you your greatest pleasures as you submit to me. To make you remember who loves you."

El gasped at Tom's statement before he immediately dove back down to flatten his tongue against her clit and lap furiously.

"Oh fuck," El moaned as her mind swirled in pleasure, unable to fully process his declaration of love.

El felt the throbbing in her clit intensifying as he worked her quickly to the edge again.

He could feel her hamstrings tighten under his palms as another orgasm neared, and her whole body tensed.

Tom lifted his tongue away just as it threatened to explode through her.

"Uhhh," El whined as she turned into a quivering mess. The need to feel that sweet release taking over, and this was only the second denial.

Tom chuckled as she winced at the loss of contact.

"That's two... Only eight more to go, El. Think you can handle it?"

"I... Yes," she said, flustered, desperately wanting him to keep going.

He chuckled darkly as his mouth attached to her clit again, and he started to suck firmly on that tiny little bundle of sensitive nerves.

El writhed under him, and Tom stopped immediately, slapping her left ass cheek this time, making her jolt up the bed. She quivered as the sting nearly made her cum.

Tom raised a curious eyebrow at her.

"Three," he smirked down at her as he watched that darkness slowly return to her eyes as it had when he had his hands around her throat. Desperately, he wanted to make her cum, but his head wouldn't let him. He needed that control.

His cock was raging as he continued to lick and nibble on her clit, thrusting his body against the bed to gain some relief from the building urge just to give in and fuck her senselessly into the mattress again.

El breathed in sharply as another orgasm threatened to take hold, and he pulled back, blowing over her sensitive clit with his cooling breath.

"Four."

Tom moved his hands around her knees and pulled her legs back down so her feet rested on the bed.

The relief El felt from moving her legs around was intense. The muscles in the backs of her legs ached and spasmed, her thigh muscles quivering from the release of the tension in them.

His fingers glided along her slit, gathering her juices before he put them against her bottom lip.

"Suck," Tom commanded.

El opened her mouth without question and wrapped her lips around his fingers, sucking them clean. She groaned as Tom ran his other hand along her entrance, slowly dipping his middle finger inside her. He felt El's walls clamp down immediately around it, drawing him further inside.

Tom slowly started to pump it in and out of her, adding his ring finger before feeling her tightening around his digits, squeezing them. He stilled before that knot snapped and sent her over the edge.

"Five."

Once he felt her relax, he pulled them back out of her pussy and licked them clean as he hummed in delight.

She was watching him as she continued to suck on his other fingers that were still in her mouth, pushing down against her tongue. She could see the flex in Tom's bum cheeks as he thrust gently against the bed.

"Mmmm... You taste so sweet, El... I could never get enough of that taste."

Again, Tom's head dipped back between her legs, and his tongue speared her pussy. He pulled his hand back from her mouth with a satisfying pop and dragged it to her breast. Pinching her nipple as he curled his tongue up inside her as he fucked her with his slippery muscle.

"Fuck," El groaned as she clamped down around it.

The sensation from her nipple added to the intensity in her pussy. She was so close and wound so tightly now that sweat was beading on her forehead.

Tom could feel her again at the edge, and he let go of her nipple, pulling back his tongue from inside her.

"Six."

Tom sat up, back onto his knees, before he reached up, pulled the pillow out from under her waist, and moved it to her under her head. He grabbed his cock and started stroking it.

El's eyes were transfixed as she watched his movements, and her hips involuntarily started to thrust at the same pace.

SMACK.

Tom's free hand made contact with only the tip of her nipple as he swiped it across her chest.

El let out a breathy moan before Tom grabbed her chin, forcing her to look at him.

"Do not cum."

El squeezed her eyes tight to push down the feeling in her lower stomach. That overly tight knot nearly burst. But because he told her not to, she just about managed to hold back from giving in as she panted underneath him.

"Seven... Good girl... That was close," Tom chuckled.

El was an absolute mess now, her hair sticking to her forehead as she opened her eyes to look up at him. Tom leaned over her as he continued to stroke his cock. His breathy moans ghosted over her lips as he placed his hand on her wrists, pinning them to the bed.

He rubbed his cock along her slit and over her clit, watching her reactions. Her pussy throbbed with fire as he used the head of his cock to massage her overly sensitive clit. Her walls were desperately clenching at nothing, and she whimpered.

"Tom," El's voice was barely a whisper as she whined, and he stilled against her before she came.

"Eight."

He lowered his mouth to her lips and kissed her, the taste of her still on her tongue as they danced together.

Tom moved one of his legs between hers. Letting go of his cock, he grabbed El's hip for leverage as he began moving her up and down, forcing her clit to rub against his thigh.

El shuddered as she fought her orgasm back down. She was going to break soon.

Again, Tom stilled.

Again, he pulled back from her before he let her release.

Tom was enjoying this torture and control far too much. He was incredibly close to cumming as well and didn't know if he was going to last much longer.

"Nine."

His eyes darkened at the feeling of control over her. "Such a good girl... Only one more, my love," he purred.

El was vibrating across her entire body. The intense feelings she had of her pleasure building repeatedly, only to be denied, was the most fantastic feeling she had ever had. It set a blaze in her body that only Tom could quench. She knew she would explode in pleasure when he eventually deemed it fit to give her. She never knew she would enjoy this lack of control so much, even as tears welled in her eyes.

Tom worked his way down her body, kissing and licking her sweaty skin. He loved her taste. The mixture of salty and sweet drove his mind crazy.

With how close El was now, this final denial only needed Tom to lick her clit once, and her walls clamped around the invisible feeling of having him inside her.

Her whole body trembled as she fought to push her orgasm down because he hadn't given her permission to let go.

El may have thought she had given up her control, but at that moment, she was the one who had complete control over her body. The power to not give in to her desire.

"Ten."

Tom's voice was breathy as he looked up at her from between her legs. The fine sheen of sweat covering her forehead and chest, the look on her face, the lust in her eyes. He never wanted her to look at him any other way.

He had ensured she would never want anyone else to make her feel like this, and she knew it, too. She would only ever crave him.

Tom moved up to kneel between her legs as he ran his hands across her thighs, massaging them to release some of the tension in her muscles.

"Such a good girl... You deserve this," he purred as he moved his hand down to stroke his stiff length. "Tell me how? How do you want me to make you cum?"

"Your cock... I want your cock inside me. NOW!" she commanded.

El could see how close he was as she looked down at his balls squeezed tight by his scrotum, his cock twitching with anticipation. El wanted him to feel his release as well. He smirked at her before he licked his lips.

"You're absolutely dripping, El. Are you sure you want this?" Tom looked up and met El's eyes.

El gritted her teeth, frustrated that he wasn't already fucking her.

"I said your cock, Tom. So, fuck me already!"

Tom may have thought he was in complete control of her. El was the one tied up, after all. She was the one he had denied. But now, she was in complete control of him, and he'd do anything to please her. He was her willing servant, worshipping her in every sense of the word.

Tom leaned over and took hold of her wrists, quickly undoing the ribbon. His hands travelled down her arms and around her back to pull her up with him as he sat back up.

El placed her arms around his neck as he lifted her up, her legs wrapping around his waist as she sunk immediately onto his waiting cock. Her walls were so swollen and so tight because of all the edging that it was almost painful to feel so full again.

She moaned slowly at the feeling of him stretching her fully as his groans mixed with hers.

Tom was now the one standing at the edge. The feeling of her wrapped around him was the most intense thing he had ever felt.

El cupped his face, putting her forehead to his.

"Don't you dare cum," she breathed out.

Tom nodded his head at her command.

El had kept hold of the ribbon and now had it between both hands behind Tom's neck. She leaned slowly backwards, and Tom could feel the pull of the material against the nape of his neck as it dug into his skin. She wrapped it around each hand as she leaned further back.

Tom only supported her ass cheeks, his fingers digging into her flesh. She rolled her hips up and then down onto his cock, making her walls tense around him.

"Fuck!" Tom's cock throbbed inside her as he moaned out, closing his eyes.

"Open your eyes, Tom."

He did as he was told and met her gaze.

"How many people have you fucked?" she snarled at him.

"Fifteen."

El watched his eyes intently and saw no lies in them.

"Did you love any of them?" she questioned, afraid of his answer. His pupils dilated slightly, and she knew even before he said it.

"Yes."

El's breath caught in her throat as her stomach plummeted with sorrow.

"How many?"

"One."

El thought she would see the sadness in his eyes, but there wasn't any, only that darkness lurking in the background like it wanted to scratch its way out.

Tom's eyes glazed over for a moment as they both stilled.

He pictured the memory of *her* eyes filled with fear, distorted by the air bubbles she spurted out of her mouth and nose as she tried to hold them in her lungs. The look she had when she took that first lung full of water as he held her down under the water in the lake in France.

His first kill.

The realisation in her eyes that he was going to kill her thrilled him, and he bathed in her awareness of it, savouring every last squirm before her body stilled. Her pupils fully dilated, staring back at him in horror and disbelief. Only then did he take his hands from her shoulders and release her.

He watched her body as it sank into the dark water, being swallowed up by the deep.

She had cheated on him. He had watched her do it through the caravan window.

The holiday crush he thought he loved and felt loved him in return had crushed his heart and turned it black.

El rolled her hips, groaning against the jealousy building in her before she stilled again.

"Did they love you?" her voice was quieter now, edged with trepidation.

El could cope with it if this mystery person didn't love him too. If they did, El was worried that deep down, Tom would still love them too.

"No," Tom's voice was more profound as he said it.

El swallowed as she watched him. A little bubble of relief burst through her.

"Do you love me?" she asked nervously.

"Yes," Tom said as he thrust up into El, causing her head to lull backwards in pleasure and a moan fall from her lips.

He needed her to know that she wasn't like *her*. This wasn't like that at all. It was Tom's darkest fear that El wouldn't love him. That El would run rather than fall for his possessiveness, obsessive tendencies, and compulsion to be with her.

Tom moved one of his hands to the back of her head, bringing her back to look at him as he thrust into her again. "Do you love me?" he asked, staring into her eyes.

"Yes," she didn't hesitate in answering him. She didn't need to. Deep down, she knew from the moment he had come and held her hand as she stood in the sea that she loved him.

El rolled her hips as Tom thrust up into her, but they didn't stop this time. They couldn't. Their breathy moans mixed together as the sounds of their skin slapping against one another filled her bedroom.

Tom was bathed in the moonlight streaming into El's room through the cracked blinds.

El was illuminated in it. A halo almost cast around her body like some ethereal being of light and shadow.

Tom knew as he gave himself to her entirely that he would have to tell her everything.

He wanted to, but it frightened him.

El could feel the intensity of her dark side taking hold as she fucked him back with as much force as he was fucking her.

The yellow ribbon now cutting into his skin.

El pulled herself up and let go of it. It fell onto the bed, the edge soaked in Tom's blood, staining the yellow, red.

El wrapped one hand around his throat as she leaned back, the other resting on the bed, as she bounced on his cock.

Tom's hands wrapped around her waist as he pounded up into her, and she matched him back.

"Oh fuck, El... You're so fucking hot... You're beautiful, El... That's it... You're such a good girl... My good girl."

El tightened her hand around his throat as her orgasm neared, ready to rip through her, cutting off Tom's air.

El didn't think his pupils could get any larger with the darkness consuming them, but they were almost entirely black. She was getting sucked into it as her dark desires took hold of her.

El's eyes were just as black as Tom's.

He felt he was falling into a void as they continued staring at one another, chasing their release, only seeing each other as the world was shut out around them.

The pleasure burst within them both as Tom tried to gasp for air, releasing his load into her, as El gushed down his cock, coating his legs in her juices as she came.

Her grip tightened on both his neck and the bedsheet as she rode her waves of pleasure just as his fingers dug into the skin of her hips, leaving marks.

They were both going to end up with bruises by tomorrow.

El sat up and released her hold on his throat, pushing her fingers into his hair as her other arm draped across his shoulder.

They both leaned forward, their foreheads touching, as they caught their breath.

Neither of them had ever orgasmed so intensely before, and it was a craving that they both wanted to chase again.

El wanted to tell him everything about what had happened the night of the accident. She didn't feel ashamed or guilty about it anymore. She wanted to show Tom her true self just as much as he wanted her to glimpse his.

When you don't have to hide who you truly are, the dark side shines through, sucking everything and everyone into it.

20.

El sat mesmerised, watching the flames burning the wooden logs in the fire pit at the end of the garden as she absentmindedly rubbed the scar on her arm. She was at her Nan's home with her mum. She was transfixed as the heat from the flames distorted the air around the whispering glow of light.

It was August and should have been a relatively warm night, but the breeze from the sea air brought a chill to the air. This was why she had started the fire pit in the first place, to bring some warmth back into her bones without having Tom there.

This day had been strenuous enough already without having Tom there to comfort her. She missed him when he wasn't near.

El's mind drifted in and out of thought with the new information she had discovered today. Everything swirled in her head like the flames wrapping around the charring logs, clambering to take centre stage before the next one was pushed out of the way and consumed.

She still couldn't accept that this house was now hers or that any further information her Mum had divulged was true.

It was all so overwhelming.

When she arrived with her Mum this morning, they looked around the house, trying to decide what to pack away first. That had been the reason why they had come here today. It was about time to sort through everything. But as they had both stood in Enid's old bedroom, they just couldn't bring themselves to do it. They decided to leave it as her Nan had left it.

El didn't want to pack away anything. It felt like they were trying to forget her if they did. She wasn't ready to pack away her Nan's life into cardboard boxes for storage as if it was in the way.

El looked around her Nan's bedroom, remembering all the times she had found herself waking up in her bed after she had crawled under the covers next to her in the night. Her nightmares during those first few weeks after the accident terrified her, waking her up, her throat sore and hoarse from screaming out. She always felt more exhausted when she woke in the morning after those terrible nights.

As El stood in front of her Nan's old dressing table, tracing her fingertips over the edge of the old oak wood as she savoured the smoothness of the worn texture, rubbed smooth from years of wear, she noticed that things were missing.

Some of her Nan's personal possessions were gone.

Enid's jewellery box, some of her antique trinkets and a painting that took pride of place above Enid's bedroom dresser. A piece titled Market Day, The Pantheon, Rome, by Jean-Victor-Louis Faure.

The details within the painting captured Enid's imagination. She adored Rome. The images transported her back to one of her favourite places. She had promised to take El there after she finished university. A trip that they would now never be able to take together.

El had called out to her Mum when she noticed the things that had disappeared, her heart pounding in her chest as anxiety stirred.

"Mum? You haven't moved anything, have you?"

"No... Why's that?" Betty was downstairs fixing a salad for dinner later, as she called back up to El before she washed her hands and headed up.

Betty paused in the doorway to the room as El looked at her with a worried expression before El's eyes darted around the room.

"Nan's jewellery box, the snuff boxes, and the painting are missing." El gestured about as she looked around in case anything else was gone.

Betty stepped into the room and looked around with a frown. "That's odd... I don't think anyone's been in here since the..." Betty drifted off, remembering who had disappeared for a while after the news of El inheriting nearly everything broke. Betty stilled her movements as she let out a suffering sigh. "Mark was up here."

El furrowed her brow. "What? Dad? He wouldn't take anything, would he?"

Betty's body lurched as she let out an uncontrollable sob, her hands covering her mouth as the realisation hit. Her husband, El's own father, probably had stolen them.

El wrapped her arms around her mum to comfort her as Betty cried into her hands, and her body shook with sobs. They had hardly spoken about El's dad and what had happened after he had pushed Betty and knocked her out.

El had never seen her mum in such a state, which immediately worried her, filling her with concern.

Betty was always strong, putting on a brave face. She was the one they relied on to be the comforting figure. Betty couldn't afford to break with two girls to look after. Even when El nearly died, she remained optimistic, denying any negative comments as bad luck. Betty found the positive in everything.

"Shhh... What's going on, Mum? You can tell me," El spoke against her shoulder as she held her.

Betty juddered in El's arms as she tried to control her breathing and calm down.

"Let's go downstairs, and I'll pour you a scotch," El said.

Betty sniffed. "You sound just like her."

El leaned back and smiled at her Mum/ She wrapped her arm around her shoulder and guided her back downstairs to the living room.

Betty sat down with a sigh on the oversized, comfy couch as El appeared with a large tumbler glass and an expensive bottle of scotch.

El didn't drink anymore. She couldn't stomach it after the night of the accident. Even the smell brought back too many bad memories.

El set the bottle and glass on the coffee table in front of her Mum and let her pour herself a large drink.

Betty knocked the scotch back in one hit, swallowing down the burning liquid as if it were nothing.

El gasped at her Mum's behaviour. She'd never seen her drink like that before. Betty was always a wine-spritzer kind of woman.

"Bloody hell, mum... Good job, Dotty's not here. You'll become her new drinking buddy."

Betty chuckled as she poured another large measure and sat back on the sofa, swirling the amber liquid inside the glass. "El... I don't want you to have this burden as well as everything else, and what with the anniversary in two days..."

El sat beside her Mum and took hold of her free hand. "I'm stronger than I look, Mum... You can tell me... You need to talk to me and tell me what's happening with Dad. Something is obviously very wrong, and you're making me worried."

Betty squeezed El's hand, turning slightly to face her. "Your Dad's business is in trouble. It has been for a couple of years."

Mark owned an accountancy firm that employed around ten staff members. El had no idea that it was in trouble. It was doing so well, or at least it looked like it was from the outside.

"But that doesn't make sense... He's still employing people... He still took you on holiday this year. He still bought that new car not long ago too."

Betty exhaled a deep sigh. "That's what I thought too, but it was all just for appearances, for show for clients. That was until Mum passed away. It all came out then in an argument we had, and when I looked into it myself, he's been syphoning money from people's accounts to pay for his gambling addiction."

"What!?!" El exclaimed as her eyes widened.

El was stunned; she had no idea her father gambled, let anyone that he was addicted to it, and it seemed her mum didn't either until recently.

"That's why he thought he was quids in when Mum died. He could repay all the stolen money by selling this house and everything in it. No one would know what he had done. But then all the money went to you. All the properties went to you. I begged him to stop wasting money on gambling... That it was destroying our family. But he couldn't. I didn't even know that our home belonged to Mum either."

El's brow furrowed in confusion at this new information. "I don't understand... Our house in Cambridge was Nan's?"

Betty nodded, confirming it. "In the letter, Mum left me. It explained it all. Mark had re-mortgaged our house twice to pay back some of the money he had stolen from the accounts, but then he went to Mum to borrow some more. She told him she would keep a roof over our heads, but that was it. So she bought our house, and I didn't even know. Mark must have known she had more money than she let on as she paid for our house straight out in cash... just over four hundred thousand." Betty started to cry again, causing the scotch to slosh in the glass as she held it in her hand. "That's why your Dad was so distant with you. He knew you'd find out and tell me as soon as you looked through that property portfolio. His secret would be out."

"Hold on... So, I own our house?"

Betty wiped her nose with the back of her hand and nodded solemnly. "I'm sorry I didn't tell you sooner, El. I didn't want to burden you with more crap with what's going on."

El pulled her Mum into a hug and held her tightly as she continued to sob against El's shoulder.

Something else was going on. El could feel how tense her Mum still was as she hadn't fully relaxed after divulging that information.

El gently rubbed her hand up and down her mum's back to try and soothe her as her mother had done to El as a child. El's body automatically started to rock back and forth as she closed her eyes, getting lost in the comforting motion.

"What else is happening, Mum? You don't seem yourself at all sometimes. And you changed your mobile number, what's that about?... Has he been harassing you?"

Betty stiffened before she released El slowly and sat back, looking down as she fidgeted with her hands. She looked nervous as she spoke. "Your Dad kept phoning me..." Betty said quietly. "Telling me how sorry he was that he pushed me... That he loved me. That he wanted us to talk it through. I kept declining his calls after he started threatening me. Telling me he would break into the house. He told me he would be waiting for me, and I couldn't do this to him. It was all my fault."

El held her Mum's hands to stop her from viciously picking at her fingernails and let her keep talking.

"I changed my number, hoping he would stop, but the letters started arriving..."

"What letters?" El asked, confused as she furrowed her brow. El tipped her head down to catch her mum's gaze and make her meet her eyes.

"Nasty ones, El... You don't need to know what was in those," Betty shook her head as she looked away sadly.

A rage started to build in El, one she knew she had to shove down in her gut and keep hidden. She couldn't let this out now. She felt like smashing something and setting it on fire to watch it disintegrate to ash just so she could stomp on it and crush it to nothing below her feet.

"Why didn't you tell me sooner? I could have helped you. Tom would've helped you."

Betty shook her head. "Mark was waiting at the house for me one day. Luckily, the neighbours were out in the garden, so he couldn't do anything without them seeing... but he did talk to me. Well... it was more at me than with me."

El grit her teeth and clenched her jaw before taking a deep breath.

"What did he say, mum?" she asked.

"He warned me to keep you away from Tom. That Tom was only after your money. I said to him that he should take a look in the mirror. Then he said he knew what Tom did. He remembers Tom holding that bottle to his throat. That look Tom had in his eyes... like he'd done that before. Your Dad told me I have to keep you away from Tom to protect you. That Tom's dangerous."

El swallowed down the lump that was now in her throat. They had yet to go to trial for the assault charge; they were still waiting for a court date as her mum was insistent about pressing charges.

What if her Dad says this in court?

"But Tom didn't do anything. Dad slipped," El stated, immediately going to Tom's defence as her fingers tightened around her mum's hand.

Betty frowned at El and shook her head slowly as she took a few deep breaths and rubbed her thumbs across the back of El's knuckles.

"I saw him, El. I saw what Tom did."

El stilled as her stomach dropped, and she felt like she couldn't breathe as a lump formed in her side, not letting her catch a lung full of air. All the times she had asked her mum about this, her mum had said she couldn't remember anything after hitting her head. But now everything stopped as panic rushed through El as she let her mum continue speaking.

"I saw him grab hold of your Dad and stop him from hurting you. I saw you intervene when Tom pushed that bottle to his neck. I saw him shove Mark away so hard that he slipped over, and I saw you hit him over the head with that vase."

El's nostrils flared as she tried to catch her breath, preparing to defend Tom as much as possible. El couldn't believe her mum had lied to her about what she remembered. But right now, the lie didn't matter. Defending Tom if she needed to was El's priority.

Betty could see the panic in El's eyes. She could feel the tension seep through her grip as she held her hand and continued speaking, revealing the truth. "I told the police I couldn't remember anything... that I was unconscious on the floor. But I saw El, and do you know what I thought after?"

El swallowed down her fear before asking her mum, "What did you think, mum?"

"That I wished you hadn't stopped Tom."

There was an echoing silence around that living room. All the air seemed sucked from it as El stared at her Mum. Her confession left El completely surprised and unsure how she should respond.

21.

El felt a presence in the garden next to her as she sat bathed in the glow of the fire. She turned her head to look up as the familiar scent of peppermint assaulted her senses, mixing with the salty sea air, turning it sweet.

"Hey... You ok?" Tom asked as he bent over and kissed her forehead delicately.

El sighed into it as she reached over and ran her hand up the back of clothed Tom's thigh. "Yeah... Everything's all right," she said. She felt a little better now Tom was here and not so alone. "How was the drive down?" she asked as her fingertips traced the seam along the leg of his shorts.

"Hmmm... It doesn't sound like everything is all right. You're deflecting my question."

Tom nudged El slightly forward from the corner of the garden seat and sat down behind her. He moved her bum slightly to accommodate his long leg down her side and pulled her back into the space between his legs. Tom wrapped his arms around her waist and dragged her back against his chest. Resting his chin on her shoulder, he turned his head to kiss her cheek gently. Tom wrapped his arms around her middle, squeezing her protectively in his arms.

"The drive was fine, thank you. I missed you not sitting in the back criticising my driving skills," Tom chuckled, trying to lighten the mood, but

El was quiet as she continued to look at the dancing flames whilst her hands rested over Tom's.

He knew something was wrong. Tom sighed as his fingers absentmindedly traced along the ridge of a scar through El's top. "Now tell me what's wrong, El."

She sighed loudly as she tried to relax into his touch and closed her eyes, attempting to organise her thoughts into some sort of order rather than the jumbled mess that made it hard to concentrate.

"A few things, actually."

"Go on..."

El took a deep breath before she began and opened her eyes, looking into the fire pit's flames again.

"My dad is a swindling, gambling-addicted crook. He's stolen money from clients to gamble away, and it looks like he's stolen some of my Nan's things during her wake. To top that off, he's also been threatening Mum." El held back the part about Mark also making remarks about Tom's behaviour. El also didn't want to tell Tom yet that her dad wasn't quite as incoherent as they first thought. Mark remembered what Tom was about to do with the bottle and that her mum had seen what Tom had done. Before she broke that news to Tom, she wanted to gauge his reaction to those bits of information first.

El felt Tom tense behind her and huffed a breathy sigh across her neck. "The suitcase."

"What?" El asked, confused as she turned slightly within Tom's arms to look at him.

"I thought it was strange when we left that your dad put what looked like an empty suitcase in the trunk of his car."

El gasped. She hadn't even thought about it then, but now that Tom had mentioned it, the memory flashed in her mind.

"He planned to steal from the house before he knew what was in the will. That fucking bastard." It was El's turn now to tense with rage.

"What's missing?" Tom asked calmly as he rubbed his hands up and down El's arms, trying to calm her and ground himself.

"Nan's jewellery box, her favourite painting and some other antique things."

"Right..." Tom gritted his teeth as his jaw clenched. He couldn't bear the thought of her father stealing from his family. The only thing Tom had ever stolen, if you could call it that, was body parts, but technically, they didn't have a value, so he didn't consider it stealing. Well, not in his mind, anyway.

They were both tense as they sat there watching the fire, filled with a burning desire for revenge. "What has your dad said to your mum?" Tom asked suddenly.

"She wouldn't tell me all of it, but she did say..." El drifted off. She didn't know whether to tell Tom or not about her father remembering what Tom had done. Or that he had advised her mum to keep Tom away from her. Or that her mum had wanted Tom to slit her dad's throat.

That last thought was dark, but El knew what her mother and grandmother were like when protecting their children.

El chewed on the inside of her lip.

"What did she say, El?" Tom leaned forward and took El's chin, slowly turning her to face him as his thumb traced her jawline. He needed to see her eyes, to see if she was holding something back.

El could see the slow, simmering fury in his but decided just to go ahead and tell him. To hell with the consequences.

"He... He said he remembers what you did with the bottle and that mum should keep me away from you because you're dangerous." El sighed after she quickly blurted that all out and looked down at the fire.

Tom clicked his tongue against the back of his teeth as his fingers slipped from El's face.

"And what does your mum say about that?" he asked as he tried to hide his fury at the suggestion to keep El away from him.

El didn't know whether she should tell him or not what her mum had said to her. She didn't want to hide anything from Tom, but she also didn't know how he'd react to that particular confession.

"Look at me, El," his voice was full of that calm authority that she craved. Her eyes automatically raised back to look at him. That commanding voice that he used on her when he wanted her to obey him. "What does your mum say about it?"

El took a deep breath, rubbing the scar on her arm before she spoke. "She said she saw what you did. That she wished I hadn't stopped you from doing it."

Tom raised an eyebrow.

He was shocked that Betty would say such a thing. He thought she would have stood by Mark on this. Especially if she saw what actually happened.

El continued. "She told the police she was knocked out and didn't see anything."

That also sat in Tom's mind as he mulled it over. Betty was also lying to the police about his involvement.

"She saw you protect me, Tom. She saw you stopping him from attacking me. To mum, that's worth everything. That's worth more than her marriage. We have always come first." El swallowed. She was glad to get that off her chest, feeling like a weight had been lifted.

"What about the trial?" Tom asked. "They'll set a date for it soon."

El looked back at the fire briefly before she answered. "She's sticking with her story. She was unconscious, so she didn't see anything. And I'm sticking with mine."

Tom let out a breath. He was worried for both Betty and El with Mark's upcoming trial. "You know they'll cross-examine you, don't you? They'll question everything. Those defence lawyers will look for any weakness."

El looked away and sighed, "I know..." She turned her head back to face Tom. "But I won't change my mind, and neither will mum. Plus, Dad was drunk. They aren't going to trust a thing he says," she said as her eyes never left Tom's. She wanted to reassure him that both her mum and herself were behind Tom in this. They would protect him, even from El's own father.

As he looked back into El's eyes, Tom felt a swell of pride and reassurance. He couldn't believe he had found someone willing to protect him like this.

Tom wondered how far El would be willing to go to keep him safe. It had been a strain for Tom not to quench his thirst recently, especially when it came to

Mark. His hands twitched with the need to be covered in blood. To see it. To smell it. But El had proved to be enough at the moment to quiet the urge for death.

Tom moved one hand to cup her face, stroking his thumb across her cheek to savour her skin beneath his fingertips, silencing the beast within before lowering his lips to hers.

El moaned into the kiss. She had missed him today and wished he didn't have to keep attending so many meetings at university.

Tom had missed El too, and now it was getting closer to term starting again, he knew he wouldn't have as much time with her as he liked. Even if he had managed to secure teaching one of her lectures, Tom would still have to continue with his PhD work. They wouldn't be able to spend all day together like they had been the past few months.

Tom was still keeping the possibility of becoming her lecturer a secret for now. He wanted to surprise her. After everything with Chris and Dotty, Tom felt like a hypocrite but couldn't care less. El and Tom had gotten together before he was going to become her lecturer. This was an entirely different situation.

El pulled back from the kiss, suddenly feeling quite tired. It was late, and today had been a particularly stressful day. She and Tom had been having non-stop sex since that first time, and truth be told, she was exhausted.

She covered her mouth as she yawned.

"Sorry," she giggled softly behind her hand.

"I have been keeping you up too much, my love?" Tom chuckled.

El nodded as she rested her hands on her lap and smiled at him. "Mmhmm... But I don't mind... You know I don't mind," she wiggled her eyebrows at him as she tried to fight the urge to yawn again.

Tom smirked and kissed her temple as she turned around to face the fire and rested her back against his chest.

He started to rub her shoulders gently, relaxing her. He could feel the tension in her body begin to ease away as his fingers worked their magic, smoothing out the knots in her muscles.

"Mmm, that's nice," El moaned softly as her head rolled backwards.

Tom chuckled against her ear, the rumble of his chest reverberating through her body. "I think we had better head to bed before you fall asleep on me." Tom's hands stilled on her shoulders as El's head lulled to the side before snapping back up. "Whoops... You definitely need to sleep. Come on, sleepyhead," he chuckled.

Tom lifted her onto his lap and swung his leg around underneath her so he could carry her bridal style as he stood up.

"Woah... Tom!" El playfully swatted his chest. "I can walk, you know," she scolded.

He chuckled at her. "I know, but my queen deserves to be carried when she's this tired," he quickly pecked her temple as he began walking back to the house.

"Hmmm... Well, as long as you don't drop meee..."

With that, Tom pretended to, making her squeal as he walked back towards the house.

"TOM!!!" reprimanded El as she hit him playfully with her palm across the back of her head. She was fully awake now.

He darkly chuckled as he practically threw El over his shoulder, swatting her bum cheek.

"I thought you promised me sleep," she laughed against the back of his shoulder as she saw her opportunity and swatted Tom back on his ass hard, making her palm sting.

Tom stopped walking and slowly slid El back off his shoulder so she stood before him. He looked down at her, her body half illuminated by the crackling fire, the other half cast in shadow. The outline of her black underwear showed through the yellow top she was wearing, causing saliva to pool in his mouth.

El looked up at him, the same mixture of the amber glow from the flames and the shadows from the darkness mixed together. Tom was wearing a white T-shirt and those damn black shorts that El loved. Of course, he was commando. He always was.

Tom quickly looked around and grabbed her hand, heading towards the side of the garden behind a tree. He pulled her in front of him and pushed her back against the bark before quickly poking his head around the trunk.

"What are you doing?" El asked curiously.

Tom's eyes darted around, making sure the coast was clear. "Don't start something you can't finish, El," his voice had taken on a husky, lust-filled tone now.

Tom looked back at her, his eyes dark with desire. He quickly grabbed her by the thighs and lifted her up.

Instinctively, El wrapped her legs around his waist, pulling him closer to her. She was wearing a long, loose yellow t-shirt that came down just above her knee, which was now riding up around her waist as Tom held her there.

The bark dug into her back with a delightful sting, scraping her skin as Tom crashed his lips to hers.

Immediately, their tongues swirled with each other in a passionate kiss. This would have to be quick. Being out in the garden excited them both. The danger of getting caught was an added bonus.

Tom leaned his hips back slightly as his fingers found El's already-soaked thong, hooking his fingers under the gusset to move it to the side.

El's hands moved to grip his hair on the back of his head, her forearms resting on his shoulders. She moaned against his mouth as he pushed two fingers inside her and started to thrust frantically.

Her moans got louder as she arched her back, pushing her chest into him, her shoulders digging into the tree bark, leaving stains on her yellow top.

Tom pulled back from the kiss. "You gotta be quiet, El," Tom warned her. He withdrew his fingers from inside her and put them against her lips.

El knew what to do without question and obliged, opening her mouth to wrap her lips around them.

Tom groaned as he watched her. The feeling of her sucking his fingers was exquisite. Tom used his other hand to free himself before positioning his cock at her entrance. The silent tightening of both her lips was all the permission he needed before slamming into her.

El almost bit down on his fingers as she groaned against them. Her eyes widened and rolled into the back of her head at the sudden intrusive stretch of his cock as he filled her to the brim.

Tom stilled for a moment, watching her reaction as his hand tightened on the back of her thigh. The flare of pain in El's eyes made Tom's heart swell. He loved that he could push her to the edge only to soothe her with pleasure as she relaxed.

El nodded to him to signal she was ready before Tom pulled back and thrust into her again, knocking the wind from her lungs like the flames sapping the oxygen from the air.

Tom withdrew his fingers from her mouth before replacing them with his tongue. She tasted so good he couldn't get enough of it. The tree bark bit into his kneecap, and he moaned into her mouth, letting her swallow him.

El could already feel herself tightening as Tom continued to fuck her roughly against the tree. The pain from the scratches to the top of her ass and shoulders only added to her pleasure.

El's grip on his hair tightened as she neared her release, her pussy walls swelling and flooding with arousal. She hooked her ankles across each other, gaining more purchase on Tom's body. His fingers dug into the back of her thighs as he pounded up into her.

She broke away from the kiss, needing to take a breath, but as she did, Tom rolled his hips up, hitting her g-spot relentlessly.

"OH FUCK! YES!" El squealed loudly before Tom quickly put his hand over her mouth and slowed his thrusts.

"You've got to be quiet, El," Tom leant in, whispering against her ear as he pushed his body flush against her.

El mumbled quietly against his palm. "Mmm-hmm," she nodded against his hand as her eyes rolled back in her head.

The slowed rhythm was increasing the build-up to her orgasm. The intensity she was feeling in her core was all-consuming, making it feel like she was floating.

Tom started kissing her neck as he moved his hand away from her mouth down between them to her clit and began rubbing it in slow, purposeful circles.

El's back arched in response as Tom changed from fucking her hard and fast to making sensual love to her against the tree.

"I can't get enough of you, El", Tom started whispering against her neck between kisses. "You consume my thoughts when you're not there... My body aches for you constantly."

Tom continued his slow rhythm, drawing out every inch of pleasure for them both. This had turned from a quick fuck up against a tree to something else. He lent his head back from her neck and rested his forehead against hers. They were both staring at each other as sweat beaded on their foreheads, mixing together as they continued to make love.

Tom squeezed his eyes tightly together. The feeling of being this connected to someone was how he thought it must feel if you ate them in the literal sense.

"I need you, El... You don't realise how much," Tom said breathlessly.

"Open your eyes, Tom."

He did as she asked as El rolled her hips down. Tom's eyelids fluttered at the feeling of her squeezing his cock, milking him in the best possible way. He could feel every muscle tense in her walls, gripping him, not wanting to let him go.

"I love you, El... I love you so fucking much it hurts."

El moved her hands from his hair to cup his face as she stared back into his eyes.

Tom slowly drew back his length, leaving just the tip within her. He could feel her hole puckering around him with need, wanting him deeper again. The end of his middle finger continued to brush against her clit as he teased her, drawing out every sensation he could.

El exhaled as he pushed back into her just as slowly, filling her again.

Their eyes solely focused only on each other. Nothing else mattered when they were together.

Tom started to rota his hips, hitting every deep angle within her as his pelvis pushed his fingertip against her firmly.

El was about to break, and he could feel it as her walls clamped down on him. Tom was determined to chase it, pushing her over the edge before his own orgasm took over.

"Uhhh... I love you, Tom. I won't stop loving you," El said breathlessly.

"Cum for me, El. Let go."

Her body gave in immediately to his command, El's back arching as he slowly pumped into her.

Tom could feel her juices running down his pulsing length as he unleashed a torrent inside her, unable to hold back any longer.

El squeezed him for everything he could give her. She could feel him shake and spasm as he thrust in as deeply as he could, holding her there.

They stilled as their breath mixed in the warm August night as they rode out their orgasms, saving every last wave until the very end, and they both saw stars dancing in their vision.

Tom started to soften inside her and stepped back from the tree, lifting El up off him. He held her by her waist for a moment to ensure she could stand before Tom quickly tucked himself back into his shorts and then dropped to his knees.

El could feel his cum leaking out down her leg, and she clamped her thighs together, wanting to hold it inside for longer. She loved the feeling of him coating her from the inside out and was always disappointed when gravity interrupted it.

Tom's hands ran up the backs of her legs slowly as she looked down at him with an eyebrow raised.

"What are you doing?" she whispered.

"Cleaning you," Tom smirked as he gripped the back of her knees and gently eased her legs apart before burying his head under the hem of her top.

He ran his tongue up the inside of her thighs one at a time, lapping up every last drop of their combined juices before his tongue found its way between her folds.

El moaned quietly as her hands went into his hair, holding him there. She swayed as the feeling between her legs started to grow.

Tom shifted his grip, moving his hands around her knees and up her thighs, guiding her backwards as he pushed her back. El's shoulders now lay against the tree, allowing Tom to lift her legs over his shoulders. he moved his hands back up her legs to hold her steadily by her waist.

This was so erotic to El. She wasn't going to last long at all and was already close to a second orgasm cresting.

Tom felt it, and as she started to tremble, he wrapped his lips around her labia, forming a seal around her clit and added his tongue in a swirling motion, stroking that little bundle of nerves into a frenzy.

El's head dropped back, and she had to let go of his hair to cover her mouth. She bit down into the pad of flesh between the creases, stifling her moan as El gave in to her second orgasm, gasping Tom's name behind her hand. Her juices flowed down Tom's chin as she clenched around nothing.

Once she was bathed in her second orgasmic afterglow, and Tom had finished lapping her clean, he gently placed her legs back on the floor, moving the crotch of her thong back over to cover her and stood up in front of her, supporting her with his hands on her waist.

El went to her tiptoes and licked up Tom's neck, chin and lips. She moaned as she tasted herself and him on his lips. The heady mixture of sweat and arousal made her hum in delight.

Tom was starting to get hard again, but he could see in El's eyes how exhausted she was and ready to drop where she stood. He wrapped his arms further around her waist to hold her to him.

Once El was satisfied she had cleaned his skin sufficiently, she kissed him, mewling against his lips. Tom pulled back from the kiss. He was almost holding her up now.

"Time for bed now, my love," he stated.

El whined. "Can't we stay in the garden? I like outside."

Tom smirked down at her. "Not tonight... I have something planned for tomorrow, though."

El smiled at him, her eyes heavy as she felt her body start to give in to its need for rest.

"Come on." Tom scooped her up again, carried her towards the house, and straight upstairs.

Betty was already asleep in bed. She had drunk quite a lot of alcohol and had headed up before Tom had arrived.

He carefully navigated the stairs, and when he got to El's room, he laid a fast-asleep, softly snoring El down on the bed.

Tom sat beside her, carefully moving her hair from where it was stuck to her forehead.

He couldn't find that lock of her hair anywhere and was disappointed he had lost it. He was tempted to cut another piece as El was asleep but couldn't bring himself to do it, even though it pained him not to have a piece of her with him when they weren't physically together. Tom had her now, but he still craved constantly having her with him. He'd ask her in the morning if she'd let him cut a lock. It was a romantic gesture to want to have a lock of your lover's hair. Old fashioned, perhaps, but still romantic.

Tom lay down beside her, and El unconsciously snuggled into him. He loved how she would seek him out even in sleep, just as he did her. He sighed contentedly as he watched her for a few more minutes before drifting off.

22.

"N...N...Noo...NOOO... St...STOP!"

Tom immediately jolted awake in bed.

The noise of El's panicked, raised voice woke him from an otherwise peaceful night.

As he sat up in bed and turned to look down at El. She was still fast asleep, covered in sweat as she writhed about on her back next to him. Her arms and legs started to flail everywhere, disturbing the sparkling specks of dust as they danced in the moonlight streaming in through the window.

"El?" Tom quickly placed his hand on her arm to try to calm her and stop her from hurting herself.

"GET OFF ME!!!" El screamed out as she retched her arm back from under his palm.

Tom pulled his hand away and froze, not knowing what to do. His heart thrashed in his chest with panic. He'd never seen El have such a violent nightmare before.

"STOP IT!!!" El screamed out in terror before something switched in her, and she sat bolt upright in bed, still fully asleep, but her eyes were wide open.

Her body pushed through the swirling effervescent particles, parting them like a curtain as if presenting herself onto a theatrical stage for the first time. El took a deep breath as her head bowed down, the air calming around her like a tranquil sea before a storm. She started sniggering quietly before it got louder, becoming the most terrifying, menacing laugh as her shoulders shook. She didn't sound like El at all.

Tom sat perfectly still next to her as he watched her.

"That'll teach you to touch what isn't yours."

Her voice was completely different, deeper and darker. Gone was her sweet, sing-song voice that sounded almost angelic. This was rougher and full of spite like it was coming from somewhere within her that had been unlocked, setting it free.

Tom had heard that voice before when she first switched as she spoke about Dotty in her rage. He cautiously watched her, unsure what to do.

Sweat beaded and ran down El's bare back, catching the gleam of the moonlight. Her forehead and chest glistened with the sheen of her exertion.

Tom's heart raced as his breathing stuttered in shock, unsure whether this was all a dream or perhaps a nightmare of his own. He moved around the bed to kneel next to her, his knees dipping into the mattress as he kept his hands on his lap, ready to move them swiftly should he need to restrain her if something happened.

As she lifted her chin slowly, El's face turned sinister as she smiled before she threw her head back and screamed again as if in pain. Tom's hands raised swiftly of their own accord, hovering in the air but hesitant whether to touch her whilst El's hands clutched onto the sheets below her, turning her knuckles a trembling ghostly white.

Tom felt a stir of something within himself as he watched her, his panic turning into fascination edged with desire.

He liked this.

El's head slowly lulled back forward and tilted to the side. Her eyes were open but vacant, like looking into a deep, dark, bottomless pit. She licked her lips, gathering the line of sweat from her top lip before speaking, her voice barely above a whisper as she hissed.

"I like watching you burn."

...

"How's your head, mum?" El looked up from her bowl of fruit to see her mum wincing as she came downstairs into the morning sunlight as it streamed in through the kitchen window.

"Urgh... Next time you provide the alcohol, El, make sure you remove it after I've had two..." Betty groaned as she rubbed her temples, trying to relieve her dreadful headache.

El chuckled to herself as Tom appeared through the back door, returning from a morning run.

Well, that's at least what he'd told El he'd gone to do.

It was partially true. Tom did run to the co-op in Yapton to grab a few bits for his surprise later.

It was the closest shop to them, as Atherington had no grocery shops; it was only a tiny village. Tom had then quickly hidden everything in the fridge in the summer house, with a plan to sort it all out later whilst Betty distracted El with a spa trip to Bailiffscourt. Well, that was the idea he had devised as long as El went along with the suggestion to have a relaxing spa day with her mum.

"Good morning, Betty." Tom greeted her cheerfully.

"Oh... Hey, Tom," Betty just about managed to greet him before plopping herself down on a barstool and burying her head into the crook of her elbows.

Tom smirked at Betty, holding back his chuckle at her hungover state as he walked over to El.

"Hey... How was your run?" El asked as her eyes followed Tom.

"Good... Phew... It's getting warm out there," huffed Tom.

El smirked at Tom before she rolled her eyes. "Well, I did tell you to leave earlier because you'd get too hot."

"Well, I like to have a good sweaty run... Ya'know... Feel the burn." Tom smirked as he flexed his arms.

"Sunburn, you mean," El sniggered under her breath.

"Hmmm, well... perhaps if you joined me", Tom raised a questioning, sweaty eyebrow.

El chuckled. "No thanks... I get enough exercise."

Tom walked around and stood next to her, leaning down on his elbow, as she sat at the breakfast bar. El inhaled the intoxicating smell of his sweat as he bent closer to her ear to whisper. "I could always use some more *vigorous* exercise."

She turned her head to face him, their lips almost touching. El could see the beads of sweat running down his face. She desperately wanted to lean forward and catch them on her tongue before they fell.

Tom watched her eyes as she followed the trail of one of the droplets. You wouldn't think El's beautiful eyes were hiding a hidden rage behind them that seemed to be unleashed last night again whilst she slept, but Tom had.

It was as if it was trying to claw out of her.

Tom hadn't said anything about what had happened in the night. He didn't want to dampen El's day and didn't know how to ask her about it either.

After she had turned into some kind of demon last night, that was the best way to describe it; she had laid back on the mattress and stilled back into a dreamless slumber. She had snuggled back into Tom's side when he lay beside her and gently started snoring against his chest.

El obviously wasn't some sort of possessed demon, but Tom didn't know what else to call her dark side. He wasn't even sure El was aware of her sinister rage that reared its head when she lost control of her temper. She was seemingly oblivious to it whilst both conscious and dreaming.

Tom lay there, watching her breathing for the next couple of hours as he held her close, stroking her hair. He was afraid that if he let her go, she'd disappear back into her nightmare.

There was definitely a lot more to the accident than she had told him, and he wanted to know what had happened to her. He just didn't know how to ask her.

If Tom was truly honest with himself, he was turned on by that darkness in her. Something called within him to want to draw it out more.

Tom didn't want to tame it. He wanted to bathe in its savagery with her.

Tom slowly leaned back from the breakfast bar, smirking at her suggestively.

"I could do with a shower."

With that, Tom winked at her, turned and left, heading upstairs.

El quickly jumped down from the stool and followed after him, knowing exactly what would happen if they had a shower together.

Betty shifted her head from her elbow and laid it against the cool counter, staring at the kettle, wishing a mug of coffee into existence with sheer willpower.

El suddenly rushed back into the kitchen and leaned beside her mum's ear to whisper.

"Coffees in the pot, mum."

El quickly kissed her on the cheek, then grabbed the remainder of her breakfast bowl before rushing back upstairs.

"You're an angel...ooooww," Betty called out before she winced in pain from calling out too loudly to her.

...

Tom gripped her waist with one hand as he eased himself into El.

She pushed her hands up against the tiled wall of the shower, bracing herself as he took her from behind. Her hands slipped on the wet tiles as she tried to stop her feet from sliding on the slippery shower floor.

Tom's hand wrapped around her wet hair before he pulled back, making her arch her back and raise her ass higher.

It was hard and fast as he pounded into her.

El had to muffle her moans with her own hand as she moved one from the tiled wall and bit down into her fisted knuckles, leaving red bents in her skin.

Tom bent over her, stifling his groans into her shoulder as he bit down on her skin, leaving more tooth imprints on El's body.

They were both completely out of breath after their swift, vigorous shower sensation as Tom clung to El's body, and she supported them both against the wall.

It took them a few moments to recover before Tom removed himself from El and stood back up. He turned El around slowly and smiled lovingly at her, wholly sated from what they had just shared.

El looked up at him with the same look. She loved everything about this and was very happy that she had invited Tom to come to Atherington this week with her.

Tom gently washed El with her favourite jasmine and vanilla body wash before she washed him with his peppermint one. They took their time exploring every dip and rise in each other's bodies as they had countless times before becoming more than just friends over the past few weeks.

El loved the feeling of her fingertips running up and down over the definition of Tom's abs and the ridges of his v-line. She could spend all day just touching him and getting lost in those smooth valleys.

She loved to watch Tom's eyes slowly close as she did it. His breathing changed with the relaxation and comfort she brought him with her touch. And she especially loved the little moans that escaped his mouth when she touched his neck, the inside of his wrists and thighs. That deep-throated groan he made when she carefully washed his hair had his head lulling in satisfaction.

After they finished showering and drying each other off, El lay on her bed with Tom beside her.

Out of nowhere, El started talking about her scars as she pointed to each one, Tom intently taking mental notes in his head.

"This one was from them removing my spleen," she explained.

It was one of her longest and deepest scars that ran from her belly button up the middle of her abdomen to just under her ribs on her left side.

Tom traced it lightly with his fingertips before he bent over her and kissed every inch of it.

"Why did they have to remove it?" He asked as he whispered against her skin, and El ran her fingers through his hair.

"It was torn, and they couldn't repair it, so it had to come out." El's voice was quiet as she continued to run her fingers through Tom's hair.

She felt the ridge of the scar on the back of his head. She had been wondering where it had come from, and now seemed like the perfect opportunity to ask.

"How did you get this scar here?"

Tom swallowed before moving his head back to rest the side of his face on his open palm as his elbow supported his head, making El's fingers slip from his hair. He couldn't tell El the truth about this. Not yet anyway.

"Oh… I, err, fell out of a tree as a kid," he chuckled softly. "Anyway, we are talking about you, El. Not me. Tell me more," he smiled softly at her, directing the conversation back to El.

El smiled back at him and continued describing the story of each mark. "This one is from a piece of wood sticking out of me."

This scar looked like a round bullet hole on her body. It sat on her left side, in the middle between her seventh and eighth ribs. Tom rolled El to her side so they could face each other, tracing the scar with his fingers before placing a delicate kiss against it.

El giggled. "That one kinda tickles..."

Tom stopped and pulled back. He knew she hated tickling, but she smiled at him as she traced his jawline with her fingertips and sighed. She took hold of his hand and placed it on another operation scar as she moved onto her back. Her fingers guided his as they traced it together under the right side of her ribs.

"This one is from another operation to repair my liver. This is the one that almost killed me." El stated matter of factly.

Tom's eyes widened as he watched their fingers running across her body together.

"Does it hurt?" he asked quietly.

El shook her head. "No... it's the scars you can't see that hurt the most," she whispered as her eyes followed her fingers.

Tom was quiet for a moment as he absorbed El's words as he traced the raised edge of scar tissue with her. "Was this the worst one?" he asked with almost a child-like curiosity as he continued to try getting her to open up.

She nodded her head.

"Mmhmm... They thought it was just my spleen that was damaged, but after a few hours, I started crashing again. The branch had punctured my liver as well. They hoped it would stop on its own, especially as they had already removed my spleen. They thought my body was too weak to take another operation, but they had to. I survived by some miracle, and I don't know why."

Tom gradually pulled his fingers away to cup her cheek as a tear began to run down her cheek. He leaned in and placed his lips to it, kissing it away.

El closed her eyes, savouring his touch before she pulled her head back.

"I'm a bad person, Tom... I don't deserve to be here," she said sadly as her chin tilted down.

Tom's brow creased.

"You're not a bad person, El. You are sweet and kind and always know the right thing to say. You're full of wisdom and fire and passion and love."

El shook her head and opened her eyes to look down at her hands as she swallowed.

"There's something dark within me, Tom... a rage... something that's always there simmering in the background... When I get angry, I can feel it. It pulses in my head and my chest. I can't control it." El shook her head sadly before she continued trying to explain what she felt. "It's like it takes hold of me and boils through my blood... corrupting me...I just want..."

She stopped herself and looked him in the eyes. She was afraid if she said what was really on her mind, he'd be frightened of her and leave. He wouldn't want to be around such a monster if she told him the truth.

Tom leaned in, running his fingers through her hair, and gently kissed her forehead as he spoke quietly.

"I know, El. Believe me. I know."

23.

Tom waited patiently on the beach next to everything he had prepared as El appeared over the crest of shingle at the top of Atherington Beach. He couldn't help the smile that spread across his face as his dark blue eyes met hers.

El had spent the afternoon with her mum getting pampered at the spa. El had even been persuaded to have her hair and makeup done, leaving her with a gorgeous natural look for her makeup and elegant waves of hair. Her mum told her to put on something special when they returned to her Nan's house before she needed to leave and head to the beach to meet Tom there.

El wore a yellow summer dress that fanned out just above the knee. It tapered in at the waist, with a sweetheart neckline covering the tops of her breasts and beautiful ruffled half-cut sleeves that pulled in at the elbows.

El's face beamed with delight at what Tom had done as she looked down from her vantage point.

Tom had staked some oil lamps into a little section of shingle, with fairy lights joining them together. A wooden table and two chairs, with a blue and white checkered tablecloth, sat on top of it. Candles in jars occupied the middle of the table in a beautiful display. He even had their food prepared and under those metal cloche things.

Tom stood in a pair of black fitted suit trousers and waistcoat, with a black and navy blue striped tie and a white dress shirt. His sleeves rolled up to the elbows, exposing his forearms. His usually unruly mop of auburn hair was slicked back, and he had the sweetest smile. Clutched between his hands was the most enormous bouquet of sunflowers El had ever seen. It looked like something out of a movie scene.

The sun was still sitting just above the horizon to their right, casting the most gorgeous red and purple light across the clouds.

El cautiously made her way down the peaks of shingles as the small stones crunched below her feet.

Tom met her halfway and leaned down, placing a tender kiss on her lips. El hummed into it as she rested her hands on his biceps. Tom pulled back slightly and rested his forehead against hers.

"You look stunning, El."

"So do you." El smiled up at him as he took her hand, stood up straight and gave her the flowers.

She wrapped her hand around his and gently ran her lips over the soft pellets. She loved their softness against her skin.

Tom held his breath as he watched her. He could picture himself running those pellets across her body. He had to clear his throat to break out of his lustful thoughts. They were here to eat dinner that was already getting cold.

"Would my lady allow me to escort her to her table?" he asked.

El chuckled. "Why, of course, sir."

Tom guided her over to the table and pulled out the seat for her.

El placed the flowers on the table and bowed her head slightly as thanks as she tried to hide her little snigger at this formal display.

El took her seat, but Tom couldn't resist touching his lips to her bare shoulder as he pushed the chair in slightly. He took a deep breath, savouring her jasmine scent that permeated his senses whenever she was near. El bent her head to the side to give him better access to her skin, but Tom pulled his mouth away slowly before whispering against her ear. "If I don't stop now, you know we won't eat."

El lightly chuckled. "It would be a shame to waste your wonderful cooking skills, my love." She turned her head to his and lightly kissed his lips before Tom stood again, clearing his throat and lifting off the cloche to reveal the most beautiful-looking steak, rocket salad and new potatoes in garlic butter. El's favourite meal.

Her mouth instantly salivated. It may have been a simple dish, but she loved it.

"Oh, Tom, you remembered," she gushed, looking up at him with a brilliant smile.

Of course, he remembered. He remembers everything about El. All the little details that others would miss are what he focuses on.

"This looks wonderful... Thank you."

She took his hand and placed a delicate kiss on his palm as she looked up at him with doe eyes.

Tom's pupils dilated with desire.

He could have dropped to his knees right then, kissed her and ravaged her over the table, but this night wasn't about him. He wanted to give her some good memories around this time of year and not think about tomorrow's anniversary. He had something extra special planned for tomorrow.

Tom kissed El's forehead before stepping back and moving around the table to take his seat and lifted his own cloche off his plate.

They sat, ate and chatted about Tom's research and what his future plans were with it. El even offered to help him with what she could around her own studies. He adored the idea of her buried in research papers, lying on her stomach, her legs bent at the knee as she swished them around in the air above her body whilst concentrating. He got lost in his lustful thoughts about what he'd then do to her as he watched her eating.

El liked her steak rare, and the blood oozed from the centre as she cut into it. Tom watched as her pupils dilated slightly at the sight of it. Time seemed to slow as she slowly put the bloody meat into her mouth. A tiny droplet of blood lingered on her bottom lip as she savoured the metallic taste in her mouth. Her tongue dipping out to lick the blood from her lip was all Tom could focus on. It kept replaying in his head as he sat motionless, holding his fork mid-air with a piece of potato jammed on the prongs.

"Tom? Tom?"

El reached across the table and took his hand, causing him to blink his eyes out of his trance.

"Hey... There you are... Where did you go?" chuckled El.

"Hmm?" Tom raised his eyebrow as he quickly popped the piece of potato into his mouth.

El smiled at him. She couldn't resist that eyebrow raise. "I lost you for a moment."

Tom swallowed. "Eh-heh... Yeah, sorry... You're very distracting when you eat," he admitted.

"When I eat?" El tilted her head curiously.

Tom nodded as he smirked back at her. "Mmhmm."

El's eyes widened as she smiled. She could have some fun with this.

"So... You like watching me?"

Tom's lips parted as he watched her slowly sink her fork into the meat on her plate, piercing the flesh to hold it steadily. El dragged her silver knife through it, slicing her steak knife across the succulent meat before bringing it to her lips.

The whole thing had Tom's throat bobbing as he thought about what El would look like slicing through human flesh.

El continued, thinking the next part was the most seductive as she purposefully stuck her tongue out further and slowly placed the meat onto it, curling the edge of her tongue up around it before pushing it into her mouth. Her lips wrapped around the fork to hold the flesh on her tongue as she pulled the fork back.

She watched Tom's eyes on her mouth and the slight adjustment he had to make as his glutes tensed, raising him from the seat to wiggle his cock free from between his legs. The way his forearm flexed as his hand adjusted his length under the table to accommodate it hardening in his trousers.

El was taking her time and enjoying teasing him. She chewed the meat slowly, subtly pushing her arms together to push her breasts up and out more. The noises of pleasure El had from eating that juicy, delicious steak were increased tenfold. She purposefully wanted to make Tom know how delectable that meat was with the moans and mewls she let pass her lips.

Tom swallowed as he continued watching her cut another piece. His food now sat cold and barely touched on his plate as it was forgotten.

El ramped up her game, making sure this next piece of meat was dripping as she brought it to her mouth, allowing a droplet of bloody meat juices to drip onto the curve of her breasts.

Tom practically threw his chair back as he stood abruptly and, in one stride, was there with his tongue against her skin, lapping it up like a predator grazing its tongue across their meal.

El moaned as Tom's hand slid up her back, holding her to him as his lips and tongue continued their assault on her chest. Her hand dropped the fork onto the table as El's eyes fluttered for a moment at the feeling of his lips on her chest.

Something caught El's attention in her peripheral vision as her head dipped back, snapping her head towards it. She placed one of her hands on Tom's shoulder, the other in his hair and quietly whispered. "Someone's watching us."

Tom didn't care who was watching at this point, but then he heard the shingle crunch and turned his head towards the approaching noise.

The form of an older woman appeared from out of the gloom and into the light cast by the fairy lights around them, clearing her throat loudly.

"You know this is a public beach, right? You can't be having sex out here in the open." The older woman sounded pissed off as she continued to rant at them. "It's disgusting and inappropriate!"

Tom felt the sharp intake of El's breath as her chest swelled with it. "Excuse me... We are not having sex." El argued back.

The woman gasped loudly. "You are... He's got his head buried in your chest," she said, flustered as she gestured towards them.

El scoffed. "Do you even know what sex is? Because clearly, you aren't getting any. Do you see his cock buried in me at all?" she asked angrily.

Tom slowly eased himself back from El as she stood up and turned to face the woman entirely. He was going to enjoy watching her rage.

"Excuse me?" the woman asked, shocked as she placed her hand against her chest.

"You heard me," El spat.

"You are a very vulgar young woman!" the woman shouted back at her.

El gasped irritatedly as she gritted her teeth and her nostrils flared. "I'm rude? You're the one sneaking up, watching people. You're obviously jealous." El told her as she slammed her hand on the table, wrapping her fingers automatically around her steak knife. El leaned towards her as the knife glinted in the candlelight.

"Jealous?"

"I can guarantee that dusty old cunt hasn't seen any cock for at least thirty years." El's voice was full of venom as she stepped around the table, pointing the knife towards the woman.

The woman stepped back slightly. "Excuse me... I am a happily married woman," she protested.

El placed her empty hand on her hip, taking a wide stance as she went off on a torrent at the nosey busybody. El started to gesture wildly with the knife in her hand as she spoke.

"Are you, though? Because clearly, you enjoy poking your nose into other people's business. Surely if you were happily married, you'd have your mouth wrapped around your husband's cock instead of being out here alone, spying on others and probably getting off on it."

The woman gasped loudly in shock, her face paling.

"Uh!?! I have never..."

El immediately cut her off, speaking over her. "I saw you. I saw you watching us from the moment you noticed us sitting here, enjoying each other's company. I saw you edge closer. I saw your thighs clamp together when he started kissing me. I saw the glazed look in your eyes as you remember finding your husband cheating."

The woman stuttered, unable to say anything back before she spun around on her heel and scurried off sobbing.

"El? What was that all about?" Tom asked.

El chuckled and turned back to face a curious, almost proud-looking Tom, placing her knife back on the table. She hadn't even realised that she'd picked it up. But she wasn't about to deal with that now.

She looked up at him as she came to stand in front of him. "Nan fucked her husband. She caught them down here on the beach. I recognised it was her. The village busybody. Too busy poking her nose in everyone else's business rather than sorting out her own life."

Tom's eyes darkened. He craved that fire in her that was now coursing through her body. He could see it in her eyes just as El could see the desire in his.

She placed her hands flat on Tom's chest and backed him up to her chair, guiding him into position and making him sit down as the back of his legs hit it. She hooked her dress up and straddled his lap before turning slightly, reaching over the table and grabbing his plate and cutlery.

"You've hardly eaten."

She shuffled back, placed the plate on her lap, and started cutting into his steak. She pierced a piece of meat and brought it up to his mouth.

"Open," El commanded with a smirk.

Tom did as he was told, and she placed the fork into his mouth. His lips caressed the metal of the utensil as his teeth sunk into the steak.

El's mouth gaped slightly as she watched him. It wasn't just her mouth that was salivating. She could feel her pussy throb, begging to be filled with him.

She cleared her throat and pulled the fork back to get him another piece. This one, she made sure, was extra moist with juices. As she put it to his lips, he didn't open them and kept them closed. He smirked at her, so she smirked right back.

El pushed the meat firmly against his lips before circling the steak around them, coating them in the bloody juices before she pulled the fork away. El leaned forward and ran her tongue across his lips, licking the juices clean from his mouth. She felt Tom's cock twitch against her inner thigh as he filled with excitement.

"Mmmmm," El moaned as she leaned back, placing the fork back onto the plate on her lap. "I like you tasting of blood."

El swallowed, suddenly realising what she had just said. Her eyes widened with a hint of fear as her body tensed with shock at the words that had tumbled from her mouth so effortlessly.

Tom picked up the plate and moved it back to the table before pulling her forward against him. He cupped her face with his hands, but she didn't meet his eyes.

"El... Look at me."

Her eyes slowly came back to meet his gaze. She was embarrassed that she had let that dark fantasy slip out.

"You don't need to hide your true thoughts from me. I'm not bound by rules in the way that I love you. If you told me to stop, even if you told me, you don't love me anymore, El... I wouldn't be able to stop loving you. I can't..." Tom took a deep breath. " I won't shy away from you. Just as I hope you won't shy away from me." He leaned in, his breath ghosted over her lips as he spoke. "I love you. I love all of you."

Tom gently placed his hand over her right eye, hiding her dark chestnut iris and only showing her ice aqua blue left eye, focusing on it.

"The light," he whispered before his hand swapped to cover her other eye. "And the dark... You have both of them in you... Just as I have." Tom's hand slowly slipped away to cup her face again as he pushed his lips gently to hers, his fingers pushing into her hair, holding her to him.

El moaned into the kiss as she wrapped her arms around his neck, deepening the kiss. She felt a wave of acceptance washing over her as Tom's words fully sunk in, and her embarrassment washed away with his kiss.

Their tongues fought against one another as they became lost in each other again, being swept away in their emotions and the metallic, coppery taste lingering in both their mouths.

El's heart was hammering in her chest. She wanted him. She wanted to show him what he did to her.

She shifted her hips back, her hands running down his body to find the button of his trousers, quickly undoing it, followed by his fly. Her hand sunk past the material, immediately finding his stiff cock and setting it free.

Tom groaned against her lips as her fingers slipped around his velvety shaft. He could never get enough of her and what she did to him.

El broke the kiss and let go of Tom's cock to lick up her palm, soaking it with saliva before she wrapped her fingers back around his firm length, pumping him slowly.

Tom's head tipped back as he groaned out her name, his fingers tightening in her hair, pulling on the roots. She loved it when he did that. She loved to hear him groan and grunt and moan her name, like a prayer falling off his tongue as he held her with a vice-like grip.

El's free hand found its way between her legs, and she started to rub her clit in slow sensual circles. She moaned as she touched herself, causing Tom to look back at her with blown pupils.

"Fuck El," he groaned. "You had no panties on? You naughty girl," he scolded her playfully.

El giggled slightly between her moans. Of course, she wasn't wearing any knickers. They inevitably weren't needed when she was with Tom, and it saved time.

Tom moved a hand to touch her, and El grabbed it, stopping him.

"Don't. Just watch me. I want you to watch me," El said in a low sultry voice.

Tom's hands slipped from her hair to wrap his hand over the top of hers that continued to stroke him, guiding her as she bit down on her bottom lip.

El's moans got louder as the pressure started to build quickly in her lower stomach, her pussy flooding with arousal that seeped out and began to

coat her ass cheeks.

Tom's other hand pushed her dress up further and lifted her leg so he could get a better view. El was illuminated by the soft lights surrounding them. Her hands moved quickly, bringing them both pleasure, but Tom just couldn't see everything he wanted, leaving him frustrated.

He stopped pumping his hand and leaned forward quickly, pushing everything off the table and smashing the plates onto the shingle below their feet, not giving a damn about the noise or the wasted food.

Tom then wrapped his hand around El's waist with his other, lifting her ass onto the edge of the table, causing her hand to slip from his cock. She whined until she realised what he was doing.

El spread her legs wide as he placed her feet on the table's edge, letting her knees fall open as far as she could.

Tom had a fantastic view of El as she continued to rub her gleaming clit in the light of the oil lamps.

She lifted her other hand to his mouth and put two fingers on his lips.

"Open."

Again, Tom did as she asked, and she guided both of them into his warm, wet mouth. Tom ran his tongue around them, soaking them in his saliva before she pulled them back out with a pop and pushed them inside her drenched pussy. Her back arched as she fucked herself slowly with them, Tom watching every movement intently.

Tom could control the loud groan that fell from his open mouth as he started to pump his cock slowly at first, matching El's movements as her fingers sunk inside her.

El moved to sit up more, shifting her ass back slightly but keeping her feet firmly placed on the table with her legs spread wide to get a good view of him as he jerked off. It only made her wetter, seeing and hearing him do it.

Her fingers started moving faster and harder as she felt her walls tightening around her digits, that delicious impending snap closing in as the pressure built in her lower abdomen.

Tom's own strokes started to get frantic as he watched her.

"Uhh... Oh fuck... Tom, I'm going to... Uhh," El's body shuddered as her knees started to tremble.

"Don't stop, El... I want to see you clenching around your fingers. I want to see you soak them," Tom groaned as he kept his eyes focused on her hands.

El started trembling as she pumped her fingers furiously inside her, curling them just right to hit the spot she needed whilst her other fingers rubbed her clit faster.

"Cum for me", commanded Tom. His eyes widened as he watched her pussy clenching and pulse with every thrust as her back arched. She let out a guttural moan as her head tilted backwards.

El rode out her waves of ecstasy, Tom watching her so intently, only adding to the eroticism of the whole situation. His hand tightened around his cock as he pumped faster, and his thighs flexed in his trousers.

As El returned from her high, she snapped her head forward as she watched Tom. She could see his jaw and neck muscles tense as he neared his release.

El dropped her feet from the table, slipping off it and sank to her knees before him. The shingle was biting into her kneecaps, but she didn't care.

She snaked her hands up his clothed thighs before she wrapped her lips around the head of his cock and licked across his slit. Tom shuddered as she hollowed out her cheeks and started to suck, bobbing her head back and forth. His hands moved to push his trousers down to his knees as his glutes tensed under his palms.

"Oh fuck, El... You're such a good girl... That feels so fucking good... That's it... Yes," Tom moaned loudly as words tumbled from his mouth. His hips thrust forward as her head started to bob faster, drawing him further into her mouth.

El grabbed Tom's wrists and lifted his hands to place them in her hair. El then put her hands back onto his bare thighs, digging her nails in slightly. The pain only added to Tom's pleasure as crescent-shaped dents were created in his skin.

His grip tightened at the roots of her hair as he started fucking her mouth, pushing his cock deeper until it hit the back of her throat.

El groaned as he pushed in further, feeling that delicious burn in her chest as she fought for air. She loved the feeling of him using her, and her groaning only increased his pleasure as her throat vibrated around the head as it rammed into the back of her mouth.

Tom was on the edge of bliss, ready to give in as his thigh muscles tightened and tremored. He groaned loudly into the salty nighttime sea air.

"Fuck El... You're going to swallow every fucking drop, right?"

El swirled her tongue around the head of his cock and hummed in agreement as Tom neared his release. He pulled her almost entirely off before sinking her head back down as deep as she could go, pushing against the back of El's throat, making her swallow him.

With a loud growl, Tom started to spurt down her throat with long hard pulses, his cock throbbing against her tongue as he held her captive. His fingers dug into her scalp, pulling at the roots of her hair as he spasmed, squirting every rope of cum down her throat.

El swallowed down every last drop he gave her before his fingers relaxed in her hair, and his hands slipped away as he fought to catch his breath.

El pulled her head back slowly from him, savouring his taste as she ran her tongue back over his slit, making sure she didn't miss anything.

They were both breathless as they looked at each other.

Tom stood above her as El knelt before him. They gave themselves a moment to catch their breath before Tom gently took hold of El's hands, removing them from his thighs and helping her stand back up on shaky legs. He wrapped his arms around her waist, pulling her to him before their lips crashed together in a deep, passionate kiss.

El's darkness was starting to show much more frequently, and Tom loved every second of it.

In fact, he was beginning to crave it.

24.

El woke herself up with her own screaming. Her throat was sore and dry, her face wet with tears, and her body covered in sweat. She looked over to the side, but Tom wasn't there.

The early morning hazy sunlight was just starting to grace the world with its presence, the sun not quite cracking over the horizon yet, turning the sky into a glowing ember ready to burst into flaming colours with the return of another dawn. The corners of the room were darkened with shadows where the bedside lamp light only illuminated portions of the room in a soft glow, much like El's panicked mind. Like a cancer growing with corrupted cells, numerous dark patches were expanding in El's head, shrivelling her kindness like a leaf in autumn, leaving a void.

This awful day was packed with disturbing memories that she tried to brighten with light and push back, shutting them away in a box, but they kept clawing their way back out, swarming her.

It was the day she had been dreading for the past month. A day she hoped to forget, but it seemed her mind had other plans as it took up every available space in her head, pushing out the luminescence and replacing it with gloom.

El sat shaking on the bed, clutching her side, her knees pulled up to her chest. The memories of that stick sticking out of her, the gravel burns on her legs and arms. The pounding in her head from smacking it hard onto the tarmac as she rolled and rolled. The fire of pain in her abdomen before a clarity washed over her, focusing her on that driver's seat. The adrenaline rush that made her take that step forward was all rushing through her mind and body as she relived every terrifying moment.

The bedroom door creaked back open, and Tom entered the room with a glass of water. He stopped mid-step as he saw El just rocking back and forth. He quickly rushed over and wrapped his arm around her shoulders as she began to sob.

"Shhh, it's alright," his voice was calm and level as he rocked with her. Her breathing started to calm instantly, and her body relaxed at his touch as she leaned into him. "I went to get you some water... Here." He lifted the glass to her lips and helped her take a few sips.

"Thank you," she said gratefully as her arms relaxed around her knees and she held the cool glass of water.

He smiled at her as he sat stroking her hair. It was a comforting feeling for El as she leaned into him and sighed. She watched the condensation on the outside of the glass run down the side of it, following a random path as it fell. El was starting to feel like she was plunging into something, hoping that Tom would be there to catch her before she lost herself entirely.

"Tom?"

"Hmmm?"

"I... I need to go and do something," El replied quietly.

"Oh... ok..." Tom shifted his arm from around her shoulders and tilted his head forward to look at her.

Her eyes were red and puffy, with dark circles under them. Tom traced his finger around the edge of her hairline on her forehead, moving her hair from her sweaty face and tucking it behind her ear.

"Whatever you need, El." Tom smiled reassuringly at her.

El smiled back at him briefly before she turned to focus on her violin case. Tom took the glass of water from her hand, placing it on the bedside table as El slipped from the bed and walked over to go and get her violin to bring back to the bed with her. Tom moved around and sat with his back to the headboard as he watched her, intrigued.

El hadn't played it yet, hadn't strung it yet, and now she needed to. She had a compulsion in her to do it.

She popped the latches one at a time and slowly opened the case, inhaling the smell of the Italian spruce and maple wood of the violin.

Her fingertips glided over the smoothness of it as she wrapped her fingers around the neck to lift it out.

She paused as she looked at the picture of her and her Nan together at the beach that Tom had placed in the lid of the case before the corner of her mouth twitched into a small smile.

Tom watched, fascinated, as El took each string out of the paper wrapping and very carefully and precisely began to string it.

Her fingers glided expertly over each piece of catgut as she threaded it into the tuning pegs and twisted them slowly until taunt. Her fingertips drifted over every part of the instrument, ensuring each of the four strings fitted perfectly. She adjusted the E string slightly with the adjuster until she deemed it perfect. El then lifted the violin to her shoulder and tucked it under her chin as she plucked each string individually and slightly adjusted the tuning pegs to make each note flawless. She took her time and closed her eyes as she concentrated on the tune of each note.

Tom swallowed as he leaned forward. This was starting to get more than fascinating to watch. He was beginning to get turned on from just observing her. Her dextrous fingers worked with an efficiency Tom had never seen before except when he used a knife to part flesh from bone, cutting through the tough connective tissues to sever it from its anchor as he dismembered a body.

El had drifted into autopilot mood, complete muscle memory as she strung and tuned the violin. She hadn't played since her Nan died, but it was like she had done this every day without fail as her body fell into a familiar rhythm, shutting out all the awful memories from today.

Tom adjusted himself as El's tongue dipped out again, her eyes closed in concentration as her fingers gripped the tuning pegs, turning each one by mere microscopic adjustments.

Once El was satisfied, she placed the violin back in the case, unhooked the bow, and took out the paper package that contained the length of horse hair inside it. She passed the hair through her fingers, stretching it slightly before concentrating on taking the bow apart at its delicate ends to slot in the hair and tighten it into place.

Once satisfied, she picked the violin back up, placed it under her chin and drew the bow across it, making sure it sounded faultless.

The room echoed with the violin sound, and El smiled, enthralled as the familiar sound wrapped around her like the comfort of an old friend.

El looked down with a look of contentment as she lovingly placed it back in the case and clicked the latches shut to secure the lid.

She got off the bed and went to the bathroom to wash her face and body with cold water and rid herself of the sweat and tears that had coated her skin. She wanted to be fully awake for this and needed the shock of cold water to help. She didn't want her nightmares to follow her for this next part, and washing off the sweat caused by them was part of that.

El returned to the room to find Tom dressed in grey joggers and a black t-shirt. She smiled at him lovingly but with a hint of trepidation.

"You don't have to come with me... It's very early still," she said.

"I don't care... I'm coming with you... If you're going to do what I think you are..." he replied excitedly as he approached her and cupped her face, leaning close to her lips. "Then I'm definitely coming... I haven't heard you play yet." Tom pecked El's lips before standing back up to his full height.

El smiled and quickly got dressed into a black, off-the-shoulder flowing dress, her feet bare and her hair tied up into a messy bun. She was relieved that he wanted to come with her, and it settled the trepidation in her body to know he wanted to hear her play.

The dress was a little too formal for five in the morning, but she wanted to do this right. She was meant to have done it all those weeks ago at her Nan's funeral, but as she had smashed her old violin, she couldn't even if she wanted to.

Tom held the violin case for her in one hand and held out his other for her to take. El smiled at him as she accepted it, and they left the house together, holding hands and heading for the beach.

The waves crashed into the shingle, making a cracking noise as the small rocks tumbled and bumped into each other. Seagulls were screeching overhead as the sun rose quickly, bathing the sky in red and orange light.

Tom handed El the case, and she placed it on the table he had left there the night before. She took a deep breath, opened it up, and took out the violin and the bow before turning on her heel and heading straight down to the water.

El walked with purpose, ignoring the painful stab of the shingle crunching under her feet, only stopping her legs from moving once her feet hit the water.

The frothy white edge of the waves wrapped around her ankles as she took a stance. Her feet were just wider than her shoulders, planted firmly into the beach, her toes curly around the tiny pebbles and sand that slipped between her toes.

El stood, stock still for a moment to compose herself, taking a few deep breaths to ground herself.

Tom stood a few yards behind her, off to the side, to give her a private moment, watching her as she closed her eyes and lifted the violin into position.

El rolled her shoulders and head as she got comfortable, stretching her fingers out before her grip tightened around the neck of her instrument. The bow in her right hand, out to the side, the end, almost touching the water but not quite like she was teasing it, daring the sea to wet it.

El took another deep breath and opened her eyes before she spoke out into the open sea air, focusing on the horizon bathed in flaming colours as dawn crested above it, chasing away the darkness.

"I'm sorry I couldn't do this on the day, Nan... But I'm here now... I hope, wherever you are... You can hear this... I will only ever play this for you..."

El took a shuddering breath before she brought the bow string up to the violin, resting it gently against the strings. She took another deep breath and immediately began to play, drawing the bow across the strings, closing her eyes as she swayed with each movement of her right arm, getting lost in the music as she played.

Tom's mouth dropped open. He had never seen anything so entrancing as El playing. The music she played invaded his ears like a drug, pulling him towards her, like an addict chasing their next hit, a moth to a flame, a predator drawn to the smell of blood, the earth spinning around the sun. She was like gravity, and Tom was the falling object, tumbling towards her without realising. He couldn't stop himself. His legs had a mind of their own as he began to step towards her.

El's passionate playing drowned everything else out. Her dress blew in the wind, the edges of it getting wet with seawater. Her hair started slipping from the tie, holding it up, but she didn't stop. She continued playing as her hair wiped around her face, billowing in the breeze.

Tom was now standing only a few feet away, completely captivated by her. Her playing was flawless. Her body movements, her features, her hands and arms. Every part of her, he was committing to memory. He didn't want her to ever stop playing. She was the most beautiful sight he had ever seen. El was creating the most beautiful music he had ever heard as she was bathed in the early morning sunrise, casting her in a halo of light as it caused her hair to sparkle.

He swallowed as he took his phone out of his pocket and hit record, holding it close to his thigh to film her secretly.

El played continuously until her arms ached. Her fingers felt like they were bleeding from where she hadn't played for so long, and her callouses had softened.

The sun was much higher, the sky now blue, the waves pulling back as the tide retreated, and El stopped playing. Her shoulders and elbows felt like they were on fire as she winced, dropping her trembling arms by her sides.

Tom was there in a flash, taking hold of her arms carefully. He could feel her muscles trembling as they started to spasm with cramps.

"Bloody hell, El... Here... Let me take those," he said, concerned.

Her hands shook as she let go of the violin and bow as Tom took them from her. He hooked his arm up under hers, draping her arm across his shoulder and wrapping his hand around her waist to guide her back to the table and chairs on the beach. He sat her on the chair, then carefully put the violin back in its case with the bow.

El started laughing as her hands trembled. She shook her head as she looked down at her red fingertips.

"That'll teach me for not playing for so long."

Tom crouched next to her, placing his hand on the table and the back of the chair, trapping her in the seat. This reminded her very much of that time in the library.

"El..." Tom didn't know what to say. He had too much to say that he couldn't process it to form words.

She smiled at him as he looked at her worriedly. Her hands were still shaking and looked incredibly sore. He knelt down and took them into his own. The warmth of his hands eased the tension of her muscles, letting her hands relax.

"You play... So beautifully." Tom's voice was so quiet as he met her eyes. He had tears in them. He was so emotional.

"Hey?... What's wrong?" El asked worriedly. She pulled both her hands back from his and cupped his face. He closed his eyes as tears fell down his cheek, and she wiped them away with her thumbs. He leaned into her touch more, turning his head to kiss her palm softly before he looked back at her and opened his eyes.

"I... I've just never heard or seen anything as stunning... graceful... talented, or exquisite as you. You are like watching a goddess play, like Euterpe herself. I'm captivated by you, El. You make me feel things I can't even put into words... It scares me how much I need you... How much I love you."

Tears started to fall from El's eyes, and Tom leaned in to chase them away with his lips. The saltiness from her tears and the fine dusting of sea salt El had lingering on her cheeks caused Tom to hum in satisfaction as he licked his lips. He leaned his forehead against hers as he cupped her face.

"Your Nan would be very proud of you today, El. I know it... because I am."

25.

"Why do I need an overnight bag?" El groaned as her head fell back against the headrest.

"Because it's over five hours away driving, and the clue is in the name El... Overnight bag, i.e... we're staying overnight," replied Tom as he concentrated on driving.

El leaned forward in her seat, resting her hands on either side of her legs.

"What is this surprise?"

Tom chuckled as he heard the eagerness in her voice. "It wouldn't be much of a surprise if I told you now, would it?"

El huffed loudly in the back of the car as she slumped back into her seat and crossed her arms over her chest like a scolded child. She stared out the window for a few minutes before looking at Tom's reflection in the mirror. She loved his concentrating face whilst he drove, but this trip irritated her. Not even Tom's tongue dipping out to wet his lips every now and then could break her out of her mood.

"Pleeeease tell me," she whined.

El had been complaining about the drive, the travel time, and why Tom wouldn't tell her where they were going since they had gotten in the car. Everything irritated her. She was just in one of those bratty, impatient moods. It didn't help that she hadn't slept well or that the early morning beach trip had worn her out. Plus, today was the anniversary of her accident. Her mind had been struggling to relax and live in the moment rather than in the past.

El hated today.

"Why don't you try and get some sleep, hmm?" Tom tried to be patient with her and kept his voice level as he spoke. He knew she was only irritable because of the anniversary, but his patience only went so far.

"Sleep? But I'm too grouchy to sleep," she groaned. "Please, Tom, just tell me what county you're driving to. I'll make it worth your while..." El looked at him in the mirror as she bit her lip and wiggled her eyebrows suggestively.

Tom could see what she was up to in the mirror's reflection. He clenched his jaw as his hands tightened on the steering wheel. She was making this drive nearly impossible.

"El..." There was a warning tone to his voice as he tried to focus on the road. But his eyes kept drifting back to her reflection in the rearview mirror.

"Pleeease..." El pouted, "please, baby." El leaned back in the seat and started to run her hand down over her breasts. She knew exactly what she was doing as she watched his reaction in the mirror.

El hoped that by using her irresistible charms, Tom would give in and tell her.

Tom swallowed as he tried to concentrate back on the road, shifting in his seat and rolling his shoulders.

"Are you determined to kill us both? I can't concentrate, El, if you keep doing that. You do realise how distracting you are without having to..." his eyes drifted back to her reflection.

El sniggered as she continued her teasing and caused Tom to lose his train of thought.

His cock swelled in his trousers as she slowly ran her fingers over her breasts, pinching her nipples and sucked her bottom lip into her mouth.

"Tell me where we are going, and I'll stop," El said in a sultry tone as she parted her legs and sunk her teeth into her bottom lip, making a soft moaning sound as she tweaked her nipples into stiff peaks.

Tom let out a shuddering breath.

She knew his weaknesses and used them to her advantage to get what she wanted. But he was about to call her bluff as he signalled to pull over in an approaching layby.

Before the car had even stopped, Tom already had his seat belt off. He quickly yanked the hand brake up, causing it to make that awful ratching noise and jolted the car forward as he turned the engine off. Tom spun around in his seat; the expression on his face was of pure feral lust as El smirked back at him seductively.

"Tell me where we are going, Tom and this..." she gestured down her body, "is all yours to do with as you please."

It was barely past lunchtime, and there was a lot of traffic on the road, zooming past them.

El backed herself into the corner next to the door after unclasping her seatbelt, her right hand on the grab handle above it, her other on the top button of her yellow shirt, covering her left breast.

Tom practically growled, looking like a dark and dangerous jaguar as he clambered his long limbs over the seat, stalking his prey as he edged closer to his meal, getting ready to pounce.

El put her foot on his chest to stop his advance.

"Tell me where we are going, Tom," El demanded.

He chewed on his lip thoughtfully, weighing up his options.

Tell El, and the surprise is ruined, but he gets to do what he wants with her or don't tell her and try to survive the next three hours of driving with El pestering him and a hard cock in his trousers, making it incredibly uncomfortable to drive.

It was an easy choice, really.

Tom narrowed his eyes at her as his fingers tightened on the back seat cushions.

"I'll tell you the county... But that's it, El... No other information," that was his bargain.

"I can live with that," she stated as her toes curled in her trainers, pushing more into Tom's chest to emphasise her intent. "Where?" El asked as she tilted her head, watching him.

"Cornwall"

"Hmmm..." El's eyes drifted off thoughtfully before Tom pounced on her, causing her to squeal in delight.

He grabbed her ankle, which was still on his chest and yanked her towards him, wrapping her legs around his waist.

Tom was now between her legs, and his mouth attached to her neck.

El was moaning loudly with her eyes closed as he sucked her neck in that spot he knew she loved. His hands roamed her body, and as he ground his stiff cock into her clothed pussy, she felt her wetness leaking out in anticipation as it soaked into her knickers.

All the teasing she had done to herself had created a horny monster on the backseat, one which would have given in anyway, even if Tom had refused to tell her anything. But Tom didn't need to know that.

El's eyes flew open just as Tom's hand travelled down her legs to her knee, pushing it further out. A flashback from two years ago echoed in her mind as her body tensed and her heart started to race with panic.

The feeling of the leather car seat behind her, the faint smell of petrol and oil, the noise of the other cars zooming past, she froze, but Tom was too lost in his desire to notice. He started scrambling to undo her jeans button and zip, ripping them down once he got them open by grabbing her back pockets, exposing her knicker-clad ass.

"Stop", El's voice trembled quietly.

Tom's hand was already in the gusset of her knickers, his fingers gliding between her wet folds.

"Stop," her voice was barely a whisper, her grip tightening on the grab handle and back seat until her knuckles blanched white. Her heart was ready to burst out of her chest as her adrenaline soared.

Tom leaned back, pulling her knickers to the side with one hand whilst undoing his trousers with the other.

In such a small, cramped space, he was so focused on the task that Tom didn't see El's eyes glass over. He didn't feel her whole body tense as her fight or flight kicked in.

Tom had his cock in his hand as he grabbed her thigh and lined himself up.

SMACK.

El slapped him hard across his cheek with her open palm. Tom's head snapped to the side before he slammed back into the door as she brought her legs up and kicked him in the chest, forcing him backwards.

El yanked her jeans back up and managed to open the car door behind her before scrambling out backwards.

She fell on her ass as her body tumbled out of the door, but she quickly got up and took off, running into the trees that lined the layby.

As the sharp sting across his cheek settled into a painful throbbing sensation, Tom suddenly realised what he'd done.

"FUCK!" he shouted as he slammed the side of his fist into the headrest. He quickly pulled his trousers back up and climbed over the back seats to follow El out of the open back door.

Tom called out frantically as he ran through the trees, jumping over black bags of strewn fly-tipped rubbish, his eyes quickly shifting from left to right, looking for any trace of her.

"El! El!... I'm sorry I didn't think... El!" As he called out her name, he looked for any sign of her. "El! Where are you? I'm sorry!" Tom was panicking, he couldn't find her.

He skidded to a stop as he reached the other side of the trees, an open field in front of him and spun frantically around. His eyes scanned everywhere, desperately looking for a glimpse of her, as his heart raced.

Any other time, he would have enjoyed this chase. He had even thought about asking El if they could play this game, one where if he caught her, he could have his way with her in the woods, taking her on the floor or against a tree again.

The last time Tom had chased someone through the woods, he had a shovel in his hand and ended up driving it right through the back of her head.

Louisa Higgins was her name. She was a second-year law student at Cambridge.

Tom had seen her whilst in his first undergraduate year of university. She was pretty and knew it, using it to get what she wanted.

Tom took a chance one night whilst Louisa was walking home to introduce himself to her. She had screwed up her nose at him and refused to acknowledge him with nothing more than disgust that he had dared to approach her.

Tom was just being friendly, but she took it as something else.

It made his blood boil with that itching feeling to satisfy his need to watch her striking ice-blue eyes turn red as the capillaries around them burst and the life drained from her blown pupils whilst he choked her.

Tom started to follow her until he saw an opportunity he couldn't pass up.

Lousia had been sleeping with her best friend's boyfriend at any chance they could get. This enraged Tom further, and he couldn't help himself once the opportunity presented itself.

Lousia was going to meet her friend's boyfriend when Tom grabbed her from behind, dragging her down a dark alleyway with his hand over her mouth to stop her from screaming. She had been lying to everyone where she was going, and her lover had been doing the same. This meant that Tom could take her without anyone realising where she actually was. Tom was convinced her lover wouldn't reveal their rendevous as he hadn't left his girlfriend for her, keeping their affair a secret.

Well, that was Tom's hope, at least.

Tom had ended up hitting her over the head with a claw hammer to knock her out. He needed somewhere private to do what he wanted with her and had stuffed her into his car's boot to drive to some secluded woods a few hours from Cambridge.

Once there, he had opened the boot, but Louisa was now fully awake, taking the opportunity to trick Tom.

She pretended to still be knocked out until he turned his back, and she hit him across the back of the head with the clawhammer he had thrown in the boot with her by mistake.

Tom stumbled forward, falling to his knees as he grabbed the back of his head and groaned in pain as Louisa clambered out of the boot and ran into the woods.

This had only been Tom's third attempt at murder; he was still new to it and made mistakes, which he learnt quickly from. He never turned his back on a victim again unless they were fully secured to something.

Tom stood back up from the floor, slightly dazed, shaking his head before grabbing the shovel from the boot. He had planned to use it to bury her body before he took off after her with the shovel in his hand.

Lousia was easy enough to track, even in the dark, as her laboured breathing was loud enough for Tom to follow in the otherwise quiet wood. Her stumbling steps cracked branches below her feet, giving away her position as Tom got closer.

She screamed as she saw Tom emerge from behind a tree, the whites of his eyes glistening in the dappled moonlight as he looked at her and smirked.

"Hide and seek isn't a game I wish to play tonight, Louisa," Tom had called out as she took off again through the trees, running in the opposite direction.

Lousia inevitably tripped on a tree root as Tom rushed up behind her, his long legs giving him a massive advantage over her in speed.

Just as she scrambled to her feet, Tom swung the flat side of the shovel blade across the back of her head.

Her body slumped forward against a tree with her arms limp against her side, dropping the clawhammer that she had taken with her.

Louisa was barely conscious as her body scraped across the tree bark, scratching her face in the process before she fell to the floor.

Her face was buried in damp leaf litter, making it harder for her to take the laboured breaths that her body was fighting to draw into her lungs as she gasped and choked.

Tom stood over her, waiting for her to move, his feet planted on the floor on either side of her thighs.

Louisa's right arm twitched as her chest heaved. Her body was still desperately trying to cling to life as her adrenaline kicked in, forcing her to try and get away.

She turned her head to the side and saw the shining blade of the shovel glinting in the moonlight before it was driven into her face just below her cheekbone, severing her head in two.

Tom let out a satisfied breath as he crouched down closer to Louisa's face, watching as her pupils dilated slowly and her body twitched as her nerves fired for the last final seconds.

He gently ran his fingers through her hair as blood seeped into the ends that sat at the back of her head.

It took a little effort to retrieve the shovel from her skull as it was now also buried in the dirt below Louisa's mutilated head. But once Tom had pulled it out, he decided to just continue to chop up her body into pieces where she lay.

He was far enough into the woods that the forecasted rain would wash away any traces of blood the next day, and they weren't near any of the footpaths that crossed through it.

Tom buried Louisa's body parts in various scattered graves around the woods. It took most of the night, but he was satisfied with his work as he returned to his car with Louisa's nose in a plastic bag in his pocket.

The chase this time wasn't going to end satisfactorily with a kill for Tom. His panic increased tenfold as he continued to look for El, dreading that he wouldn't be able to find her.

El had been faster than Louisa and wiser as she sat with her back against a tree, her knees tucked up to her chest, her hands flat on the floor as she pushed herself further against the bark, trying to hide away.

She couldn't catch her breath but wasn't making any gasping sounds, merely opening and closing her mouth silently like a guppy.

But El wasn't running from Tom because he was going to kill her. She was running from the situation that reminded her of this awful day's memories.

El couldn't speak as Tom rushed past her about ten feet away. She felt like she was choking, like Andy's hand was back around her throat, squeezing the life from her as she relived her nightmares.

She didn't cry.

She didn't sob.

El shut down like she had so many times before. Her mind went into self-protection mode, stopping her from feeling anything and blocking everything out.

Tom couldn't see her across the field, so he searched back through the trees, his head looking left to right. As he ran through them, jumping over tree roots and scattered rubbish, back towards the road, his eyes scanning everywhere, he saw a flash of yellow against a tree and called out to her in relief.

"El!"

Tom ran as fast as he could towards her, skidding onto his knees in front of her when he reached her.

She was looking straight ahead, straight through him again.

"El?"

Tom's voice was quiet and trembling as tears ran down his face in both relief and anguish.

He was relieved that he had found her but terrified of the vacant look that had returned to El's face.

It was like all their progress over the last few months had been wiped away to nothing as El sat on the floor.

"El, I'm so sorry... I wasn't thinking."

He didn't know if he should touch her, but his intuition took over, and he placed his hand over hers on the ground and lightly squeezed it. He gently put his other hand under her chin to try to get her to focus on him.

"El?... Ethel?" his voice was louder now as he tried to bring her back.

He ran his thumb across her bottom lip, and she blinked. That glassy look slowly disappeared from her eyes as she focused back on him. He felt her squeeze his hand back. She carefully brought her other hand up to wipe his tears away as she continued to look at him, holding his gaze.

Tom leaned forward, their foreheads touching as he moved his fingers from her chin to the back of her neck and tangled them in her hair.

"I am so sorry, El... I wasn't thinking... I should have known better," Tom shook his head as he apologised. "Please forgive me."

She shut her eyes and took a deep breath, leaning back against the tree away from him. El could feel herself returning to the present as she focused on breathing and the comforting scent of Tom.

Clarity washed over her as she opened her eyes and looked directly into Tom's, meeting his worried gaze.

El swallowed.

It was now or never.

She took a deep breath before she let her confession that had been clawing at her throat for weeks tumble from her mouth.

"I murdered him, Tom."

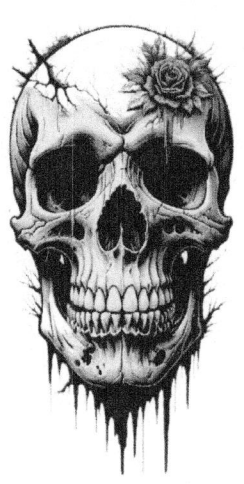

THE OBSESSIVE SERIES

This story follows the growing relationship between El and Tom and how far they are willing to go for each other as they descend into darkness and murder.

Book 2 is set for release in late 2024.

Book 3 is set for release in 2025.

MY KILLER CAPTURED

Book 2 in the Obsessive series follows directly after El's confession to Tom about what she did on the night of the car accident.

Their journey together develops as Tom contemplates telling El the truth about himself as well.

Will El stay once she knows who Tom really is, or will she run?

Sneak peek

MY KILLER CAPTURED

CHAPTER 1.

"I murdered him, Tom."

El was expecting Tom to pull away from her, to be shocked, to want to run for the hills when she told him her darkest secret as tears ran down her face.

Instead, he rubbed small circles into the back of her neck with his fingertips. Almost as if he was coaxing more out of her.

They sat silently for a few moments on the damp floor of the small wood, surrounded by strewn rubbish, the smell of petrol fumes lingering in the air and the distant sound of cars driving past on the motorway.

El took a deep, steadying breath. It was now or never.

Tom would either run or stay and look at her differently after she confesses, giving him the gruesome details of what she did that fateful night.

Well, that's at least what El thought would happen.

There's no way he'll stay once he knows how depraved I am.

El was scared and hesitant to say any more as her mind wandered to the what-ifs.

Her nan, Enid, had been the only other person she had told the whole truth to.

Enid had sat, listened, and squeezed her hand after she had managed to get El to start opening up.

She never pulled away from El, she never tutted, and she never judged. She gave her all the space and comfort she needed to tell her what had happened that night as she sat and listened to her without interruption.

To El's surprise, her nan's face had filled with so much pride as she told her what she had done, putting her mind a little at ease, if only for a brief moment, as El stayed in the bubble of safety and security her nan had created.

Enid told her after El had finished revealing the truth that she was strong and brave and that if she had been in El's position, she would have done more to that bastard than El had.

El felt a connection to her nan that she had never felt with anyone else, and when Enid started to tell her parts of her own dark past, El felt even more connected to her. They were one and the same, not just in appearance but in mind, body and soul.

There was a weight lifted off El's shoulders. It made her feel better, and like she wasn't carrying the burden of her guilt alone.

But when her nan died, that guilt had felt like a lead weight slamming back down onto her as her moral conscience, the one that told her she should feel guilty and that she was a murderer, had almost crushed her under its weight.

Tom lightly squeezed El's hand as he waited patiently for her to see if she would say more. He moved his hand away from her neck to take her other hand in his.

El leaned back against the tree and met his eyes, her flushed cheeks stained with tears. The rough bark caught strands of her hair as she lifted her head more, tilting her chin up to gauge Tom's reaction.

His eyes were soft and kind, full of love. Not what El was expecting but what she had hoped for.

El chewed on the inside of her lip as she built up her courage to break through the lump that had formed in her throat. That lump of guilt that made it hard to breathe, let alone speak.

El swallowed again as her hands squeezed Tom's. "You don't have to stay with me, Tom," she said solemnly.

"Why wouldn't I stay?"

"Because..." her voice trembled as she spoke. "Because I'm a murderer. I'm a horrible, awful person."

As she looked at him, tears filled El's eyes, threatening to spill down and run along the shining trails the previous ones had made along her cheeks. She dropped her chin, looking down at their conjoined hands.

"You're not a horrible, awful person, El. Far from it," Tom said softly as he moved one hand to lift her face.

"But I could have helped him. I could have saved him. But I chose not to. I chose something else," El's voice strained as she spoke.

Tom smiled at her, a genuine smile filled with love and understanding. He knew exactly what she would have felt at that moment. That choice between the light and the dark.

But for Tom, there was never a choice. He always knew what would happen as his rage consumed him. He would always choose the darkness because he was drawn to it.

It always won.

The only time he had ever stopped was when El's touch brought him back, her light guiding him away from ploughing that broken glass into her father, Mark's neck.

The feeling of wanting to confess his own sins clawed at his chest, but he couldn't bring himself to let the words tumble out. Tom didn't know if El could love him back once he told her his darkest secrets. He had told her already that his love wasn't bound by rules, but was her love for him conditioned to them, to those unspoken moral codes that humanity was governed by?

The thoughts terrified him, especially with how El was right now, but he buried them down and locked them away.

This was her moment, not his.

Convincing El that she could still love a serial killer after she knew everything was a plan that Tom needed to formulate. He needed to ensure that El needed him more than anything before he told her the full extent of his truths.

Tom's thumb stroked along El's jawline before travelling higher to wipe her fallen tears away. He watched her closely as she leaned into his palm. His heart remained steady as he waited for her to open up.

El sighed before she spoke quietly, keeping her gaze locked on Tom's.

"I'm guessing Dotty told you she took me out, and I got drunk. And that he said he'd take me home. Dotty's boyfriend?... and then, for some reason, the car crashed into a tree and caught fire?"

Tom nodded slightly, "Yes... That's what she told me."

"Ok, well... That's mostly true. I did go out drinking with Dotty and her friends to celebrate... But I wasn't that drunk. I just had enough and wanted to go home. Dotty was the one-off her face and didn't want to leave. We had an argument. I can't even remember what it was about... Dotty can't remember us arguing. But if she does, she hasn't told me." El swallowed before taking a deep breath, her hands trembling slightly. "But *he* told her he'd take me home, that *he'd* look after me."

El sighed loudly as Tom moved his hand from her face to join his other in holding her trembling hands. She looked off into the trees behind Tom as a single tear ran down her cheek.

"I should never have gotten in that car with *him*." El's voice was bitter as she spoke about him, about Andy.

Tom tilted his head to get her to focus back on him, and her eyes met his. He gently wiped her tears with his thumb before retaking hold of her hand again, trying to ground her and not let her drift off into that void that seemed to want to drag her back down at every opportunity.

"As soon as we pulled out of the car park, he sped off... I laughed... I actually laughed at the excitement of it, the thrill... I was a fucking fool... A stupid little girl..."

El tensed, angry at herself for trusting Andy. Her eyes started to glaze over.

Tom ran his thumbs over her knuckles to bring her back, making her blink through the haze of memory and focus back on him. He wanted her to continue, but he didn't want her to get lost in her memories.

She felt him grounding her and relaxed again, taking another calming breath.

"After a while of us laughing, the atmosphere changed," El swallowed again as her heart rate pounded in her ears, but she was determined not to stop now. She needed Tom to know.

"He put his hand on my knee, rubbing my thigh. He told me how pretty I was. How he'd watched me. How he was jealous of his friend sleeping with me." El scoffed a humourless laugh as she looked at Tom. "I was kind of a hoe back then," she swallowed down her embarrassment as she told him.

Tom took a deep breath, his tongue darting out to wet his lips, trying to keep his composure. He didn't want to think of her with anyone else. He could feel his heart rate quicken as he fought to remain calm. But his fingers flexed around her hands, tightening just enough to ensure El knew she was his.

Tom nodded his head once to get her to keep talking. He needed her to continue.

"He told me his friend had told him all about me. Shown him the video he'd taken," she sighed loudly as her eyes dropped away and shook her head. "I didn't know he'd filmed us. I didn't know he'd done it," El's voice wavered as she lifted her head to look at Tom with pleading eyes.

Tom's grip tightened on her hands immediately. The rage building in him threatened to take over at what El had just said.

He wanted a name.

He wanted an address so that he could find him. So that he could pummel his fists into this fuckers face before he would cut his cock off and force it down his own throat, watching him choke on it.

The only downside to that plan was that he'd probably bleed out before he succumbed to lack of oxygen.

Unfortunate, Tom thought. But necessary.

Tom had to force himself to blink and not succumb to his blind rage. He felt El squeeze his hands back. He needed her to ground him just as much as she did him.

"He said he wanted a taste... He said *he* knew I'd put out. I told him no. That *he's* Dotty's boyfriend. That I wouldn't do that to her. *He* laughed at me." El dropped her head but continued talking in a hushed voice as everything tumbled out, like water bursting through a broken dam.

"He moved his hand higher up my leg and under my skirt. I grabbed it and told him to stop. I didn't want to. He pulled his hand back, grabbed my hair, and pushed me into the window. He kept driving, holding me against the glass. Telling me I was going to love it and that I wanted it," El swallowed as Tom moved his hand slowly up her arm. "I kept screaming at him to stop, but he wouldn't. He yanked me towards him and switched hands, grabbing my throat and pushing me back into the seat."

"El..." Tom's voice was barely above a whisper, but El looked up at him. Tears welled in her eyes as Tom's hand rested on her shoulder, rubbing his thumb across the ball and socket joint.

"The car started to serve as I struggled against him. I managed to grab the steering wheel, and the car served more. He let me go immediately to stop us from crashing, but then he laughed again before punching me in the face. My head hit the window with so much force. It hurt so much that my head spun. I felt myself flopping forward as I tried to focus. He just kept laughing. Telling me how I was going to enjoy this. That I wanted it really." Her eyes darted side to side as the fear started to wreak havoc through her, but she couldn't stop now. Tom had to know.

"I could feel the car speed up... So I... I unclipped my seat belt. I didn't care anymore. I just wanted out of the car, so when he went to grab me again, I shoved him back and opened the door."

Tom took a deep, sharp intake of breath through his nose as his hands tightened on her shoulder and hand.

El had jumped out of a moving car just to get away from that fucking rapist prick. She could have died just from doing that.

"I rolled and rolled across the tarmac and down a bank. I heard the car skid and crash. He must have lost control, and the car went sideways straight into a tree. When I managed to stand up, I had a piece of wood sticking out of me. I must have rolled onto it when I fell down the bank." El paused. This was when she could feel the change within herself. The fear turned to rage as it overtook her body. Now, it was doing the same as it had that night, scratching at the surface, clawing to get out.

Every inch of El's trembling body stopped and focused. She looked deathly calm as her face softened into a mask composure, hiding the devil beneath with its fiendish smirk.

"I felt this fury in me, Tom... This blind rage took over me. I managed to stand up and stumble over to the car. I looked into it from the passenger side. He had blood down his face, and the airbag had gone off, but other than that, he didn't look that hurt. He opened his eyes slowly, turning his head to look at me. I could smell the oily smoke before I saw the fire. His eyes looked at the noise as it crackled around his feet. He fumbled with the seat belt, screaming at me to help him. I grabbed his hand to stop him. The flames climbed higher up his legs, and they started to burn my arm. But I didn't care. His screaming was music to my ears."

That darkness in El's eyes was back as the mask of composure cracked, revealing a slither of the monster beneath. It took delight in that memory that ironically was burnt into her mind.

"He started thrashing, the heat getting too much for me. I let go of his hands and punched him in the face before stepping back. The flames were up to his chest now. The heat was incredible. I stepped back more, watching him claw at the seat belt and scream. He screamed and screamed as he was getting burnt alive. I could smell it. His burning flesh. It smelt like burnt pork fat. His clothes melted and stuck to his skin. I watched his skin bubble and pop as it blistered across his hands and face, peeling off and melting. The flames, charing his body black before the screaming stopped."

El licked her smirking lips, her body fully relaxed as she revelled in her savage memory.

Tom let go of her hand, moving his hands to cup her cheeks as his thumbs stroked her cheekbones as he leaned forward more. His legs were now on either side of hers as he moved position to get closer to her, drawn to the darkness.

She leant to her left, into his touch, and her eyes softened as she finished her story.

"I stepped back as the car was engulfed in flames, the petrol igniting and exploding. I don't remember much after that until I woke up in the hospital... They told me what had happened, asking me if I remembered. I was meant to feel guilty for surviving and for his death. But I didn't feel the guilt like that. Not for him. I felt guilty because I didn't... I didn't feel anything for him. It was easier to shut everyone out than face what I had done. Who I was."

A single tear fell down her face as she blinked, and the monster slipped back inside.

Tom had sat and listened, taking in every little detail. He wanted the name of the guy who filmed her. He wanted to find him and punish him. Deep down, he was hoping El would want that too, but as he watched her, he saw the struggle within herself. The inner turmoil.

Tom had always accepted who he truly was after killing someone the first time.

He loved it.

He sought it out.

He craved that feeling of control.

It was addictive, holding someone's life in your hands, like snuffing out a candle flame. You could blow lightly, watching the fire waver and struggle to maintain its heat as it clung to the wick, but then you could blow just that little bit harder and watch as it disappeared, turning to smoke as it died.

But with El, she hadn't yet accepted that the monster was part of her.

"You have nothing to be ashamed about, El... He was a pig and deserved everything and more... If I..."

Tom drifted off. If he had been in El's place, the police would have known it was a murder.

He wouldn't have left a piece of that fucker intact.

El took a deep breath.

"If you don't want to be with me... I'll understand," her voice was quiet as she spoke.

Tom furrowed his brow and moved his hand under her chin, making her look him in the eyes. His eyes softened as they met hers. He always melted under her gaze.

"El... Whatever you did... Whatever you do... It wouldn't stop me from ever loving you or loving you less... This doesn't change anything... If anything, it makes me love you more."

El furrowed her brow at him. "I don't understand how you could love me more."

"You shared this with me. That means something, El... That means you trust me enough to tell me the truth. I've told you that you don't need to hide from me. I love all of you. Both sides of you."

He ran his finger along the edge of her jaw and down around the back of her neck. His lips parted as his eyes dropped to her mouth.

El moved her hands up from her lap to cup Tom's face. They leaned forward simultaneously, resting their foreheads against one another and savouring the moment as they kept eye contact.

They breathed each other in as El felt relieved to reveal the truth to Tom. She trusted him wholeheartedly and knew he would never tell anyone the truth about what she had done.

As far as El knew, they both now held a secret about each other. El had revealed her darkest secret and had kept Tom from getting in trouble about almost killing her father. El just didn't know that Tom had far more dark secrets than she could ever imagine.

As they looked at one another, their eyes moved to their lips, moving their heads slowly to press them together. The kiss was slow and passionate, full of meaning.

El poured her heart into it. She wanted Tom to know how much she appreciated him. How much she loved him. And Tom wanted El to understand how much he accepted her. All of her.

About the Author

Louise Wilder lives in a seaside town on the Kent coast, in the UK, selling comic books and all things nerdy, with her husband, son and dog.

She has a degree in Marketing and Human Resources and started writing fan fiction as a hobby whilst being a Zookeeper. This developed into a passion for writing original stories of varying genres before settling on dark romance.

For updates, including new books, please follow her TikTok, Facebook and Instagram @LouiseWilderAuthor

AUTHOR NOTE

If you have gotten this far, thank you for reading this book.
I hope you have enjoyed it as much as I have writing it.

It has been a long process to get this far, taking about two years of waking up at 5am most days whilst working a full-time job to be able to write this and get my dark thoughts down on paper.

If you decide to leave a review, thank you for doing so. Reviews help to get books noticed and allow authors to keep writing, knowing that our stories are getting read and that people hopefully find some pleasure in them.

I hope you decide to continue the journey with El and Tom.

If you thought it was dark now, you haven't seen nothing yet.

Printed in Great Britain
by Amazon